Love and other Responsibilities

LEXXIE COUPER

DEDICATION

To the father of my daughters. My husband. My true-love story. My happily ever after. Thank you, Nigel. For being my everything.

ACKNOWLEDGMENTS

The Author (a *very* Aussie Australian) would like to thank the following awesome people for making certain her American characters sounded American, and that her American school system was accurately represented:

Val Meglis, Sharon Bridwell, Fedora Chen, Tamara Yunker and Jenna Underwood.

You are all amazing.

CHAPTER ONE

D*amn, that's a fine back. And fine shoulders. And arms.*
     In fact, *everything* about the man standing in the line for the Tornado Whirl fell into the delicious-eye-candy basket. Of course, Randi had yet to see the *front* of the man, only the back, but she'd been drooling over the sublime view of his back ever since she'd caught up to him at the foot of the stairs on the final level of the waterslide. The beads of water on his smooth, bronzed skin glistening in the San Diego summer sun only emphasized the sexy view.

All toned and sculpted and yummy.

Good grief, what would all those muscles feel like?

A hard jolt from behind knocked her off-balance.

"Move, Aunt Randi."

Grabbing at the railing to steady herself, she fixed her nephew—fifteen and way too smart for his own good—with an exasperated grin. "Okay, Chuckles, I get you're impatient, but can you lay off the body slams for a while. We're almost at the top, and I can't go any farther forward."

Charles, AKA Chuck, AKA Chuckles, smirked and flicked a pointed look at Mr. Back-Like-A-God. "I was just trying to help. Make you move forward, that is."

Randi cocked an eyebrow at her well-meaning but highly inappropriate nephew. "Keep that up, Chuck, and I'll toss you over the side." She leaned toward the steep mesh separating the top level of the waterslide's walkway from the view of the ground a good sixty feet below. "And"—she gave him a smirk of her own—"I don't think you'll bounce."

Chuck rolled his eyes and shoved at her shoulder a little, enough to make her panic about her boob's containment in the skimpy triangle of purple material calling itself a bikini top. Why the hell had she decided to wear it again? She was thirty-five, for Pete's sake, not twenty-five. "C'mon, Aunty R. Get a move on."

Surreptitiously checking that her cleavage remained in the PG-13 category, Randi turned back to face the direction of the Tornado Whirl and got an eyeful of Mr. Back-Like-A-God's incredible thighs and calves a few feet farther up the walkway.

Oh wow.

Mr. Incredible Back Shoulders Arms Hips Thighs *and* Calves turned slightly sideways at the mouth of the slide, one foot on its rim, one hand gripping the handle overhead.

Holy crap, his full-body profile was just as exquisitely sexy as the rest of him.

"It's okay, Daddy." A small child no more than six grinned up at him, her hand firmly clasped in his, her strawberry-blond hair a mass of wet ringlets streaming down her small back.

Daddy? Well, there goes that fantasy. Infidelity was a no-go, even in her imagination.

"Don't be scared," the little girl went on. "I'll look after you."

He chuckled. *Goddamn it, he even has a sexy laugh.* "Doing my best, hon," he answered.

Randi groaned. *Oh God, he has an Australian accent and a sexy voice.* It was as if someone had tapped into her Chris Hemsworth fantasy just to torture her.

Why the hell did I suggest Wet 'N' Wild Water Park for the day's fun?

This is what she got for putting her work as a teacher and her studies ahead of her social life. If she'd actually *had* sex in the last six months, she wouldn't be lusting after a man way out of her league on a waterslide far too scary for her own adventure limits. She should have started dating again after things ended with Professor Jerk-wad instead of plunging into a master's—

"Hurry up, Randi." Chuck nudged her in the back. "You're next."

She stumbled forward and whacked her knee on the last step.

"Shit," she burst out.

Shit? She slapped her hand over her mouth and looked up at the man perched at the entry of the slide not four feet away.

His gaze connected with hers, an expression of disapproval falling over a face so goddamn gorgeous it was ridiculous. "C'mon, Sasha." He placed his hand on his daughter's shoulder and turned away, presenting Randi his delicious back again as he guided the kid into the opening of the slide. "Our turn."

The little girl—Sasha—gave Randi a mischievous grin before disappearing behind her father's torso.

"On the green light," the slide's attendant, a teenager who couldn't be any older than Chuck, said to the man and his daughter, "you pull yourself forward. Make sure you hold her the whole way down, sir."

The Australian god nodded. "On the green light." His shoulders bunched as he slid one arm more firmly around his daughter's body, holding her against the protection of his. "Ready?"

"Ready!" Sasha crowed with a jubilant laugh, a second before the red light above the slide's mouth turned green.

The muscles in the man's back rippled with latent strength,

and then he launched them both into the jet of water surging through the slide.

A squeal of delight filled the air, as did a booming laugh, and then father and daughter were gone from sight.

Rubbing at her throbbing knee, Randi climbed the last step and took her place at the mouth of the slide. *Whoa, is that my pulse?* Adrenaline. Had to be. She hadn't been on a water slide since she was sixteen, after all.

Yeah, right. More like Mr. Hot Dad.

"On the green light, pull yourself forward."

She shot the attendant beside her a quick look. "Already? Are you sure?"

The kid scratched at a cluster of pimples on his right cheek and frowned at the light currently flickering between red and green. "Er"—another scratch—"sure."

Randi met his frown and challenged it with one of her own. She was familiar with his ilk. The kind of teenager who put their brain in neutral when they shouldn't. "I think it's too soon. Does the light do that often? If I go now I'll run into the—"

"Go," the kid pressed his hand to the small of her back and shoved.

Three things happened at once, in perfect sync and vivid clarity: Randi's damp fingers slipped from the support rail at the mouth of the slide, Chuck burst out laughing behind her, and the light stopped flickering between green and red to glow red. Bright, adamant red.

Oh shit.

Before she could do anything to halt the inevitable, the powerful jet of water slammed at her butt, gravity grabbed at her with equal enthusiasm, and she was plummeting down the wet blue tube.

Heading straight for the hottest guy she'd ever seen and his young daughter.

Even as Brody Thorton laughed his way down the slide, hugging Sasha to his body as they twisted and banked up and down its wet sides, a part of his mind kept returning to the woman in the purple bikini.

Hell, she was pretty. All that long, dark hair and ice-blue eyes, and those curves. Fair dinkum, something about her had—

"Watch out!"

The cry, frantic and terrorized at once, sounded behind him, a second before something slammed into him.

Something warm and soft with legs. Legs that suddenly appeared on either side of his hips. Long, feminine legs.

"Oh God," the warm, soft thing with legs gushed behind him.

Is that... Hell, is that...

"I'm sorry, I'm sorry."

Yep, the warm soft thing pressed to his back was the woman in the skimpy bikini, her legs damn near wrapped around his hips, her hands clinging to his shoulders.

And shit, her breasts were squashed against his back, and her wet skin slipped and slid against his, a friction way more evocative than his brain was prepared for.

He hugged Sasha as she laughed with excitement at their abrupt acceleration. Twisting as much as he could to look over his shoulder, he saw the woman in the purple bikini clinging to him, eyes squeezed shut, a mortified look of dismay twisting her face.

He opened his mouth to say something—who knows what. *Hi, I'm Brody*, maybe—but they hit one of the slide's notorious hairpin curves, and any hope of doing anything but ride out the g-forces and splashes of water was destroyed.

Sasha shrieked with joy again, no doubt on an adrenaline high. The woman let out a strangled "Eep," her arms wrapping around his torso with desperate strength. Her breasts mashed to his back again, warm and soft and undeniably there, and her thighs pressed at his hips. Brody ground his teeth at the contact and fixed his stare on the rush of water and blur of blue tubing ahead of him.

It's that or—

Another hairpin bend whipped the disturbing, unfinished thought from his mind.

All three of them banked up the side of the slide, Sasha laughing the whole way, the woman in the purple bikini slipping against his back, her apologetic cries echoing through the tunnel. Cries that became giggling squeals as they continued their rapid, wet decent.

Bloody hell, they're infectious.

Despite the situation, his unsettling response to the woman pressed against him, and the fact that all three of them were moving way too fast for his peace of mind, he found himself laughing as well.

Laughing and giving himself over to the rush of it all.

Their laughter filled the narrow tunnel. At every whiplash-fast bend, the woman's thighs gripped him tighter. At every banking corner, her arms squeezed him closer to her. On every straight, she laughed out one apology after the other.

And then, in an assault of sunlight and hot air, they were flying through the air, momentum impelling them from the end of the slide into a shallow pool. They hit the water in a tangle of arms and legs and skin sliding against skin.

Damn, that was fun.

His feet hit the bottom of the pool, and he stood, holding Sasha tightly to his torso and seeking out the woman in the purple bikini as he did so.

Where is she? Where is—

She erupted from the water beside him, a laughing, coughing mess of tangled hair, glistening skin, and jiggling boobs. "I'm sorry," she spluttered, lurching sideways, face half covered by thick strands of wet hair. "I'm sorry. I told the kid up there it was too—"

"*Incoming!*" a boy's voice shouted, a heartbeat before a blur of color slammed into her, knocking her to her knees.

"Can we do that again?" Sasha burst out, squirming in his arms as he watched the teenage boy, who'd just arced from the slide, lever himself off the woman in the purple bikini.

"Daddy, let's do that again."

"That was *epic*." The teenager whooped, slicking his hands over his face as he grinned at the woman currently trying to regain her footing in the thigh-high water. "Let's do it again."

"Yes! Again, *again!*" Sasha grabbed at Brody's shoulders and shook him with as much strength as her six-year-old muscles would allow. "Let's do it again. All of us. Me, you, and the lady, too!"

The woman laughed, her balance still not altogether sound as she raised a hand to her wet-hair-covered face. "Oh, wow, I don't think—"

"All of us, Daddy," Sasha cried, still shaking him. "Please?"

The woman pressed her palm to her forehead and smoothed the hair from her face, lips curling into a happy smile.

A beautiful smile.

Damn it, there wasn't a hope in hell he could agree to Sasha's excited request. Not with the way he was reacting to the drenched woman grinning in front of him. Not with the way his mind noted her incredible breasts and lush curves and... *Bloody hell, is that a belly ring?*

Yep. A bloody belly ring. He had a thing for belly rings.

Belly rings and bikinis that barely concealed curves that spoke of a love of exercise *and* a love of food...

His body reacted with interest, and he turned away.

Shit. Think of something else. Think of something—

"Brody, are you going to get out of the pool soon?"

Shit. Again.

Forcing a relaxed smile to his face, he directed his attention to the willowy woman in the blindingly white bikini watching him from the edge of the slide's pool. "Sorry, Alicia. We just had an incident."

Alicia arched an eyebrow, her red-glossed lips pursing. *"We?"*

Before he could stop himself, he turned back to the woman in the purple bikini.

She grinned at him, her eyes dancing with fun. "We did, didn't we?"

Every molecule in Brody that ran on testosterone noticed how she looked. Noticed and wanted to catalog it.

Stop it.

Brody jerked his stare back to Alicia, now regarding him not only with pursed lips and arched eyebrow, but with folded arms and a jutted hip. "There was some confusion with the gap between riders on the slide," he said, threading his fingers through Sasha's. His daughter looked like she was about to make a beeline for the lush bundle of laughing sexiness in the purple bikini. Alicia would have a fit if Sasha did such a thing. "We got tangled up altogether mid-slide."

"Hmm." The eyebrow arched higher as Alicia slid a steady stare to the woman standing near him in the pool. "Did you now?"

"It was awesome!" Sasha burst out, swinging Brody's hand in wild circles. "We're going to do it again, Alicia. Now. Aren't we, Daddy? Aren't we, lady?"

"Miranda." The vision in skimpy purple laughed. "My name's Miranda. But almost everyone but my mother calls me Randi."

Brody couldn't stop himself shooting her a look. Randi. Talk about the perfect name.

She grinned at him again. And yet, something about the way she fidgeted with her bikini top and ducked her head told him she was feeling…what? Unsettled.

"Please, Daddy?" Sasha played tug-o-war with his hand some more, the beseeching tone in her voice equally as powerful as her tiny grip on his fingers. "All three of us."

"Yeah, Aunty R." The teenage boy behind Randi gave Brody a wide smirk as he nudged Randi's shoulder with his own. "All *three* of you."

"Brody?" Alicia's cool voice sounded over the water, loaded with barbed opinion.

He turned his stare to her, unable to miss the judgment in his sister-in-law's gaze as it ran over him.

His gut clenched. "Where's Will?"

Alicia shrugged. "Snapchatting, I think."

He ground his teeth. *So much for a family day out. At least Sasha is having fun.*

And so am I. Even more now Randi—

"Daddy!" Sasha laughed. "Let's go."

"Go for it, Aunty R," the teenager encouraged.

Alicia cocked her eyebrow higher. At the rate of its ascension, the immaculately shaped feature would soon join the immaculately groomed hair on her head. "Really, Brody?"

Fixing Alicia a level stare, Brody scooped up his giggling daughter, deposited her on his hip, and swung to the goddess in the purple bikini. "Game to go down with me again, Randi?"

CHAPTER TWO

R andi was pretty certain she'd missed something really important he'd said as they climbed the stairs to the top of the slide together.

Must have.

Somewhere between the, "G'day, I'm Brody," in the landing pool and the halfway point of the climb to the beginning of the slide, Mr. Hot Dad must have mentioned who Alicia was. He didn't seem like the kind of guy to go off with another woman in front of his partner/date/whatever Alicia was. Maybe he was divorced and this was a mutual-ground meet-up?

God, please let him be divorced.

A hot finger of guilt stabbed at her, and she gave herself a mental slap. Seriously, she needed to get a hold of herself.

It was hard not to feel guilty about going down the slide again with a maybe-divorced man. It was harder still not to ignore his little girl, Sasha, who was too damn adorable for her own good. Randi was enjoying chatting and laughing with her way too much to stop and think about what she was doing.

Surely that was the case. Surely that's why she'd agreed to do the slide again even with Alicia studying her like a hawk.

What a little cutie.

Sasha, not Alicia. Even though she didn't speak with an Australian accent like her father, there was no denying she was his daughter. They shared the same eyes, the same mischievous smile. The same predilection for the word "crikey."

"…to San Diego?"

At Chuck's loud question, Randi started paying attention to the conversation between her nephew and Mr. Too-Sexy-For-Words.

Of course he'd joined them on the adventure. He was Chuck. He knew how to track down an awkward situation like a bloodhound. He'd stuck out his hand to Brody as they'd begun to climb the stairs again, said, "Hi, I'm Chuck, Randi's nephew. I live with her. 'Cause she'd die without me," and then proceeded to talk about the physics involved in water slides. And *now* it seemed he was grilling Brody. *Damn.*

"About seven years ago," Brody answered, a warm smile on his face as he looked down at Sasha holding his hand as they climbed another step. "To be closer to the maniac here's grandparents."

"Are they from San Diego?" Charles gave Randi a surreptitious nudge to the back.

Brody nodded, lifting his smile from his daughter. "They are. Although they're currently two months into a year-long, round-the-world trip. Gray nomads we call their like back home in Australia. Oldies who travel. Who said seventy-year-olds don't know how to live, eh?"

Clearly, nothing like her own parents. Her mom and dad had ventured no farther than the universities they both lectured at for decades. When they'd retired, they'd both written book after book on the academic process, on raising gifted children, and just about any other subject that put a spotlight on their superior intellects and achievements.

"That sounds wonderful," she said, giving Sasha a grin. "And adventurous. Not typical grandparents, then?"

"Not typical at all. But then, they never have been. Sasha's grandmother still owns an art gallery in Old Town, and her pop is a children's book author. I.R. Fenchurch. The author of the There's a Dragon in My Soup series."

"Wow." Charles nudged Randi on the back again, this time with nothing close to surreptitious force. "Did you hear that, Aunty R? You could go hang out with them both."

A rush of heat flooded Randi's cheeks, and she pivoted to cast him a what-are-you-*doing* face.

"Aunt Randi," Charles went on, "is an art teacher."

"You know, I *can* talk for myself, Chuckles."

"So do it."

She opened her mouth and closed it.

No part of, "I'm a thirty-five-year-old teacher embarking on an insane master's degree in Creative Narrative Through the Visual Image and Written Word," was sexy.

He's a dad. Which means there's a mom. Which means he's off-limits.

Besides, she was still smarting over the failure of her relationship with Professor Jerk-wad. Finding him in bed with one of his students was a cliché she never thought she'd have to experience. But experience it she had, along with the humiliation of once again being the biggest failure in the Lockwood family, and her parents—God love them—pointing it out to her, followed by her brother's condolences, and her sister's placating sympathies. Yes, the last thing she should be doing was trying to make her life sound sexy to a married man with a family of his own.

Guilt lashed at her.

Good grief, I'm pathetic.

Brody cleared his throat. Sasha looked at her, waiting...

"So," Charles said, "Aunt Randi is an art teacher and she's doing a master's in Creative Story Telling Through Pictures and Words." He paused, his grin stretching wider. A conspirator's grin through and through. "Or something like that."

Heat flooded her cheeks. "I don't think he cares."

"No, no." Brody held up a hand. "I do. If only Tinder was this informative."

Randi blinked. Tinder? Surely he couldn't be on Tinder? Maybe she needed to un-delete the app on her phone.

Really, Miranda? Really?

Brody grinned. "Kidding. Sorry. I have a shocking sense of humor, apparently. Or at least, one that doesn't translate that well over here."

"I love your sense of humor, Daddy." Sasha beamed up at him.

"That you do, kiddo." He tapped her adorable nose. "Your sister, however…"

Sister? Two little girls? Tinder, and daughters and…

There's still a mother somewhere in the picture. Even if they're no longer together, do I really want to get involved with someone who has that kind of…of…baggage?

"So, what's your master's in?"

She drew a deep breath, her pulse rapid. Damn it, maybe she should just ask him outright where his ex was.

"Creative Narrative Through Visual Image and Written Word." She really needed to regroup. And find her brain. "Which of course, is going to land me an awesome promotion and a well-deserved raise at work that will totally erase my student loan within a month." She rolled her eyes. "I wish."

Brody chuckled. "Ah yes, the joys of higher educations. Know that feeling. Both my wife and I had student loans coming out our…" He stopped. Flicked his daughter a quick look. "Coming out our noses."

Sasha giggled up at Randi. "Daddy almost said *arse*." The Australian pronunciation of the word sounded weirdly perfect mixed in with her normal speech.

"All right, all right, maniac." Brody swung her hand in a gentle arc. "That's enough of that."

"Arse, arse, arse," Sasha sing-songed, devilish light dancing in her eyes.

"Sasha," Brody intoned, frown promising punishment.

It was obviously all an act. The love radiating from Brody for his daughter could power the entire West Coast.

Sasha grinned up at him. "*Ass.* Is that better?"

He nodded. "Bloody oath, love."

Randi couldn't help but laugh, even as she fought back a groan. God, was it possible to fall in love at first sight? Or in this case, at first water-slide-stair climb?

Good grief. Fall in love with a hot married Aussie with two daughters only six months after being dumped? So I have *become a cliché. And a masochist.*

"Where's your wife now?" Chuck asked, flicking Randi a quick look. "She not a fan of water slides?"

A still quiet fell over Brody. At his side, Sasha grew equally calm. "It's just us now," he said, giving his daughter a gentle tap under her chin with his fingers. "Me, Sasha, and Will, my elder. Bridget passed away two years ago."

Oh man.

Ice sheared through Randi's chest. God, and here she'd been wanting him to say he was divorced a few moments ago.

"Ahh, crap, dude," Chuck muttered behind her. Consternation turned the words to a strangled apology. "I'm sorry."

Brody raised his head, his smile warm. "No worries, mate. Honest. We're all good."

Sasha gave Randi and Chuck a nod. "Mommy is with the angels. Probably telling them to make their beds."

Randi's heart clenched. A lump the size of the Rock of Gibraltar filled her throat. She gave the little girl a wobbly smile. "And to wash their hands before eating?"

Sasha answered with a cheeky smile, and yet there was no denying the pain behind the curled lips. "Yep."

"So who's Alicia?" Chuck asked. Just like that. She was going to kill him later.

"My sister-in-law," Brody answered, his gaze holding Randi's for a second before he let out a dry grunt of a laugh and shrugged at Chuck. "She's all right. Bit uptight sometimes."

"Sister-in-law." Chuck grinned at Randi. "Cool. Cool, cool."

Brody cleared his throat. "We're almost at the top. We should figure out how we're going to do this."

Dinner at Denny's, followed by the latest Pixar movie at the closest AMC with a bucket of popcorn between us.

The ridiculous notion flashed through Randi's head in a rush of glorious Technicolor images and Hallmark-cheese, at once terrifying and way too wonderful and appealing for words.

Holy crap, what the hell am I thinking? What kind of person am I?

"Er…" she croaked, staring—no, gaping—up at Brody.

"I know I know!" Sasha jumped up and down between them, damp strawberry-blond curls bouncing around her cherub face. "I'll sit in front of Randi, Randi can sit in front of you, Daddy, and Chuck can sit behind you."

Chuck burst out laughing. "I think the limit is three to a group." He winked at Randi and then gave Brody a grin. "Damn it."

Randi swallowed.

"Poo bum," Sasha protested before beaming up at Brody. "Just us three then. It can be like a huggy train."

A less-than-wholesome image of Brody's legs hugging her hips replaced the image of euphoric domesticity in Randi's head and, before she could stop herself, she dropped her gaze. Of course, it landed on his crotch.

For God's sake, Miranda, stop it. Be a grown-up.

"And I'll shoot down all by myself after, laughing my a— butt off." Chuck smirked.

Brody shuffled his feet. "Maybe Randi might not feel comfortable sitting between my…"

He trailed off. Heat flooded Randi's cheeks.

Sasha frowned. "Sitting between your what, Daddy?"

He cleared his throat and flicked Randi a glance.

It was all she could do not to groan.

Yeah, definitely too long since she'd had any kind of social or sexual life. Her body was getting out of hand.

Sasha looked at both of them. "It'll be little, big, bigger!" she declared, pride in her voice as she decided whatever he was going to say in his sexy Aussie accent wasn't worth the wait. "Perfect!"

An enigmatic expression filled Brody's face. Did he *want* her sitting between his spread thighs?

Goddamn it, a water slide was never meant to be this traumatic.

"Maybe you should ask Randi if that's okay, Sasha."

Wide, innocent blue eyes swung up to her. "Is that okay, Randi?"

Chuck laughed behind her. "Of course it's okay."

She wanted to elbow her nephew in the stomach. Instead, she found herself trapped by Brody's stare.

A complicated monologue was taking place in his eyes, one she wished like hell she could translate.

Was he regretting going on the slide with her again? Was it even *possible* to replicate the unexpected joy of their first time going down together? Was he going to get in trouble with the woman—what was her name? Alicia? And just *who* was Alicia to him anyway? His sister-in-law? Is that what he'd said? Then what was with all the Tinder jokes?

The knot in Randi's belly twisted.

"You don't have—" she began.

"Let's do it."

Sasha let out a whooping *yay*, jumping up and down. Chuck whacked Randi on the back, his laugh altogether too knowing for a fifteen-year-old.

Randi gave Brody a sheepish smile. "Looks like we have a plan."

Brody's jaw bunched again. "Looks like we do."

"Next!"

They both startled at the slide attendant's cracked-voice shout.

Sasha grabbed Randi's hand, her grip stronger than expected, and with another jubilant cry of delight, yanked Randi forward. "Come on!"

There was no time to argue. Or think about what was going on.

One second Randi was staring up into the eyes of the sexiest guy she'd ever met, a man with two daughters and a heart-wrenching history, the next she was being towed with gusto up to the mouth of the slide.

Randi couldn't help but laugh. What the hell? One more moment of lunacy. What with the way Alicia was glaring at her earlier, she would no doubt take Brody away the second they were out of the water anyway.

She squeezed Sasha's hand. "Let's do this."

Sasha *yay*ed again, even as Randi prepared herself for what was to come. How on earth she was going to survive Brody wrapping his almost bare legs around her hips was beyond her.

Oh. Boy.

Time—and the pimple-faced slide attendant—didn't allow Brody to retreat or rethink what he was doing.

Neither did Randi's nephew, a boy who seemed to be quite adept at matchmaking machinations.

With a smirk, Charles "Randi calls me Chuckles" slapped Brody on the shoulder and told him to hurry the hell up and get on the slide at the exact same moment the pimple-faced slide attendant did.

In the space of four canon-shot heartbeats, Brody took in the grinning teenager and the growing queue behind him. He saw the upturned faces of his daughter and Randi, with their respective excited and apprehensive expressions, and then he was gripping the support bars on either side of the slide's mouth and swinging his legs either side of Randi's hips.

Every blood cell in his veins charged south.

He heard Sasha laugh with joy, heard Randi let out a gasp, and then the slide attendant's palm slammed into the center of his back, and the world became a wet blur.

They rocketed down the twisting tube in a laughing train of limbs and laughter.

Every time they banked up the walls of the slide to take a bend, Brody's thighs instinctually tightened on Randi's hips, and his hands circled her waist.

Every time *that* happened, every time his palms slid over her smooth, wet flesh, base male desire flooded his body.

Hell. Hell. Think of something else. Think of—

Nope. He was damn near wrapped around the wet, semi-naked body of a gorgeous woman with gorgeous curves and a gorgeous smile whose very laugh made his heart beat faster. How *could* he think of anything else?

The faster they slid down the slide, the hotter and more flustered he became, and the more he tried to distance himself from Randi.

Of course, it was physically impossible. He may have spent most of his time during high school physics trying to figure out how to get into Shellie Anderson's pants—unsuccessfully, as it turned out—but he knew enough about gravity, velocity, and speed-to-weight ratio to know a 202-pound Australian male was incapable of going backward up a waterslide no matter how much he wished he could.

It didn't help that the g-forces on their bodies meant Randi kept leaning back into him.

Shit, there went his hands again, slipping up her wet rib cage. His fingers came close to brushing the swell of her incredible breasts, and he forgot how to breathe.

Bloody hell, I'm in trouble.

When he should have been totally submerged in the fun of the slide, in the sheer joy of his daughter's squeals, he was thinking about how amazing it would be to slowly peel Randi's bikini—

The slide vanished.

Replaced by the sensation of soaring through nothingness for a split second, a nothingness filled with Sasha's and Randi's happy screams.

And then, with his legs still wrapped around Randi's hips and his hands still precariously close to her breasts, all three of them hit the water of the pool.

A rush of cold enveloped him, arse first, then his balls, his cock, and the rest of him.

Somewhere between breaking the surface and being completely submerged, his brain—ever helpful—registered his hands had slipped up over the swell of Randi's breasts and skimmed their perfect round form as he plummeted into the water.

Heat flooded his body, rivaling the cool water surrounding him and, with an awkwardness he'd not possessed since he was a teenage boy still growing into his lanky limbs and size-thirteen feet, he lurched upward and backward.

As fast and as far from Randi and her amazing curves as the water would allow.

Which wasn't far or fast enough.

In a mess of thrashing arms and legs, their bodies collided. His inner thighs slid against her hips, her thighs. Her elbow connected with the plane of his stomach just below his navel, and her shoulder rubbed up the length of his inner arm.

The fingers of his right hand tangled in the floating curtain of her hair.

Fuck a fucking duck.

He burst up through the surface of the pool, towing Randi with him.

Somewhere nearby, muffled by the water in his ears, Sasha's delighted cries danced on the air.

"Again, Daddy! Again!"

Instinctually, he went to swipe away the drops of water dribbling into his eyes, and proceeded to yank Randi—by her hair—smack-bam into his chest.

Wet lush, soft breasts mashed against him.

Her belly followed, the tiny circle of her belly button ring a wicked friction against his lower abs that his brain had no right registering in the ludicrousness of the situation.

But it did. Registered. Noted. Catalogued away for future sexual torment.

Staggering back a step, Brody could only groan as his heel slipped on the pool's bottom. Could only grab on to Randi tighter with his free hand as he began to tumble backward, his right hand still knotted in the wet strands of her hair.

Shit. Her arse.

Of course, it would be her arse he blindly grabbed. Her gorgeous, round arse that yielded to his reflexive grip in the exact way a woman's arse should.

Once again, his brain catalogued the sensation. Randi's backside was that exquisite combination of toned muscle and padding that a man could spend a lifetime squeezing and grabbing and kneading.

Ah, fuck no. He did *not* need an erection right now. He did not—

He bit down, hard, on the inside of his mouth.

Pain sheared through him. And still, all the blood in his veins surged south.

What the fuck? What the—

Gravity snatched at both of them. He fell back into the water, Randi flat against him, her bare stomach rubbing against a growing bulge no one could miss no matter how chaotic the situation.

In the space of ten minutes, the stunning American he'd

known for hardly any time at all had experienced his hands on her boobs and his semi on her belly.

Way to make a first impression, dick—

Water enveloped his head, poured into his nose.

Underwater. They were both completely underwater.

They were both—

Warm lips found his.

A bold tongue stroked at the slight opening of his mouth, and without thought or hesitation, Brody surrendered to the need surging through him and kissed her back.

Even as he planted his feet on the pool's floor, tightened his grip on her arse, and propelled them both upward with a powerful thrust of his legs.

They broke the surface kissing, burst from the cool embrace of the water into the bright, humid afternoon fucking each other's mouths with their tongues.

CHAPTER THREE

"D addy?"

Sasha's shocked gasp yanked Randi away from the most incredible kiss of her life.

Guilt flooded through the desire turning her blood hot and her breath shallow.

Holy crap, I kissed him.

And Brody had kissed her back, and for wild seconds, nothing had mattered except his tongue sliding against hers. Nothing had *existed* except that kiss and his hard length rubbing against her stomach and his hard fingers squeezing her ass and his fist balled in her hair.

Nothing. Not even the splash and wake of Chuck's arrival in the pool.

Nothing.

Until Sasha's cry.

Spinning to face Brody's daughter, Randi opened her mouth.

And closed it again.

What did she say?

The little girl stared up at her, eyes wide, mouth a perfect *O*.

Behind her, Chuck cleared his throat. "Whoa…" Awed disbelief cut through the impressed approval of her nephew's exclamation.

Randi gaped some more at Brody's daughter. "Sasha…" The name was barely more than a croak. "I didn't—"

"*Yay!*" Strawberry-blond curls bounced around Sasha's wet cherub cheeks as she leaped up and down in the water, a smile splitting her face. "You and Daddy kissed! Wait till I tell Will!"

Before Randi could move—or process Sasha's reaction—the little girl burst into laughing *yays* again.

Randi blinked. *Okay, was not expecting that.*

Shooting a look at the silent Australian standing but a few feet away, she swallowed. The memory of his erection rubbing at her stomach taunted her, and she had to stop from dropping her stare to his groin.

Loud kissing noises filled the air, punctuated by delighted little-girl giggles and more kissing noises.

Randi forced her attention on Brody's face.

Motionless, he watched his daughter with an array of expressions Randi couldn't decipher flickering across his face.

"Okay, okay, maniac." He chuckled—finally—and moved his hands in the universally recognized parental gesture for *time to settle down.* "That's enough."

Randi swallowed again. Her stomach knotted and churned and generally behaved like she was about to sit her SATs all over again.

Oh God, I kissed him. And he kissed me back.

Hard. Fast. And hungry. And it was so goddamn good she wanted to do it a—

Snap out of it.

"I'm sorry." The apology burst from her with the same level of premeditation and contemplation as her earlier possession of Brody's lips—zero. "I'm really sorry, I didn't mean to—"

"Daddy's got a girlfriend," Sasha sing-songed, splashing

toward her father in the water, her smile now an open grin of pure mischief. "Daddy's got a girlfriend."

"Whoa," Chuck repeated behind Randi. This time, there was less disbelief and more admiration in her nephew's voice. "Way to go, Aunty R."

"I really didn't mean to kiss him," Randi continued, determined to bring the situation back under control.

Sasha froze in the water, tiny fists on her hips, an indignant frown knitting her eyebrows. "Didn't you *like* kissing Daddy?"

"It was the best kiss of my—"

She slapped her palm to her mouth. Far too late, if Chuck's delighted laugh told her anything.

Incapable of any other action, Randi slid her gaze to Brody.

Their stares met. Held.

Randi's stomach churned some more, this time, however, it had nothing to do with the guilt and disbelief of her actions, and everything to do with the raw desire she saw in Brody's eyes.

Desire she understood completely.

If it weren't for the fact that they stood in the middle of a public pool with dozens of people around them, not to mention Brody's adorable, innocent daughter, she would throw herself at him this very second and mount him like a—

"What the *hell* is going on?"

Randi flinched. The woman from earlier once again stood at the side of the pool. The woman with the haughty glare, disdainful inspections, and disheartening lack of cellulite.

That haughty glare was fixed firmly on Brody, who now—Randi noticed—was hitching Sasha up out of the water and onto his hip.

"Did you see?" Sasha wriggled about, wrapping her tiny arms around Brody's neck and swinging her legs back and forth next to his torso. "Daddy and Randi kissed." To emphasize the observation, she made fresh kissing noises.

Kissing noises Brody silenced by tickling her ribs, turning them into a fit of hysterical laughter.

"No, Daddy! No!"

"So now you're kissing her, Brody?" Alicia arched an eyebrow shaped to an arc so sharp it could be used to cut wheat. "Not just 'going down' with her?"

Chuck—ever the debauched teenager, despite his advanced intellect—burst out laughing behind Randi.

Alicia turned the power of her eyebrow on him.

He silenced his chortles with his hand and a turn of his head.

Randi regarded the woman. Something about the way Alicia ran a slow inspection over her suggested Brody's sister-in-law certainly didn't see him in a very sisterly way. If ever she'd seen a direct challenge in a woman's eyes before, it was now.

Prickling heat razed up Randi's spine and crept over her scalp.

She drew a slow breath. She didn't intimidate easily. What high school teacher did? But this woman…

"What I'm *doing*," Brody answered, an enigmatic calm to his voice, "is none of *your* business, Alicia."

Alicia crossed her arms beneath her breasts. For a surreal moment, it dawned on Randi that *both* of Alicia's boobs would probably fill one of Randi's cups.

"I think it is my business, Brody. Given you've just made a total fool of yourself in front of Sasha with a complete stranger." Alicia snapped her stare to Randi. "Unless *Randi* here isn't a stranger. Unless this whole trip to the water park was just a cover so you could meet up. And here I was thinking you were still in mourning—"

"Enough."

Brody's flat command seemed to echo across the water. A weird silence claimed everyone around them.

Heart racing, throat tight, Randi stared at him.

Rage broiled in his eyes. "That's enough, Alicia."

On his hip, Sasha squirmed. "What's wrong with Aunty Alicia, Daddy?"

Damp fingers hooked around Randi's upper arm, and she jumped, jerking about to find Chuck almost crouching behind her. Uncertainty etched his young face. "Think we should go, Aunty R."

Her stomach knotting, she nodded. As incredible as the kiss was—and holy crap, was it incredible—she didn't want to expose her nephew to this kind of dispute between strangers. Even if one of the strangers had turned her core to a molten puddle.

Shooting Brody a quick glance, she burned his gorgeous looks into her memory, thankful he was still focused on Aunty Alicia.

She was about to turn away when Sasha's gaze connected with hers.

The little girl, still wrapped around her father's hip and torso, gave her a small smile. A melancholy smile, one that very clearly said she didn't want Randi to go.

It broke Randi's heart.

Stay. Stay for her. And…

"Aunty R?"

At the tug on her hand—Damn, how stressed was Chuck to actually take her hand in public?—Randi offered Sasha an equally sad smile and then hurried from the pool.

A part of her, a powerful part she couldn't name, told her to go back. To tell Alicia to stick her indignation up her nose, to grin at Sasha, tweak her nose, and then kiss Brody with such passion his knees gave out.

Damn it. Why shouldn't I?

What stopped her were Chuck and Sasha. It was all well and good to piss off a condescending woman she'd never met before, but she didn't want to upset her nephew or traumatize Brody's little girl with the melodramatic machinations of adults.

That wasn't fair to either of them.

Reaching the side of the pool, she forced herself not to look over her shoulder at where Brody and his daughter no doubt still were. Instead, she dragged her hands through the wet strands of her hair and watched Chuck launch himself out of the water and up onto the pool's edge.

The sound of splashing behind her sent a ribbon of nerves and hope through her.

Damn it, she wanted Brody to come after her.

After just one kiss she was damn near aching for him to come after her.

To grab her arm, swing her about and silence her startled gasp with a bone-melting—

"Good grief, woman," she muttered, shaking her head and planting her palms on the pool's edge. "Get a—"

A strong hand wrapped around her wrist, and before she could say anything more, someone spun her around.

***

This is bloody lunacy, mate. Lunacy.

The mental reproach had no effect on the raw desire controlling Brody's body. And his mind.

There was no other way to describe what he was doing but acting on instinct, and at this very moment in time, his instinct was telling him to kiss Randi again. To kiss the hell out of her.

A life of living in the absolute moment had never led him astray. In all his forty-two years, never once had he second-guessed any decision he'd made, no matter what.

And now Brody's gut instinct was telling him not to let Randi—a woman he'd known for a bugger-all amount of time—get away.

His gut, his very soul, was telling him there was something about her. Something…right.

Brody Thorton always listened to his gut.

Or was it his dick? It had been two years, after all. Two years without—

No. He never listened to his dick. It was his gut.

His gut was telling him to kiss her. So he did.

And as before, the moment his lips touched hers, a charge of elemental electricity shot through him, detonating a bloom of warmth in his very soul. He hadn't experienced a reaction like that since the first time he kissed Bridget.

Right. So right…

On his shoulders, Sasha giggled out an *eew* sound.

Brody smiled against Randi's lips. He didn't stop kissing her, though. There was nothing porn-film about the kiss, no matter how deeply he wanted to explore Randi's mouth with his tongue. That would come later. When his youngest wasn't perched on his shoulders. For this moment, Brody needed to feel Randi's lips move against his.

To discover if the kiss they'd shared earlier, one far more frenzied and hungry, was a one-off.

To discover if, for the first time since Bridget passed away, another woman had the ability to touch his heart and soul.

Sasha wriggled on his shoulders a heartbeat before Randi pulled away from him.

The American woman's gaze connected with his for a second, an indefinable emotion in her light-blue eyes, and then she was smiling up at Sasha. "Was that you tapping the top of my head, little one?"

Sasha squirmed about with such enthusiastic glee, Brody had to quickly grab her ankles to stop her tumbling off his shoulders. She giggled again, the sound a delightful mix of shy mischief. "Yes."

Brody couldn't help but smile. It seemed he wasn't the only one enchanted with Randi.

Enchanted? Is that the term you're going with?

It was. For the moment.

"Would you like to have dinner with me?"

The request passed his lips without hesitation. Surprisingly, his heart thumped faster in his chest with each word uttered.

Randi caught her bottom lip with her teeth, an action he found thoroughly sexy. "Dinner?"

Behind him, on the opposite edge of the pool, he could feel his sister-in-law's glare drilling into his back. Alicia had never approved of her younger sister marrying an Australian graphic artist, a fact Brody found curious given her own parents were heavily entrenched in the U.S. art scene and Bridget owned an art gallery in San Diego. Alicia had made it clear from the start she didn't think Brody was good enough for Bridget.

Bridget had thought the whole thing hilarious, telling Brody with a laugh and a smile Alicia was just jealous she was happy. Brody had thought the whole thing ridiculous. Thankfully, Alicia lived on the East Coast, on the opposite side of the country.

Since Bridget's death, however, Alicia had taken it upon herself to "fill the void" in his daughters' lives. She'd moved to San Diego, acting as a mother figure whenever she could, pointing out Brody's shortcomings as a father with equal regularity. This "family" outing she'd organized was a classic example. Since arriving at his house that morning, Alicia had criticized the food he served his girls for breakfast and the snacks and lunch he'd packed to bring with them. If he heard one more "Vegemite is vile and disgusting and not fit for human consumption," he feared he'd be responsible for the destruction of the U.S./Australian relationship.

He let his smile curl wider, nodding at Randi. "Dinner," he repeated. "With me."

On his shoulders, Sasha giggled.

Randi gnawed on her lip some more. Behind her, standing on the pool's wet edge still waiting for her to climb out of the water, her nephew grinned. "Of course she will."

"Chuck!" Randi spun to face him.

Her fleet-footed nephew skipped backward as she swiped a hand at him.

Sasha giggled again.

"I'm outta here," Charles laughed. "See you around, Brody."

With another grin at Brody and a wink at Randi, he took off in a loping gait particular only to teenage boys.

Brody moved his gaze to the back of Randi's head. "So? Is he right? Will he see me around?"

For a moment, she didn't move.

He drew a slow breath. His head roared. What if she said no? What if his gut was—for the first time—completely misguided?

Randi turned back to face him. Her teeth were no longer worrying her bottom lip. Instead, she flicked Sasha a quick look before meeting his stare. "Depends," she said.

Brody swallowed. "On what?"

"On dinner."

Warmth flooded through him.

"And what you think of the Oakland Raiders."

Brody laughed. "If I say I don't think they're as good as the Sydney Swans, do I still stand a chance?"

Randi's lips curled, and a devilish light glinted in her eyes. "With me, yes. With Chuckles? I can't promise anything."

Heart pounding fast, Brody reached for Randi's hand, threaded his fingers through hers, and gave her a gentle tug toward him. The water lapped around his hips. Her thighs brushed his beneath the surface. On his shoulders, Sasha wrapped her arms around the top of his head.

"In that case, they're *definitely* not as good as the Sydney Swans."

Randi gazed up at him, the hint of a dimple in her right cheek teasing him. "Who are the Sydney Swans?"

"They're a—"

She kissed him. A quick brush of her lips on his.

Just that. But it was enough to steal his train of thought. And his breath.

"Tell me over dinner," she said, that mischievous light in her eyes again.

"Tell you what over dinner?" he murmured.

"Cheer, cheer the red and the white!" Sasha burst into the Sydney Swans' official football song above his head, wriggling on his shoulders once more. *"Honor their name by day and by night!"*

Randi laughed.

Brody chuckled. "Okay, okay, maniac." He gave his daughter a gentle jiggle on high. "The whole world knows you're a Swans fan."

Sasha hugged his head tighter. "Go the Swans."

With another chuckle, he gave Randi an apologetic smile. "What can I say? She may be a born and bred Yank, but she's an Aussie at heart."

Randi grinned, reaching out to squeeze Sasha's toes as she did so. "And an utterly adorable one."

"Ah, you haven't heard her sing the 'Star-Spangled Banner' to the Australian national anthem yet."

On Brody's shoulders, Sasha started singing the American national anthem to the tune of the Australian one. At the top of her lungs. Off key.

Randi's mouth fell open.

"And on that note"—Brody reached above his head, snared his giggling daughter around her tiny waist, and pulled her down into an inverted bear-hug—"we're going. Before we're thrown out of the park for public nuisance. Or even worse, Will sees us and dies of embarrassment." His elder daughter could be such a teenager sometimes, and he had no clue how to deal with it.

Hauling Sasha back up so she balanced on his right shoulder like she was flying, he took a step backward in the pool. "Can I call you later? Or text you?"

Randi nodded.

He continued backward through the water, watching her. "What's your number?"

She frowned. "My phone number?"

"Yep."

She gave it to him.

He cast Sasha a contemplative inspection. "You got that?"

Sasha, fully in adorable cherub mode, repeated it—also to the tune of the Australian national anthem.

Randi laughed.

"You're going to scare her, Sash," he chided with a melodramatic sigh.

"Scared," Randi called, her lips twitching, "is not the word that comes to mind right now."

CHAPTER FOUR

"Will?" Hell, was that girl ever getting out of the bathroom? "Will, we're going to be late."

Where are my keys? And my phone? "Maniac, do you know where my keys are?"

Sasha shook her head and continued to munch the peanut butter and banana sandwich she'd insisted on having for breakfast. "Fruit bowl?"

"Hurry up, Will!" Nope, no sign of his keys in the fruit bowl. Why would there be?

Because when you got home last night you'd been too busy thinking about Randi to put them where they were meant to be?

"Can you go get your sister out of the bathroom, please?"

Taking another bite of her sandwich, Sasha rolled off the kitchen counter and ran from the room. "Willow! Get out of the bathroom now!"

He chuckled—bloody hell, she had a bellow on her—and returned to his search for his keys.

He shouldn't have spent most of the night thinking about Randi, and guilt was beginning to take great big bloody bites out of his conscience. That and the fact he'd almost sent her a text just before midnight suggesting a possible coffee date. It was tamer than the original text he'd drafted. *That* one had come very close to falling into the sexting category of electronic communication. The first finger of guilt had traced up his spine as he'd reread *that* text. Thank bloody God he'd deleted it. And the coffee-date proposal.

He was a forty-two-year old dad. Sexting shouldn't be a part of his playbook.

Hell, he shouldn't even *have* a playbook.

He still wanted to send her that coffee-date text, though. Or maybe ask her out for a drink.

"Drink." He rolled his eyes and shook his head. "That's right, you idiot."

He pivoted on his heel and yanked open the fridge.

His keys sat on the top shelf, next to the bottle of milk.

He'd grabbed himself a drink last night when they'd all arrived home. The argument with Alicia about the *pool incident* before leaving the park hadn't helped the headache he'd had brewing, nor had the follow-up argument in the parking lot about it being time for them to have an *adult conversation* over dinner to sort out his life.

The last thing he wanted or needed was a lecture from her.

The drive home had been equally fun. He'd lectured Willow on not having fun at the water park, she'd ignored him, and Sasha had pestered him—again—about getting a puppy. He'd walked into the house tired and distracted, crossed to the fridge and sculled who knows how much milk straight from the bottle.

Willow had voiced her disgust and disappeared to her room. Sasha had *eew*ed at him and continued her arguments for why they needed a dog.

Apparently, he'd tossed his keys into the fridge along with the milk.

Christ, he needed to get his life in order.

"Willow says she's coming." Sasha thundered into the room

and scrambled back up onto the kitchen counter. "Can I have a cookie?"

"You mean a bickie."

Crap, he really was distracted if he was reacting to Americanisms.

Fresh guilt rushed through him and, plucking his keys from the fridge, he let out a sigh. "Sorry, hon."

She weighed him up, blue eyes far too knowing for a six-year-old. "That's okay, Daddy. *No worries.*"

He chuckled at her emphasized Aussieism.

She grinned. "So? Can I have a cookie?"

Willow walked in, and for a second, it hurt too much to breathe.

Oh God, why does she have to look so much like Bridget?

"We going?" Willow arched a dark-blond eyebrow.

Chest tight, he shoved his keys into his pocket. "Not until you have some breakfast." He nodded toward the plate of Vegemite toast on the counter beside Sasha. "I made your favorite."

Willow regarded the toast. "I'm not hungry."

Great. "Will—"

"Can we go?" She grabbed *her* phone from the dock next to the toaster and headed for the door.

"Let's go." Sasha leaped to the floor and ran after her.

Brody closed his eyes and pinched the bridge of his nose. "Pick your battles, Thorton. Pick your battles."

Pulling in a slow breath, he followed, snatching up Sasha's school bag from beside the door leading into the garage. He'd come back and locate his phone after the meeting with Willow's teacher. It was likely he'd need the time-out before heading to work anyway.

Sasha smiled at him from the back seat as he climbed behind the wheel of his Nissan SUV. "Ready?"

She nodded.

"Will?"

Willow didn't lift her attention from her phone. Of course.

"Hey." He tapped the side of her thigh with the back of his hand. "Want me to kick this Miss Lockwood's arse for you?"

Nope. No smile. Just a rolling of eyes so like her mum's.

"Or would she kick my arse?" Keep going. That's all he could do. "She's new to the school, right? Only been there for the term? You said she's a...how did you describe her? A crazy old spinster? She must be scary."

Willow sighed, thumbs tapping out something on her phone.

You've got two choices here, Thorton. Keep poking the surly teenager, or reverse out of the garage.

He reversed out of the garage.

"Daddy's going to kick arse. Daddy's going to kick arse," Sasha sang from the back.

Willow twisted around in her seat. "Shut up, Sash."

"Hey." He ground his teeth. "That's enough."

Sasha blew a raspberry at Willow.

"The pair of you." Bloody hell, maybe he should just drive to the beach and force a yoga session on them all. That's what Bridget used to do when either Willow or Sasha were out of sorts. Yoga, meditation, followed by a trip to the ice cream parlor.

Of course, him doing yoga was as successful as a roo shearing sheep. Still, better to make a fool of himself on a public beach and hear his daughters laugh than have it all continue the way it was.

If it weren't for the old duck trying to make Willow's life hell because she wouldn't return to the school's track team, he'd head straight for Mission Beach right now.

"Can I go home with Lyle today?"

He frowned at Willow's question. "Who's Lyle?"

"A friend."

Returning his attention to the road, he ground his teeth again. "No."

"But it's okay for you to kiss a complete stranger in the pool while Sash is on your shoulders? Real fair, Dad. And classy."

Fuck. The next time he saw his sister-in-law, he was having a serious word with her.

"Willow."

She turned her back to him, thumbs once again tapping on her phone.

"Willow."

She twisted farther away from him.

"I like Randi, Daddy," Sasha—perfectly indifferent to the moment—said. "I don't mind you kissing her."

A cold finger of guilt traced up his spine. "Thanks, maniac."

Willow turned and glared over the seat at Sasha. "Seriously? What do you know? You're six."

Another raspberry came from the back.

The drop-off zone for Sasha's school arrived before he could put his poor refereeing skills to use again.

Both Willow and Sasha opened their doors. "Love you, Daddy," Sasha said as she almost leaped from the back seat.

He frowned at Willow even as the car behind honked at him. "What are you doing?"

"I'll walk from here." She climbed out of the SUV and closed the door.

The car behind honked again.

Brody's gut clenched, and then he sighed as Willow lowered herself into a crouch, encouraging Sasha to jump up from the footpath and onto her back.

Willow may be angry with him, with life, but she loved Sasha. When it came to big sisters, Willow did well.

Now if only he could do well as a dad.

Since Bridget's death, he'd questioned his ability to do so.

Today's effort on that front was taking on old Miss Lockwood.

"Shouldn't be too tricky," he muttered, watching Willow piggyback Sasha up the path into Sasha's school.

The car behind honked a third time.

"Yeah, yeah, mate." He put his SUV into drive and grinned into the rearview mirror. "Hold your bloody horses."

Two blocks later, he arrived at Willow's school. He didn't think about kissing Randi in the pool once.

Okay, maybe once.

More like twice.

"Bloody hell, Thorton." He navigated into an empty parking space, guilt taking great big chunks out of him. "Get your head in the game."

He'd call Randi later tonight and somehow let her know they weren't going to…to…

"Jesus, you can't even say it, let alone—"

He killed the Nissan's engine, flung open his door, and climbed out. After the meeting he'd go home, get his phone, and call Singo. It had been a while since he caught up with the other Aussie. Maybe him, Singo, and Nate Young—the third Aussie expat he knew living here in San Diego—could hit the Irish pub later that afternoon and catch up over a beer. He needed a blast of home to clear his head, and the other two Aussies would do the trick.

"Beer with the mates and some footy on the telly." He locked the SUV's door, shoved his keys into his pocket, and headed for the school. "That's what a bloke needs."

Despite detailed directions from the woman in the front office when he signed the visitor register, it took him longer to find Miss Lockwood's room than it should have. American schools were so different from Australian ones, and even after all these years living in the States, the simple fact he was walking through one—with its rows of student lockers, banners about proms and freshman dances, and pep rallies— gave the small rural Aussie boy inside him a buzz.

His family back in Australia thought he was insane for

staying in San Diego after Bridget's death, but the city was just as much his home now as Oz.

And if you can't get your little family sorted out, Oz is exactly where we will all be headed.

Stopping, he rubbed at the back of his neck. Bloody hell, hadn't he already walked down this corridor? It looked familiar. Maybe he needed to stop one of the students and ask.

He frowned at the doors lining the corridor. "Ahh, there it is."

Room 42.

Sucking in a deep breath, he shook out his shoulders and arms, rolled his neck, and wriggled his fingers.

If the old duck inside was anything like his teachers back home, the next ten minutes or so were going to be—

"Brody?"

The familiar female voice caressed his senses.

He turned, breath tight in his throat.

Randi stood but a few feet away, staring at him like an extra head was sprouting from his shoulders. She looked gorgeous, dressed in baggy, faded denim dungarees over a black sleeveless shirt, with her black hair piled on the top of her head in a messy bun.

Jesus, how could she look even hotter than she did yesterday?

He swallowed and sucked in a deep breath.

A frown pulled at her dark eyebrows, and a little crease formed between them. That, too, was gorgeous. "What are you doing here?"

Cold fingers crawled up the back of his neck and over his scalp. *Shit. She probably thinks I'm a bloody stalker.*

"I'm not stalking you."

Okay, probably shouldn't have blurted that out quite so vehemently. Or loudly.

He threw the students around him a sheepish grin. "G'day. It's all good."

One tall boy with shoulders as wide as a doorframe scowled at him before flicking Randi a quick look. "Is everything okay?"

Randi smiled. Hell, he'd thought about that smile all night. It was as gorgeous as the crease between her eyebrows. "It's fine, Scott."

Scott narrowed his eyes at Brody. "Are you're sure?"

"I'm sure. See you period five."

Scott nodded. "Okay, Miss Lockwood. See you then."

Miss Lockwood?

Randi's last name was *Lockwood?*

The air turned hot, prickly. Willow's teacher was Miss Lockwood?

Fuck.

The old duck he was here to berate about upsetting his daughter was the woman he'd kissed at the water park, the woman he'd been trying to *not* have highly sexual fantasies about since meeting her.

Fuck a bloody duck.

Fuck, fuck, fuck.

———————✦———————

There were two possible reasons he was there at her work, outside her homeroom, at that exact time of the morning.

Option one was that he couldn't stop thinking about her and had tracked her down—both flattering and a little creepy.

Option two—that he was Willow Thorton's father—was just downright cruel.

Also cruel was how instantly her body reacted to the mere sight of him, fed, no doubt, by the countless hours she'd spent last night fantasizing about him. Hell, she'd even made little sketches of him on the sheet of paper she constantly had spread over her dining table, working from memory.

Her memory hadn't done him justice. He was just as tall, just as hot, just as…

Biting her lips, she shot the students spilling past them a nervous look. She was still considered the new teacher. She couldn't afford to be considered the weird one caught drooling over a student's father.

"Mr. Thorton?" *Please, please, please say no.*

Brody nodded, his expression unreadable.

Goddamn it.

"You're Willow's dad?"

Another nod. This time his jaw bunched, and his Adam's apple jerked up and down. It looked just as strong and sublime today—disappearing into the open collar of a black polo shirt —as it had yesterday melding into the broad expanse of his bare chest.

Now, why did I have to go and think about his bare chest? That's insane.

"And you"—Brody's eyes narrowed a fraction—"are the teacher giving her a hard time for not returning to the track team. Pushing her to do something she clearly doesn't want to do."

And the first shots are fired.

Lifting her chin—damn him if he thought she was going to crumble under all that Australian menace—she met his gaze. "Why don't we discuss this in my room, Mr. Thorton. The corridor is not the place for apologies."

His Adam's apple rolled up and down his throat again. "I'm happy to accept yours now, Miss Lockwood, so I can hurry up and get back to work."

She raised her eyebrows. "I'm not the one apologizing, Mr. Thorton."

Before he could say anything, she turned, opened the door, and strode into her art room.

He would follow, of course. He was a parent, here to discuss his child with her teacher. Nothing more.

The soft scrape of his footfalls on the room's concrete floor stretched her lips in a bleak smile.

Round One goes to me.

"Please close the door, Mr. Thorton," she threw over her shoulder as she crossed to her desk. Like most art teachers' desks, it was hidden under a mountain of various artworks, art equipment, and an ancient, paint-splattered iPod in an even more paint-splattered speaker dock. When it came to keeping a classroom of teenagers focused on their art, music soothed the savage beast.

Maybe she should hit play now? What playlist had she been listening to in yesterday's last class? Surely some Imagine Dragons would calm Brody down?

Depositing her satchel at her feet, she pulled out her chair and lowered herself into it.

"Pull up a seat."

The only seats in the room were the students' stools. He'd need to place one in front of her desk. It would give him a height advantage, but he'd also be awkward. No back, no arm rest, just a hard metal stool more suited to teenagers than a man who had to be at least six-foot four.

Six-foot four and built like a—

Metal scraped on concrete as Brody dragged a stool to her desk.

She sucked in a slow breath. She had to forget what had happened between them yesterday. Today, he was the father of the girl who'd called her a *fat cow*.

Unreadable blue eyes locked on her as Brody lowered himself onto the edge of the stool, legs slightly parted, thighs corded under khaki chinos. He crossed his arms over his chest, as if to emphasize she would never see it in all its exquisite glory again.

"Tell me why you think it's acceptable to harass Willow into returning to the athletics team," he demanded. "The track team."

Her stomach knotted. "I far from harassed Willow, Mr. Thorton."

You called him Brody yesterday. And in your head last night, while your vibrator was in top gear and your hand was bunching the sheet beneath you.

"I asked her if she'd consider rejoining the team. She set not only the school record, but the state record for long jump three years in a row. She's clearly talented in the event, and…"

She stopped. She couldn't very well say Dave Pascoe, her new principal, had *strongly* hinted her promotion to head of the arts department hung on her getting the middle school's previously impressive track achievements back. At least, that was the impression she'd gotten in her conversations with the man. Conversations about how much he *wanted* Willow back on the team, how much he *believed* having Willow back on the team was good for the school. Conversations that segued into how much Randi must be enjoying her time *at* the school, and how suited she was for a head teacher's position, especially if she *demonstrated* an ability to get the job done to a high level of satisfaction.

It didn't take her long to work out "high level of satisfaction" meant to his level of satisfaction. As principals go, he was definitely one of the more egocentric, domineering ones, that was for certain.

After the old track coach retired, and Dave had learned she was her previous school's track and field coach, he'd laid the job and the expectation of getting Willow back on the team at her feet and dangled the promotion under her nose, almost all in one breath.

"All I did," she continued, keeping her voice calm, "was ask her if she'd come along to a training session one afternoon, to see if she'd like to start jumping again."

And that's when Willow had lashed out, called her a *fat cow*, told her to stick her nose in someone else's business, and run from the room crying.

Not at all the reaction Randi had expected.

And of course, Dave had just happened to be walking past her room—or more likely lurking outside it—and before Randi knew what was going on, the parent/teacher interview had been arranged.

That was Friday. Today was Monday. In between the two days she and Brody had met, kissed, and talked about a possible dinner date.

Yeah, that's so not going to happen.

"That's all you did?" Brody's jaw bunched. A flinty steel turned his blue eyes cold.

What did I say? Why did she feel like she was in a situation with blinkers on?

"Willow's a natural, Brody."

His nostrils flared at her use of his first name.

"I watched footage of her jumping at the state championships two years ago. Her run-up is incredible, her launch is explosive, and she just flies through the air. Have you seen her compete? It's a loss of talent for her not to be jumping. Does she do any training at—?"

"Willow doesn't jump anymore." He straightened to his feet. His expression wasn't unreadable now; it was a mask of icy anger. "That's her decision, and I would ask you to bloody well back off."

He turned on his heel and strode to the door.

"Mr. Thorton?" Her heart smashed into her throat when he stopped, fingers wrapped around the doorknob. He didn't look back at her. "I'm sorry this hasn't gone well."

What am I doing?

"Please tell Sasha I had a great time yesterday."

Those broad, incredible shoulders of his slumped. A little. "I will," he said, head turning a fraction, voice deep and husky. "She did as well."

He opened the door and stepped through it. Gone.

"Well, that was a crash and burn of epic proportions," she

muttered, scrubbing at her face.

Clearly, Willow was never coming back to the team, and she—Randi—was never going to see Brody Thorton in any social situation again.

Which is good. More time to focus on my studies. And I really don't want to get involved with a father of a student.

She rubbed at her face again. "So now I just need to find another long jumper who can break the state record. Easy."

"What's easy?"

Looking up, she smiled at the blond vision in black swanning into her room. "Good morning, Miss Shelton. What are you doing over here in the creative side of school?"

Sydney Shelton, science teacher and the first member on staff to welcome Randi when she started, perched her black-linen encased butt on the edge of Randi's desk. "Was that really the Down Under Thunder I just saw leaving your room?"

"The what?"

"Brody Thorton?" Sydney picked up a lopsided, freshman-made pinch pot from the desk and turned it over in her hand. "Willow Thorton's dad. Delicious Australian widower. Top of every single female teacher's wish list."

Top of…

Wow. So I've kissed the object of desire of every single female teacher here? Yay. I may be failing at getting the track team up and running again, but at least I've achieved something.

Kissing a hot Aussie wasn't going to keep her employed, though. Or help the school reclaim its previous glory. Or get her that promotion. And if she landed the promotion, maybe the next time she spoke to her parents, her siblings, she wouldn't be the shameful failure of the family.

Maybe.

Putting on a relaxed smile, she nodded at Sydney. "It *was* Brody Thorton." Better to not tell Sydney about the weekend. Sydney was lovely and vivacious and the first real friend Randi had made since moving to San Diego, but she had no filter.

The last thing Randi needed was to become the subject of speculation and gossip. "I was hoping to convince him to encourage Willow to start competing in long jump again."

Sydney's eyebrows shot up. "Oh my God, you *went* there?"

"Went where?"

"There."

"I have no idea what you are talking about?"

Sydney grunted. "Pascoe didn't tell you, did he? Of course he didn't."

"Tell me what?" Oh boy, what was going on? Would it explain why Brody had been so angry?

"Willow's mother used to be her long jump coach. It was their thing. The woman had big plans for Willow. Huge plans. There was talk of endorsement contracts already being drawn up with Nike *and* Under Armour."

"Endorsement... Good grief, what happened?"

Sydney leaned a little closer. "Well, the rumor goes that Bridget—Willow's mom—and Brody were fighting over Willow's training regimen, about how he thought Bridget was pushing Willow too hard, when Bridget was in the car accident."

Randi blinked. Killed? In a car accident while fighting over Willow long jumping?

She went cold. *Shit. Shit, shit, shit.*

Sydney returned the student's pot to the desk and shook her head. "Why didn't you tell me you were going to ask Willow? I would have warned you it was a serious no-go zone."

Randi swiped at her mouth. Goddamn it, when had someone shoved half a desert in there? "You weren't here when Dave gave me the instruction. You were off on a field trip. Dave cornered me in the teacher's lounge and told me I was running out of time to get the track team happening, and he hinted with all the subtly of a sledgehammer my promotion was on the line."

No wonder the poor girl freaked out the way she did. If

LOVE AND OTHER RESPONSIBILITIES | 49

Sydney knew the backstory, why the hell didn't Dave?

"Oh, hon." Sydney chuckled as she straightened from the desk. "My heart is breaking for you. Pascoe is such a fan of power games. But on the upside, I guess this gives me a greater chance to sweep Mr. Oh-So-Yummy Oz off his feet. Less competition and all."

Something hot and prickly crawled over Randi's scalp. Jealousy? "You're kidding, right?"

Sydney's lips twitched. "Yes. I am. But seriously, did you *look* at him? He's every sexual fantasy a woman could have all wrapped up in one package."

And then some, especially when he's dripping wet and his skin is glistening in the sun and his bare chest and arms and legs are pressed to your—

Randi squirmed on her seat. "Don't you have a class next period?"

"I do. See you in the lounge later."

Alone again, Randi dropped her forehead onto the stack of student sketchbooks on her desk. Damn it, talk about messing up an already horrible situation. What should she do? Call Brody and apologize? Tell Dave to stick his expectations and look for a new job?

Someone cleared their throat in her room.

"I *know* I'm an idiot, Sydney," she muttered, rolling her forehead side to side on the sketchbooks. "Just leave me alone to wallow in misery for a while, please."

"I'm hoping," a deep male voice said, its Australian accent distinct and so goddamn sexy, "you'd consider coming to dinner at my place tonight?"

She jerked her head up.

Brody stood on the other side of her desk, his expression impossible to read.

"I mean *our* place." His Adam's apple jerked up and down his throat. "Would you come to dinner at our place tonight? With me and my girls? Please?"

CHAPTER FIVE

"You did what?"

Brody rubbed the back of his neck as he bumped the fridge closed with his hip. "I just asked the teacher Will is warring with here for dinner. Tonight."

Laughter spilled from his phone, loud and raucous enough he had to pull it away from his ear for a second to save his eardrum. "Yeah, thanks for the pep talk, Singo."

Adam Singleton laughed again, not as loud this time. "Mate, I've always said you're as mad as a cut snake."

"And I've always said you're as ugly as a hat full of arseholes." Brody grinned before downing the glass of juice he'd poured. "But that doesn't help my situation now, does it? I asked Randi Lockwood here for dinner. Will is going to kill me."

"Oh yeah, you're dead, mate. But ignoring that, why did you ask her to your place? And don't give me any crap about your gut telling you to do so."

Had he asked Randi to dinner on gut instinct? Or something else?

So many decisions in his life had been made on gut instinct. Take a gap year and travel instead of starting university straight out of school. Study graphic design instead of engineering. Open a graphic design company after graduation instead of working for someone else. Fly to the U.S. on a whim fifteen years ago with no other plan than to walk out of JFK airport and see where he would end up.

All gut-instinct decisions.

Where he'd ended up, as it turned out, was inside a boutique gallery in SoHo owned by Bridget Muldoon. The second he'd met her, his gut had told him she was the one. His gut hadn't been wrong. She had the kindest heart and the happiest smile. She'd become the center of his world, the reason for his breath.

Five weeks after meeting her, she'd become his wife, and a year and a half after that, the mother of his first child.

"You sure you didn't ask her to dinner because she looked hot in a bikini?" Singo continued.

Brody scrunched his eyes shut. Probably shouldn't have told Singo that little fact when he was outlining the unexpected situation he found himself in.

No. There'd been no need to tell Singo how incredible Randi looked in her swimmers, but damn, how much had he enjoyed picturing her as he did?

"I asked her here because as I was stomping out of our interview, she told me to tell Sasha she'd had a great time with her, and it made me remember just how much Sasha had come to life being around her." He placed his empty glass in the sink and rubbed at the back of his neck. "And you know how quiet and...and..."

Shit, he really didn't want to say the word.

"Disconnected?" Singo suggested gently.

"Disconnected with people Sasha has been since Bridget's death," he finished. There was a reason he and Singo had hit it off when they first met four years ago at Legoland. The engineer didn't do bullshit. He looked like a football player, had an IQ officially off the charts, and talked like a hostage-situation negotiator. The other people in Brody's life *still* tiptoed around the subject of Bridget's death, along with Willow's and Sasha's well-being, as if Brody would shatter if anything less than complimentary was uttered. Adam Singleton, however, just said it how it was with a calmness that somehow made Brody feel better.

"So, you asked the teacher your eldest daughter is fighting with—the one who is encouraging her to get back into the sport she associates with her dead mother—to dinner at your place so your youngest daughter can be emotionally elevated again." The sounds of people screaming filled the background of the call. Singo must be on-site.

He's working. Which is what I should be doing instead of planning a meal…and possible peace talks.

"I totally get why you called," Singo said.

"Because I need someone to tell me to get my head read?"

Singo laughed. "Because you need someone to tell you you did the right thing."

"Did I?" Will was going to be furious with him. And hurt.

"Yeah, mate, you did." More of that calm but commanding voice. "Willow will get over it. She's tough. A bit stubborn, sure, but she will get over it. Sash though…she's only young. And she needs to connect again, with people apart from you and her sister. I haven't seen her smile, *really* smile, since before Bridget's funeral, and she used to be a giggling monkey. Bloody hell, she almost made *me* want to have kids."

Brody couldn't help but chuckle.

"If this Randi woman is the start of Sash getting back to that, then I say have Randi around for dinner every bloody night."

There was more screaming in the background. How did Singo work with that kind of distraction?

"Bikini or not," Singo went on. "Besides, it'll tick that sister-in-law of yours off, and she needs to be ticked off regularly."

"I'm getting the feeling you don't like Alicia."

"Not at all. In fact, you need to send her a text now telling her Randi is coming to your house tonight for a pool party. And make mention of the bikini again. Just to rev her up even more."

Scrubbing at the back of his neck, Brody let out a sigh. "As fun as that would be, I'm not telling Alicia. And I'm not planning on seeing Randi in a bikini again. I'm asking her here for *Sasha*, not for…"

Me. He couldn't say it. He had no right to ask a woman out for dinner. What the hell he'd even been doing thinking about it yesterday was beyond him.

"For you?" Singo suggested. "For a date? For sex?"

"You really missed your true calling, Singo." Brody scowled. "You should have become a professional pain in the arse."

"Ah, but then who would Lego get to design and build their next life-size Marvel superhero installation here at Legoland?"

"A ten-year-old?"

"Fuck you, Thorton."

Brody grinned. "You're not my kind, mate."

"I know. Despite what you say, I'm too beautiful. Now, stop second-guessing everything you do. You're a bloody brilliant dad, and Willow knows it."

"You're not the one who's going to cop her wrath when I tell her who's coming tonight."

"Here's an idea…don't tell her."

Brody whistled. "And you reckon I'm as mad as a cut snake."

"Get back to work, you bastard. I've got an ARC reactor to implant in Stark's chest."

"You have a weird life, mate."

"That I do. And I wouldn't change it for a bloody thing. Give me a call tomorrow to let me know if you're still alive."

Ending the call, Brody shoved his phone into his back pocket.

Okay, so he would get to work. Planning dinner could wait until he took a lunch break.

The studio was empty when he arrived. Good. He wasn't in the mood to flex his waning social skills. Turning on his computer, he pulled his stool over to his drawing table and reacquainted himself with his current project, a series of posters for the upcoming Sebastian Hart/Chris Huntley film.

It had been a while since he'd worked away from home. He'd taken almost six months off after Bridget's death to focus solely on the girls, and he'd returned to working from home only four months ago. He'd reluctantly agreed to come back to the studio when the lucrative movie marketing deal had come his way.

Only during school hours. That was his self-imposed condition for coming back to the studio.

It was good to get out of the house, away from memories of Bridget, from the photos on the wall, the bottles of her perfume in the bathroom, her cookbooks in the kitchen. She'd been a good cook. Much better than...

Cookbooks. Shit, what the hell was he going to cook for Randi?

"Work. Get to work." Pulling out a fresh sheet of paper, he turned his focus to sketching out more layout thumbnails. The film was a horror movie based on a Thomas St. Clair book. Maybe if he channeled his confusion and agitation into the images, he'd nail the final one today?

The rest of the studio's creatives slowly made their appearance as the morning progressed. He nodded to them as they entered but kept his focus locked on his work.

No one bothered him. Who would bother the boss when he was working? Even before Bridget's death, most of the team of his small but highly sought-after graphic art and design studio knew not to bug him when he was at his workstation.

Catch him in the lunchroom or the common meeting room and he'd gladly "have a chin wag" as his father back in Australia would call it, but while he was working…nope.

Five minutes before two thirty, he straightened from his drawing table, cracked his stiff back, and checked out the dark and menacing image of a shadow looming over a young girl playing in a sandpit.

"Creepy fucker," he muttered with a pleased grin. He was done for the day. It was time to go get the girls from school. Tomorrow, he'd start to digitally mock up the concept ready to present to—

His phone vibrated on his desk with an incoming text message.

He swallowed.

Randi Lockwood had sent him a text.

Hi, Mr. Thorton. I wanted to make sure your invitation to dinner was still on offer.

A tight fist clenched deep in his chest.

It is, he typed. *And please, it's Brody. You have seen me shirtless, after all.*

He hit send and then scrunched up his face. Why the fuck had he typed that last bit?

"Shit. Shit."

What the hell was wrong with him? He didn't know her well enough to make that kind of joke.

"I told her yesterday I have a bad sense of humor," he muttered. "Let's just hope she remembers."

His phone vibrated in his hand with her reply.

I must admit, I don't usually call the men I've gotten all wet with mister.

He blinked. "Er…"

His phone vibrated once again.

I'm so sorry. That sounded wittier in my head.

He chuckled.

Another message flashed up on his screen. *I didn't mean to sound gross or offend you. I was trying to break the tension after our meeting this morning.*

He could totally understand that.

Another message arrived, this one accompanied by a sad emoji. *I think I failed.*

He laughed. *No worries*, he typed back. *I laughed. Trust me, you didn't offend me.*

A few seconds past. Long enough for him to realize he was holding his breath. Until his phone *ding*ed again. *Thanks, Brody. I will be there at 5:30 p.m. Do you want me to bring anything?*

Brody. She'd called him Brody.

Okay, so maybe tonight might not be so bad.

"Yeah. And Willow will suddenly forget she's angry at the world and unicorns will suddenly fill the house and fart rainbows all over the place."

She couldn't stand at the door all evening.

No, I could go home and change.

She shot the clothes she'd changed into after school a quick glance.

"What?" she muttered. "Jeans and a Vincent Van Goat T-shirt aren't appropriate attire for a dinner with a student's family?"

The Van Goat shirt—an art teacher's lame pun put into graphic logo form—was an attempt to get Willow to laugh, but maybe it was too snug. And maybe the neckline was a bit too scoopy and low?

Oh, who am I kidding? Brody's seen me in a bikini, and this is not any kind of date anyway.

Which brought her back to the closed door in front of her. On the other side was a man she was trying not to think sexual

things about, a little girl lost since her mother died, and a
teenager who'd decided Randi was the antichrist.

*Turn around. Go home. Hang out with Chuck. Help him
with his homework. Work on your thesis. Eat Thai takeout.*

She raised her hand and knocked.

"Will?" Brody's muffled shout came through the door.
"Can you get that please?"

Oh boy. Oh boy.

She set her face to a relaxed smile. Ready.

"Will?" Brody again, louder this time.

The door opened.

Willow, almost as tall as Randi, stared at her. "What are *you*
doing here?"

Crap. Brody didn't tell her I was coming?

Willow scowled and then dropped her gaze to the floor.
"Sorry, Miss Lockwood. That was rude."

Randi swallowed. "That's okay, W—"

Willow turned and strode away. Just like that.

Okay.

"Who is it?" Sasha's voice drifted from somewhere in the
house.

"Miss Lockwood." Willow didn't stop walking.

"Who?" Footsteps sounded from the direction of Sasha's
voice.

"Randi."

Randi ground her teeth. Wow, Willow sure could drag out
her name.

"Randi?" The footsteps turned to thudding stomps, and
Sasha rounded the corner. "Hi, Randi."

The smile on Sasha's face warmed the chill left in Willow's
wake.

"Hi, Sash—" Sasha threw herself up into Randi's arms.
"Oof."

"Does Daddy know you're here?" Sasha wriggled back to

the floor. "Daddy!" Her shout bounced around the front porch. "Randi's here."

Without another word, Sasha ran back into the house and out of sight.

Randi shuffled her feet. So what did she do now?

Brody rounded the corner, his smile easy, a dishcloth slung over his shoulder. "G'day, Miss Lockwood."

Her heart thumped up into her throat. Her stomach clenched. So did other parts of her that had no right clenching over a student's parent.

Run away. Now. Before you—

"Come in."

"Okay." *Five minutes. Just five minutes.* "I brought ice cream." She thrust the tub of triple chocolate fudge ice cream toward him.

He grinned. "My favorite."

Goddamn it, why was his grin so sexy? "Really?"

He chuckled, and just as it had yesterday at the water park, her body reacted to the sound. Big time. "No. I'm actually lactose intolerant. But Will will love you."

"Or at least, not hate me as much?" she suggested. Man, it was ridiculous how nervous she was.

He inclined his head with another chuckle. "Or at least that."

Taking the ice cream, he stepped to the side and waved her in.

Here we go.

She stepped over the threshold into his home.

Sasha came running at her again. "Did you bring ice cream? Awesome. Will, Randi brought ice cream."

Willow—wherever she was—didn't answer.

"Ice cream is a bit of a big deal in this house," Brody said. "I don't eat it, which means I usually don't think to buy it when I'm at the supermarket."

"Daddy buys boring things for dessert like fruit and cheese."

He pulled a mock pout at Sasha. "I thought you liked cheese."

She rolled her eyes and head. "I like ice cream more. Will likes it the best. Especially chocolate ice cream." She took the tub from his hand and went to remove the lid.

"Excuse me, maniac?" He arched an eyebrow at her.

She giggled. "Yes?"

Randi had to bite her lip. It was that or laugh.

The eyebrow arched higher. "After dinner, missy."

Sasha swung her gaze to Randi and then back to Brody. "Is Randi staying for dinner?"

Brody nodded.

Sasha's eyes widened. "Yay! Willow, Randi is staying for dinner." She turned and ran back the way she'd come. "Will, Randi is staying for dinner."

"Put the ice cream in the freezer," Brody called before shrugging. "I think she's a little excited about you staying."

And how do you feel about it?

She smiled, throat tight. She had no right liking Sasha so much. "I think she might be."

"She's *what*?" Willow's question floated to the front door.

Randi grimaced. "Willow doesn't seem to share Sasha's enthusiasm, however. You didn't tell her I was coming?"

His smile turned sheepish. "No. Now's probably the time to tell you I can occasionally be a bit of a coward." He ducked his head and rubbed at the back of his neck. "If it helps, I've made the most delicious lamb roast you'll ever eat."

Goddamn it, why did he have to look so kissable? And somehow…vulnerable?

Get the hell gone now. Tell him you have to go. Tell him this isn't a good idea. Tell him—

"It does help." She smiled. "I've never had lamb roast

before. I'm a woeful cook, and my ex was a vegetarian." And a cheating bastard, but that was neither here nor there.

"Daddy." Sasha's excited shout came from inside the house. "I've set the table."

Brody gave Randi a grin. "Now there's a first. Care to have dinner here every night?"

Before she could respond, he waved her deeper into his house.

The walls she walked past were decorated with the most incredible artworks. Pencil sketches of various sizes and subjects hung together—birds, hands, details of plants, close-ups of human eyes, animal eyes. Among the drawings were larger paintings of similar subjects along with more abstract ones. Most bore what looked like the initials BT, but a few—some of the more simplistic work—had WT and ST written on them.

Definitely a family of artists.

"Oh, wow." She stopped, stunned at the massive painting of a man's hand holding a baby's hand hanging alone on the living room's main wall.

"Bridget painted that." Brody stopped beside her, his gaze on the artwork. "Two weeks after Sash was born."

"It's beautiful."

"She was incredibly talented. And an amazing mum."

She looked around the room. Painting and sketches everywhere, quite a few of Willow and Sasha, but no photos of his wife.

Damn, how hard must it be? To lose…

"Would you like a drink?"

She swallowed. "Water? I'm a bit of a teetotaler. Woke up in the wrong state after a party back in my college days and haven't touched a drop since."

Now why the hell had she shared that little embarrassing fact with him?

"Water it is." He strode off, leaving her alone in the living room.

"So…" Willow walked into the room and leaned her hip against the sofa closest to Randi, arms folded, lower lip pouted. "Did Dad invite you here so I can apologize?"

Pulse quickening, she met Willow's stare. This conversation could make or break the night. Like navigating a minefield. "For what?"

"For calling you a fat cow."

She shook his head. "I haven't told him what you called me."

Something flickered in Willow's eyes, and she frowned. "So why are you here?"

"To see what you think of my shirt?" She held out her arms, revealing the image of Vincent Van Gogh's famous self-portrait reimagined as a goat.

Willow's frown deepened, and then she looked at Randi's shirt. Her lips twitched. For a millisecond.

"Funny," she intoned, before huffing out a breath into her bangs.

She met Randi's gaze again. "I…I shouldn't have—"

"Randi?" Sasha barreled back into the room. "Will you sit next to me at the table? Do you like mint sauce? Daddy put ice in your water. Is that okay? Do you like to eat ice? I eat ice all the time."

"Geez, Sash." Willow rolled her eyes and levered herself off the sofa. "Try to show some enthusiasm for our guest being here, will you?"

"I *am* enthusiasm." Sasha glared at Willow and then grinned at Randi again. "I like your shirt. Did you know Vincent Van Gogh cut off his ear for his girlfriend?"

"I did." *Goddamn, this kid is awesome.*

Sasha jumped onto the sofa. "Daddy changed his shirt three times before you got here. And he sprayed this stuff on that makes him smell nice."

"I'm out," Willow snarled, pivoting on her heel and stomping away.

"It was only two shirts." Brody appeared in the living room, a tall glass of water in his hand. "Ice okay?"

"Ice is okay." And yep, he definitely smelled nice. And looked nice. The polo shirt he wore highlighted just how sculpted and sublime his torso was.

What have I gotten myself into?

His eyes connected with hers and he smiled. "Shall we start?"

CHAPTER SIX

He tried to cling to his guilt. Like yesterday, he was having too good a time. He tried to tell himself to stop enjoying conversing with Randi, to stop enjoying looking at her.

And yet, he couldn't.

Sitting at the dinner table with Sasha bubbling away with joy in the seat beside Randi, it was bloody impossible not to be happy.

Hell, he'd even caught Willow smiling every now and again, although she did her best to hide it.

He also tried—repeatedly—to stop remembering just how much he'd enjoyed kissing her.

Tried. And failed.

Which brought him back to clinging to all his guilt.

All in all, it was a vicious, confusing cycle.

"Paris!" Sasha's exclamation jerked Brody away from the unsettling conundrum and back to the table. "Will wants to go to Paris, don't you, Will?"

"Do you have to, Sash?" Willow grumbled, rolling her eyes again.

"My sister loves it there," Randi said with a smile at Sasha.

She took a sip of water. "She should, though. She's the consul at the U.S. embassy."

"Wow." Willow's fork paused mid-journey to her mouth. Awe filled her face as she looked at Randi. And then she frowned, as though remembering she was supposed to be angry, and continued eating, stare locked on her dinner.

Biting back a sigh, Brody scooped up a forkful of mashed potato from his own plate. "Learning French and seeing the Eiffel Tower is number one on Will's bucket list, isn't it, Will?"

"You should talk to my nephew, Chuck." Randi turned her smile to Willow. "He taught himself how to speak French."

"You should bring him over next time." The invitation was out before he realized he'd thought it. Next time? Was there really going to be a next time?

"Dad," Willow groaned, slumping deeper into her seat.

"I like Chuck." Sasha beamed. "He was funny. Maybe he can be your boyfriend, Will."

"Oh my God!" Willow threw her fork onto her plate and buried her face in her hands.

"Okay, maniac." Brody gave Sasha a stern frown. "That's enough."

Confusion filled Sasha's face. "What?"

"It's okay, Willow." Randi chuckled softly. "Chuck assures me he's only interested in dating Gal Godot."

"Will is prettier than Gal Godot," Sasha declared, indignation ripe in her voice, a second before she frowned at Brody. "Who's Gal Godot?"

"Wonder Woman, you dork," Willow grumbled from behind her hands.

"Oh." Sasha shrugged. "Yeah, you're definitely prettier than her."

Brody prepared himself for the surly teenage explosion. Instead, Willow rose from her seat, walked around to where Sasha sat, and wrapped her in a hug.

Sasha giggled.

Willow kissed her on the top of her head and then went back to her seat.

Don't do anything embarrassing. Don't ruin the moment.

"My sister is awesome," Sasha declared.

"She is." Randi smiled, flicking Brody a quick, unreadable look.

"Did you know that Will is the best long jumper in the state?" Sasha said, sitting straighter in her chair.

"Sasha!" Willow snapped.

"Sash." Brody's chest turned to a vise.

"I did." Randi's smile was calm, relaxed. "I also know her entry in her school's new mascot competition was selected as the winner."

Willow blinked. "It was?" A smile stretched her lips. "Really?"

A smile. For someone apart from Sasha.

Brody swallowed. He could kiss Randi.

Randi nodded at Willow. "It was. But you're not supposed to know that until school tomorrow, okay?"

"Okay. Okay." Willow was almost jiggling on her seat. "I won't say anything."

"I didn't know you entered, Will." He reached across the table and squeezed her hand. "Well done."

She shrugged, even as her lips twitched with another smile. "I didn't want to tell you in case you got disappointed if mine didn't win."

"Oh, honey." He squeezed her hand again. A knot tightened in his chest. "You could never disappoint me."

"I could." She withdrew her hand and returned her gaze to her dinner. "I…"

Silence.

I did. Is that what she was going to say? They'd never talked about her quitting long jump after Bridget's death. Did she know he and Bridget had been fighting over it before the car accident, over how much training she was doing and how he thought Bridget was pushing her too hard?

"This is good lamb, Dad," she said, cutting into her dinner.

Sasha looked at her, at Brody, at Randi, and back at Willow. "Hurry up and eat it then, so we can have ice cream."

Willow laughed and proceeded to shovel food into her mouth at a rapid rate.

Sasha—always up for a challenge—did the same.

And then, with a laugh, so did Randi.

Brody raised his eyebrows at her.

"Hey," she said around a mouthful of food, "it's ice cream."

Sasha giggled.

The meal—lamb and veggies just like his mum used to make—disappeared quickly. Willow and Sasha offered to not only clear the table but to serve up the ice cream.

Sitting alone at the table with Randi, he wished he had a glass of water, a pencil and sketchbook, hell, even his reading glasses. Anything to fidget with, to lock his attention on. It was too easy to lock it on her.

Maybe if I go get my wallet? If I look at the photo of Bridget inside—

"Willow really would have found out she won the mascot logo competition tomorrow."

He jerked his stare back from the direction of the kitchen.

Randi shrugged. "Just in case you thought I'd said that to deflect the whole long jump thing."

"I didn't." He smiled. "She is an incredible artist."

"She's very talented. It runs in the family I see." She indicated toward the framed drawings on the dining room wall.

Some were his, some were Bridget's, some their girls'. "Yeah, can you imagine what games of Pictionary are like in this house?"

She chuckled. Bloody hell, he liked the relaxed sound. It made him feel...warm.

"I bet. It was chess in our house. Of course, that was only

when we weren't all being asocial individuals not interacting with one another."

He frowned.

She chuckled again. "My brother and sister are both gifted, and my parents are both scholars. I was—am—the disappointment of the family, deciding to become just a teacher, and an art teacher at that."

"Don't they realize how important art is?"

"Oh, sure. But you know the saying those that can't do, teach?"

"There is nothing about you that says you can't *do*."

A light glinted in her eyes, and her lips curled into a tiny smile. "Oh, I *can* do. I can *do* very well."

A hot tension rolled through his body. His gaze locked with hers.

Her smile turned mischievous. "We are still talking about art, right?"

"We are." So why the hell was his voice so bloody strangled?

"Do you have family over here?" She shifted in her seat, his gaze dropping to her fingers playing with the thick silver ring on her right thumb. "Australian family, I mean?"

He shook his head. "No brothers or sisters for me. Only cousins back home. Mum and Dad are still there, but the girls haven't seen them since...since the funeral."

"I'm sorry, Brody. I'll shut up."

"No, no. It's all good. It's nice to actually have a conversation."

"You don't have many conversations?" An unreadable look crossed her face. "What about Alicia? I think that was her name? You and Alicia don't engage in conversation?"

"Alicia and I don't..." How did he put this? Ever since he'd started to get his act together after Bridget's death, finally pulling the pieces of his life back together and standing on his own feet again, Alicia was behaving more and more clingy.

She'd stepped up when he'd emotionally crumbled and helped with the girls more than he probably remembered, but it was like she was having great difficulty letting go now.

A part of him felt bad about that. A part of him wondered what was the gentlest way he could tell her he needed space without sounding like an ungrateful arsehole.

"My sister-in-law and I don't converse that often."

"I try to avoid conversations with my parents." She snorted. "And my brother and sister when it comes down to it."

"What's your brother do for a living?" He smiled softly. "Apart from being gifted, that is?"

"Doctor Aaron Lockwood. The surgeon of the family. *Cardiothoracic* surgeon, at that."

Brody whistled.

She snorted. Christ, she even made *that* sound sexy. "I know, right? So two academics for parents, one of whom is a Rhodes scholar, both multi-published, a sister who's a consul in the United States embassy in France, and a heart surgeon for a brother. All of them have PhDs. I'm the only non-PhDer in the family."

"And you ended up being just a teacher, eh? That must be hard on them."

She narrowed her eyes at him. "You're messing with me, aren't you?"

He nodded.

"Lucky for you. I'm not opposed to resorting to violence if need be to defend my profession."

"Consider me warned. Don't tick off Randi Lockwood."

Laughing, she picked up her water and took a sip. "Good thing, too. The one thing I am the best at in the Lockwood family is nipple cripples." Her eyes widened. "Oh God, I can't believe I just said that."

He pressed his palms to his chest, directly over his nipples. "Randi Lockwood, you are the best teacher in the world."

She laughed again and raised her glass. "Damn straight, I am. Your nipples are safe for now." She closed her eyes and shook her head with a grimace. "I really need to stop talking, don't I? This is what happens when you live with a fifteen-year-old. Your conversations become…weird."

"But highly entertaining." He reached for his own water. "My thanks to Chuck."

"I'll tell him you said that. I'll miss him a lot when he moves out."

He frowned. "Moves out?"

She grinned. "Ah, so you *weren't* paying attention earlier. I thought so. You had a look on your face that students sometimes get. The one that tells me they've checked out and are thinking about something else. My nephew is living with me only until the school year finishes, then he's moving to Paris to be with his mom and dad. As much as I'd like to keep him, my sister, Stacey, wants him back."

"That sucks, to lose someone you love." An invisible band wrapped his chest. And yet, something equally tight bloomed low in his gut, a contentment he hadn't experienced for a long time. Sitting and talking with someone he enjoyed spending time with… It was…nice. "What will you do to keep yourself busy?"

She twirled the ring on her finger again. "Finish my master's. Got to prove to the family I'm worth putting back on their Christmas card list." She snorted again. "Definitely throw myself into my work and studies. Maybe finally get a PhD so Thanksgiving dinners won't be so humiliating."

"No social life?" *Why did you ask that?*

She shook her head. "I'm not good with the social life."

"No…dating?" *Now, why the fuck did you ask that?* "I noticed earlier you said you had an ex." *Or add that?*

Her gaze found his for a heartbeat. "I *do* have an ex. Good riddance to bad rubbish, I say. And me and dating also have an understanding."

"And that is?"

Say "I wasn't going to try it again until I met the right guy."

"I—"

"Ice cream!" Sasha ran back into the dining room, two bright-blue bowls in her hands.

Randi's eyes found his again for a fleeting second, and yet it felt like she'd penetrated right to his very soul.

"Sorbet for you, Dad." Willow placed a bowl piled high with pale yellow sorbet in front of him. "Pineapple-lime."

"I'm sorry for bringing something you can't have." Randi frowned, even as she picked up her spoon.

Christ, does she have any idea how accurate that is?

Because despite every fiber in his body craving the woman sitting opposite him, the woman sitting in the chair Bridget used to occupy, he couldn't have her.

It wasn't right or fair to his girls, or to the memory of their mother.

"Daddy?"

He swallowed, directing his smile at Sasha. "Yes, maniac?"

"Are we still going to the beach after school tomorrow?"

He nodded. He'd promised the beach adventure in an attempt to get Willow to engage on the way home from the water park.

Sasha slid a quick look at Randi and then back at him. "Can Randi come to the beach with us?"

A rejection formed in Randi's head, but goddamn it, she couldn't say it. She had nothing planned for the following afternoon. Not at all, but still… It was too much, too wonderful. This dinner, this family… It was too enticing and addictive and…well, too wonderful. "I'd love to go to the beach with you."

"What time?"

Good grief, I'm a masochist.

"After school." Sasha smiled. "We can collect shells."

A prickling sensation told her Willow was staring at her. Staring or glaring?

"Is that okay, Willow?"

Willow shrugged and dropped her attention back to her ice cream.

It wasn't a no.

"Would you like to meet us there?" Brody hadn't touched his sorbet. "Or come here first?"

"I'll meet you there."

Better that way. Less time in his company. She was already too enamored.

"Did you want to bring Chuck?"

"Oh, good idea. It'll get him off the PlayStation for a while. He's hooked on this game called *Horizon Zero Dawn.*"

"Really?" Willow looked up from her ice cream. "I love that game."

"Me too. But I'm not as good as Chuck."

Sasha pouted, first at Willow and then at Randi. "Daddy says I'm too little to play it."

"And you're also too little to be up late on a school night." Brody clapped his hands on the table's edge and stood. "So say goodnight to Randi and Willow and—"

"Aww, do I have to?"

"It's all good, Sash." Willow dropped her spoon into her bowl and rose to her feet. "I'll come with you, and you can read me a book while I braid your hair."

"Really?" Adoration flooded Sasha's face. "Yay. Goodnight, Randi. See you tomorrow." She leaped up and bolted down the hall. "C'mon, Will. Hurry up."

Willow rolled her eyes with a soft laugh before giving Randi a small smile. "Thanks for the ice cream, Miss Lockwood."

"You're welcome, Willow. And when we're not at school, you can call me Randi if you like."

Whoa, big move, Miranda.

A slight frown dipped Willow's dark blond eyebrows. "I don't think so. Bye."

She followed her sister, stopping to kiss Brody on his cheek. "Night, Daddy."

"Night, kiddo."

Silence stretched as Willow left them alone.

Randi shifted on her seat. Her skin prickled.

Brody's gaze met hers. "That went okay, right?"

His vulnerability, his hope, reached right into her soul. She smiled even as her heart pounded. "I think so."

He let out a shaky breath, part sigh, part laugh. "Phew."

She moved the melted remains of her ice cream around her bowl. "Phew."

His Adam's apple worked in his throat. "Sorry about Sasha springing the beach thing on you."

"It's okay. As I said, it'll be good for Chuck."

"And good for Sasha. I really do appreciate you coming tonight. She's a different little girl when you're around."

"Is she shy?"

"Sad. Withdrawn. Losing her mum so young took her sun away."

Don't fall in love with him. Don't you dare fall in love with him.

"I'm glad I can help."

A soft smile tugged at his lips. "Help me with the dishes?"

"Absolutely."

Brody washed the dirty dishes while she dried them. There was nothing date-like about the night. Nope. Not at all. Who washed dishes together on a date? No, this was…was…

Domestic bliss?

Good grief, I'm in trouble.

"Can I address the elephant in the room?" he asked, voice calm.

"Sure."

"We've kissed each other."

She froze, half-dried bowl in her hand. Where was he going with this?

"Twice."

She nodded. "Twice."

"And it was really good."

Her heart smashed up into her throat. "It was." Two of the best kisses she'd ever had, in fact.

"And I'd be lying if I said I didn't want there to be a third."

And a fourth, and a fifth, and a sixth?

"But there can't be."

Well, there goes all the heat in the room.

She nodded again and resumed drying the bowl. "Totally get that." *Hey, props for how calm and relaxed I sound. Go me.* "It wouldn't be wise for a teacher to be"—*in a relationship*—"involved with the parent of a student."

Involved? How was that a better word than relationship? Both were putting the proverbial cart before the proverbial horse. The sexually deprived, utterly shocked-by-the-fact-it-seemed-it-was-wanting-a-relationship-after-all-even-though-it-thought-it-really-didn't horse.

Oh God help me, I'm in so much—

"I want Willow to be on the school's track team again."

Blurting out the first thing she could think of to deflect the situation seemed like a good idea. Clearly, it wasn't. Not with the way Brody's jaw knotted.

And there goes any chance of ever being involved *with him, confused horse and rickety cart or not.*

Stare fixed on the plate he was holding half submerged in the sink, he shook his head. "No."

"But she's too good at long jump not to compete. She's ignoring a talent that could take her all the way to the top."

His jaw bunched again. His hand moved over the plate in jerky circles. It would have to be spotless by now.

"I'll gladly train her." Why could she *not* stop talking? "During lunch or after school. I don't mind."

"When she's meant to be doing her homework?" He placed the clean, wet plate on the drying rack rather than handing it to her directly. "Or being a sister?"

Abort. Abort now.

"I can arrange tutoring for her." *So much for aborting. What am I doing?* "Or I can help her."

His chest rose and fell with a slow breath. "Why do you want Will to jump again so much?"

She picked up the wet plate and started to dry it. What were the chances he'd accept her promotion being on the line as an answer?

Before she could come up with any kind of response that wouldn't make her sound desperate, he shook his head again and pulled the plug from the sink. "Will doesn't jump anymore." He dried his hands on the edge of the dishcloth she was using and then, as if realizing what he was doing, on his thighs. "I'm going to go make sure the girls are in bed."

He turned away.

"Brody?"

"Yes?" His gaze found hers over his shoulder.

"I'm sorry. It's probably better I go now."

He studied her silently.

She offered him a small smile. "Thank you for dinner. It was the most delicious lamb I've had."

He didn't move. Or say a word.

She draped the damp dishcloth over the drying rack and caught her bottom lip with her teeth. "Okay. Bye."

"Randi?"

She held her breath.

"See you tomorrow at the beach? La Jolla?"

The wise thing to do would have been to say no. No beach. No future interactions.

She smiled and nodded. "I'll see you at La Jolla."

He nodded.

A million butterflies started a dance party in her stomach. *Get out now. Before you throw yourself at him.* "I'll lock the door behind me. Thanks again for dinner."

"You're welcome. Night."

Chuck was sitting at the dining table when she arrived home, pounding away at the keys of his laptop.

"Homework?" she asked, dumping her bag on the sofa. She'd blasted Bon Jovi from her car's sound system as loud as her ears would allow for the duration of the drive home. It was that or replay the entire night with the Thortons over and over in her head. Bon Jovi only just won the battle.

Chuck shook his head. "I'm writing Mom an angry email."

"Why this time?" Her sister had a unique ability to irritate her only child from the other side of the world, usually over his grades. Apparently, being the top of his class in every subject wasn't good enough for Stacey. Of course, in the Lockwood family, being first at everything wasn't necessarily enough. You had to be so far in front of everyone else you could flake out for a month and still be first. Although Lockwoods did *not* flake out. Well, every Lockwood *except* Miranda Lockwood didn't flake out. Her family pretty much considered her art degree and her teacher's degree as flaky.

"She wants me to move to Paris now."

A cold finger drew up Randi's spine.

Chuck glowered at his laptop's screen, fingers almost a blur. "I'm telling her to stop thinking of herself and think of me."

"You don't want to interrupt your schooling." She gave him a proud nod, even as the cold finger crept over her scalp. "The teacher in me is impressed."

He stopped typing and grinned at her. "Schooling? Hell, it has nothing to do with that. You think I'm going to fly off to the other side of the world when the greatest romance the world has ever seen has just started getting good?"

She frowned. "I didn't know you had a girlfriend, Chuckles. What's her name? When can I meet her? Or is it a guy? I mean, it would be totally okay either way… Why are you laughing?"

"The greatest romance the world has ever seen is *your* romance with the Australian dude, Aunty R. You don't think there's any way I'm missing watching *this* unfold, do you?"

"My *what*?"

He straightened from the dining table and made his way into the kitchen. "I can't leave you alone when it's only just starting, can I? I mean, if it wasn't for me, you never would have even gone to the water park yesterday."

"I think you're overemphasizing your importance in the minute details of my life."

He laughed again. "Says the woman who just came back from dinner at Aussie Dude's house. How was it, by the way?"

She dropped into the closest armchair and dragged her hands through her hair. "Let's just say you're going to love what's happening tomorrow afternoon."

He frowned. "What's happening tomorrow afternoon?"

CHAPTER SEVEN

The weather destroyed the beach plans.

A wild summer afternoon storm meant only the brave and foolish attempted being outdoors. Despite being at least one of those two criteria, Brody stuck his daddy hat on and cancelled the outing.

Sasha declared she was never going to forgive him, bottom lip a wobbling testament to how he'd completely shattered her happiness.

Willow retreated to her bedroom, phone in hand, expression sullen.

"Damn it."

He'd tried to tell himself he hadn't been looking forward to seeing Randi all day. Had tried to keep his focus on his work. Had thought he'd been quite successful about it until he'd noticed he'd given the female character on the movie poster thumbnail he'd been sketching dark hair when the actress playing her had blond hair.

Dark hair, just like Randi's.

The brewing storm clouds had echoed his emotional state. The deluge of rain clearly echoed Sasha's.

Standing in his kitchen, he read the text Randi had sent

him five minutes ago, a few moments after he'd cancelled the outing. *Damn it, the rain has ruined my matchmaking plans.*

Matchmaking? Hadn't he said no more kissing?

Ah, but fuck a duck, I want to kiss her again.

His phone vibrated in his hand with an incoming message. *I meant matchmaking between Chuck and Willow.*

He chuckled, even as a jolt of tight disappointment sank into his chest.

His phone vibrated again.

I don't mean I'm trying to matchmake Willow and Chuck. I wouldn't presume to do such a thing, and Chuck would kill me. Although he did tell me today he's into girls, not boys, so there's that.

He blinked, another laugh falling from him. She was making it difficult to not—

Another message came. *I meeeeeeean the rain is messing up my plans to introduce one computer gamer to another. In a purely platonic way.*

A few seconds passed before another one arrived. *I sound like a babbling idiot. Forget this whole conversation ever happened. Better still, delete it please.*

He laughed. Warmth spread through him.

No way, he texted back. *I'm keeping it. Screen-capturing it in fact.*

Seconds passed. Long seconds. And then the three little dots appeared on his screen that told him she was responding. He grinned. What was she going to say?

Is there anything I can say or do to change your mind?

The pleading hands emoji followed.

Yep, he typed. *Bring Chuck and meet the girls and me at Phil's BBQ for dinner tonight at 6.*

He hit send.

And then swiped at his mouth. What the hell was he doing?

Asking Randi to dinner. Again.

He stared at his phone. At the three little dots now on its screen.

Sure, came the reply.

A ragged breath burst from him, one he muffled with another swipe of his hand over his mouth. "So that just happened."

"What just happened, Daddy?"

Dropping his hand, he looked up from his phone and grinned at Sasha. "Go tell your sister we're going out for dinner."

"We are? Awesome!"

"Hey." He gave her a mock hurt look. "The correct response here is 'but, Daddy, you are the best cook in the world, and I never want to eat anyone's food but yours'."

She giggled. "Fair dinkum, Daddy, your grub's bonza."

"Did your grandfather teach you that?"

Nodding, she spun on her heel and ran for Willow's room.

"Pop Thorton needs to stop teaching you out-of-date Aussie slang," he called after her with a smile. Dragging a hand through his hair, he headed for his own room. "Now what the bloody hell am I going to wear?"

"I can't believe you wore that shirt." Willow shook her head as he climbed out of his SUV.

"What's wrong with my shirt?"

"It's got a Lego Darth Vader on it."

"Your point?"

She rolled her eyes and then shook her head with a slight smile.

He resisted the urge to hug her, no matter how wonderful that smile made him feel. No way was he going to do anything that might jeopardize the fragile harmony between them.

"Table for three?" the hostess asked when they entered Phil's BBQ.

"Five," Willow said.

She hadn't reacted the way he thought she would when he told her and Sasha they were having dinner with Randi and Chuck. She hadn't exactly been ecstatic, but she hadn't been angry, either. Nor had she sat silent and sullen during the drive here. In fact, she'd almost been chatty, far more talkative than she'd been in months. Most of her conversation had been with Sasha, to be sure, but she'd been talking.

It was good. He hoped. Maybe she was lulling him into a false sense of security?

"Hi."

Hell, Randi was here. Behind him. Now.

"Hi, Randi." Sasha disengaged her hand from Brody's and took Randi's instead. "You look pretty."

Bloody oath, she did look pretty. Too pretty for his state of bloody mind. Her hair fell around her face in a floaty black cloud that kissed her shoulders, shoulders left bare thanks to the thin straps of the summery dress she wore. He had a thing for thin shoulder straps on dresses, especially when the wearer of the dress had smooth, creamy skin and beautifully shaped shoulders like Randi. What would those shoulders feel like beneath his lips?

"G'day, Charles." He shoved his right hand toward Randi's nephew, currently standing at her side smirking at him. Jesus, he had to get a fucking grip. "Good to see you again, mate."

Charles pumped his hand once. Yep, there was that devilish glint in the teenager's eye he remembered from the water park. Shit, this kid *was* smart. "Chuck. Or Chuckles," Charles corrected. "Aunty R calls me Chuck most of the time."

"Chuck, then. You've met the maniac here." He smiled at Sasha, still holding Randi's hand and gazing up at her with open adoration, before giving Willow a nod. "And this is Will. Willow."

Chuck smiled at Willow. "Hi. Aunty R says you play *Horizon Zero Dawn.*"

Willow nodded, tucking a strand of hair behind her ear before looking at her feet. A sound came from her that may have been a mumbled "Hi."

Oh, this is going to be interesting.

He rubbed his hands together and smiled at the hostess. "Let's eat."

The short walk to their table was panic-inducing. Where did he sit? Next to Randi? Would that make this more like a date than he'd planned? Should he let Sasha sit next to her? But if he did that, Willow might feel like he was forcing her to sit next to Chuck. Fuck a bloody duck, it was a logistical nightmare.

Arriving at their booth, he swiped a hand over his mouth. Shit, what did he do?

"Sit next to me, Randi," Sasha demanded as she scurried into the curved booth.

Randi flicked him a quick glance before sliding onto the bench seat next to Sasha—or maybe she didn't. Maybe he was hoping she did because he needed to gauge where she wanted him to sit. *Jesus, I'm in trouble.*

And struck by a sudden case of paralysis.

Chuck moved before he could, shuffling in beside Randi.

Relief and regret rushed through Brody, hot and prickly at once.

"Can I sit beside you, maniac?" he arched a playful eyebrow at Sasha, who was grinning up at Randi.

"No, I want Willow to sit beside me."

Okay, so he was almost opposite Randi. If he extended his legs under the table, would his feet find hers?

What the fuck is wrong with me?

Willow studied him silently before moving her gaze to Randi.

"I'm going to have ice cream for dinner," Sasha announced loudly.

"Me, too." Chuck grinned at her, unfolding his menu. "What's your favorite flavor?"

"Chocolate."

"Mine, too."

Randi laughed. Hell, he liked the way she laughed. It was relaxed, not at all self-conscious. "This is good," he said.

Willow looked at him, expression unreadable. "Is it?"

His gut clenched. Okay, maybe it wasn't.

Their waiter arrived.

After a brief argument about whether or not Sasha was in fact going to have ice cream for dinner, their meals were ordered.

Brody fought with the urge to stretch his legs beneath the table.

"How's school going, Chuck?" he asked, straightening his spine and tucking his feet beneath the booth's seat. "Favorite subject?"

Chuck laughed as he reached for his water. "I don't take after Aunty R, I'm afraid. Even my stick figures look like they've been drawn by a six-year-old." He smiled at Sasha. "No offense to the six-year-olds at the table."

"My stick figures are awesome," Sasha declared without a hint of humility. She scooped a cube of ice out of her glass with her fingers and popped it into her mouth.

Chuck laughed again. "I bet they are. Aunty R told me about the incredible artwork she saw in your house last night."

Something tight and happy curled in Brody's chest. He'd brought the evening to an end last night in such an awkward way. That Randi had gone home and talked about his home, her night with them... Yeah, it did things to him it shouldn't.

"I'm a fan of science," Chuck said. Brody couldn't miss how he kept flicking Willow quick glances. "Mom and Dad want me to study medicine when I finish school, but I'm thinking I might go into zoology. Become a zookeeper."

"Oh, Chuck." Randi dropped her face into her hands and shook her head. "Your mother will kill you if you do that."

"Why?" Sasha frowned. "Animals are awesome. I want to work in a zoo when I grow up."

"I thought you wanted to own a pizza shop." Willow said.

Sasha shook her head. "Nope. I want to work in a zoo." She smiled at Chuck. "I'll buy the zoo, and you can work in it."

Chuck stretched his hand out across the table to her. "Deal."

Sasha shook it. "Yay. Now I'm going to be Chuck's boss. Willow, you can work there, too, if you like. And, Randi, you can be the teacher who works at the zoo. Daddy, you have to make the slogos for it."

"Slogos?"

"It's logos, you dork," Willow corrected, rolling her eyes.

"All right, Will." Brody nudged her with his shoulder. "That's enough."

"So we'll all work at my zoo together." Sasha nodded her head, smile wide. "A big family."

A big family.

Brody swallowed, and this time, he couldn't stop himself from looking at Randi. She was looking at him, bottom lip caught in her teeth, a question in her eyes he doubted she knew was there.

"That sounds good," he said.

Randi smiled at him across the table.

He smiled back.

"Mom loved going to the zoo," Willow said.

Something cold and invisible slammed into Brody's gut.

Randi dropped her gaze, turning her focus to the glass of water in front of her. Chuck cleared his throat.

"Food," Sasha exclaimed, as their meals arrived. Just in

time to save Brody from saying or doing something stupid; like getting angry with his own daughter.

Another meal with the Thortons, another night of propelling her closer to falling for Brody. She had to nip it all in the bud.

ASAP.

Of course, answering yes to Sasha's invitation to a tea party on the weekend—extended during dessert when Randi and Brody were having a tea-versus-coffee discussion—wasn't exactly nipping anything in the bud.

Maybe she needed to pull up all roots and move to Paris instead of Chuck. She could just see Stacey's face. *Oh, hi, Stace. I know you were expecting your son, but he's decided to stay in the States and become a zookeeper. I know, right? Now, do you have any hot French guys over here who could keep me from thinking about this extremely attractive Australian I left back in San Diego?*

As it was, Stacey was probably going to blame her for Chuck deciding to not go into medicine. Her sister hadn't wanted Chuck to stay with the underachiever of the family to start with. Aaron had been her first choice, but Aaron wasn't available, since he was spending a year as the chief of surgery at St. Thomas Hospital in London. Another Lockwood family member succeeding in Europe.

The closest Randi had ever been to Europe was Paris, Texas.

"Aunty R?"

A solid elbow nudged her ribs, and she blinked, jerking herself back to the booth and its occupants. "Ow. That hurt, Chuckles."

Chuck smirked at her. "We were talking movies. Brody had the audacity to say *Blade Runner* is a boring movie."

She dropped her spoon into her bowl of ice cream, gasping. "He did not!"

Chuck laughed. "You're in trouble now, dude," he said to Brody.

Brody shook his head. "Overrated waste of film stock, I say."

Randi blinked. "You're kidding! It's one of the greatest examples of sci-fi ever made."

He shook his head again, lips twitching as he threaded his fingers behind his head and stretched out in the booth. Something brushed her foot beneath the table, a soft contact that detonated a ridiculous heat in her stomach. Brody's foot?

God, how old am I? Sixteen?

"It's not even Harrison Ford's best work," he said with a teasing smile. The contact was gone. If it had been his foot, he'd pulled back. "And the whole is-he-or-isn't-he-a-replicant story? Pfft. Please. Of course he isn't."

Randi burst out laughing. "Oh, you did not just say that."

He grinned. "I did." Something brushed her foot again. Was it wrong to want it to be his foot?

"What are you talking about?" Willow slid her glare back and forth between them. The only time she'd engaged in the dinner conversation had been when Chuck asked her about *Horizon Zero Dawn*. She'd come to life then. When Randi herself commented about how she'd tried the game and sucked at it big time, Willow had mentioned again how incredible her mother had been at computer games.

All Randi needed to do was ask Willow to join the school's track team again and any hope of the girl liking her would be over.

"You haven't seen *Blade Runner*?" Chuck smiled at Willow. "It's one of those *classic*"—he made air quotes beside his head —"movies oldies argue about all the time. I love it, but then, I've been living with Aunty R for a while, so she's rubbing off on me. Mom will blame her for me dropping out of school next."

Randi snapped her stare to him.

He grinned. "Kidding. Thought I needed to defuse the whole *Blade Runner* thing."

Letting out a wobbly breath, she slumped in her seat and dragged her hands through her hair. "Don't do that to me, you pain in the—" She stopped, flicking a glance at Sasha.

"Arse?" Sasha offered, Aussie accent perfect.

"And on that note," Brody said, waving over a waiter, "it's time to go. School night."

Sasha let out a moan of disappointment. Randi agreed. She was having too much fun, as foolish and risky for her heart as it was.

"An early night *is* a good idea," she said with a resigned grimace. "I've got a long day tomorrow. Not a single period free, a staff meeting at lunch, and then track and field training after—"

Shit. She'd mentioned…

"School," she finished, her stomach a battalion of butterflies.

Willow chewed on her bottom lip, looking at her with an expression Randi had no hope of deciphering before dropping her gaze to the table top.

Randi offered her a smile. "You can come watch, if you like?"

Willow didn't respond. Didn't look at her. She may as well have not even been there.

Sasha looked back and forth between them, eyes wide.

"Right." Brody turned back from the waiter, check paid. "What did I miss?"

Chuck—God love him—cleared his throat. "Er…Marvel or DC? Aunty R likes DC more, and I keep telling her she's deluded."

"Marvel," Willow said. "All the way, isn't that right, Dad?"

Brody raised his eyebrows. "I'm okay with—"

Willow smiled at Randi. "Dad and Mom went to Comic-Con once as Spiderman and Mary Jane."

The second mention of Brody's wife from Willow tonight. The message was loud and clear.

But she didn't *want* to replace Willow's mother. And Brody had said no more kissing, no more…whatever it was that had started between them at the water park, so even if she *did* want to, there was bubkes chance of it happening.

So why then was she here? Why had she gone out of her way to wear the most flattering dress she owned? And why, for the love of God and all things holy, had she almost had a mini orgasm when Brody's foot brushed hers under the table?

"Hey, I went to Comic-Con last year." Chuck grinned at Willow. He was either clueless to the tension or doing everything he could to dissipate it, and Chuck was rarely clueless. "I even met Robert Downey Jr."

Willow's mouth fell open.

Chuck let out a laugh. "Unfortunately, I was wearing my T-shirt that says Iron Man is my b—"

"Charles." Randi glared at him. Sasha didn't need to learn about *that* shirt.

"Is my what?" Sasha asked.

Chuck ducked his head. "Umm…"

"My baseball coach." Brody gave Randi a wicked smile. Goddamn it, why did he have to be so sexy?

Sasha frowned. "That's stupid. Iron Man doesn't play baseball."

Willow giggled into her hand.

Chuck nodded. "It *is* a stupid thing to have on a shirt. I don't know what I was thinking buying it."

"You know what it should say?" Sasha looked up at him.

"What?"

"Iron Man is my bitch."

"Okay, maniac." Brody shoved himself from the booth, expression stern. "We're done for the night. Say goodbye."

"Goodbye," Sasha sing-songed as she scrambled over Willow's lap.

"Ow, Sasha," Willow complained, shuffling out of the booth after her.

Sasha pointed a finger at Randi. "Don't forget the tea party. Race you to the car, Will." She ran from the restaurant.

"Bloody hell." Brody threw up his hands. "Sash—"

"We'll get her," Chuck said, running after her. "C'mon, Willow."

Willow looked at Randi. She opened her mouth, and then —at the sound of Sasha giggling in delight from the door— hurried after Chuck. "I'll get her, Dad."

Drawing a deep breath, Randi shimmied out of the booth.

"Thank you for coming tonight." Brody smiled, before shooting a look over his shoulder to where Sasha, Willow, and Chuck stood laughing together in the doorway. "Sasha really loved you being here."

"I enjoyed being here as well."

His smile grew lopsided as he turned back to face her. "You don't have to come to the tea party on Saturday if you don't want to. Unless you're really excited about being served warm water from a plastic teapot and pretend cupcakes."

She let out a mock gasp. "You mean there's not going to be pretend croissants?"

He chuckled, rubbing his hand at the back of his neck. "I'm afraid we have only pretend cupcakes."

"For Sasha, I will suffer through it all."

He laughed again. God, she liked him. A lot. The only sane thing to do would be to end it all now. Cancel the tea party with Sasha, round up Chuck, and get away pronto.

"Maybe," he said, his gaze finding hers, "I'll dig out my baking apron and make some *real* cupcakes."

"You have a baking apron?"

"I do. It's pink with hearts wearing chef hats."

"Oh, in that case, I'm definitely coming to the tea party. I need to see this apron."

He grinned. "It brings out the blue of my eyes."

Were they flirting? Surely that's what they were doing?

"Brody," she said, just as he said "Randi."

They both stopped. Both stared at each other.

He took a step toward her, just one.

"Thank you." She took a step backward, smiling even as she pretended to search the table for something. "I need to give you some money for dinner. I don't expect—"

"My shout."

She frowned at him. His expression was…uncertain. "Your shout?"

"Sorry, it's an Aussie term. It means my treat."

She swallowed. "Ah, okay. My shout next time then."

And there she went, putting the idea of more time with him out there.

"Definitely." He grinned. "Is it pushy of me to lock in a date now?"

Date. Why did he have to use *that* word?

She shook her head. Thinking about going on an honest-to-goodness date with Brody Thorton would be her undoing. As it was, she was going to spend much longer in the shower tonight than normal. With the door locked.

"I'm available next Friday night."

Friday night? That was the ultimate *date* date night. *What am I doing?*

A smile played with the edges of Brody's mouth. "Next Friday night it is."

"Daddy?" Sasha's voice wafted from the restaurant's door, loud and filled with agitation. "Are you going to kiss Randi again?"

Heat flooded Randi's cheeks. Brody dropped his face into his hands, whatever he muttered muffled by his palms.

"Oh my God, don't make me throw up," Willow's voice—stunned, horrified—reached them at the booth.

Randi bit her bottom lip, face aflame.

Lifting his head, Brody let out a shaky chuckle. "I think I better get these two home. I really enjoyed tonight."

She smiled. "Me too."

So much. So goddamn much.

A heartbeat of silence stretched between them, and then Brody turned and strode to the door. He scooped Sasha up onto his hip, said something to Chuck, who laughed in return, and then he, Sasha, and Willow walked away. But not before Willow looked back at Randi, expression unreadable.

What is she thinking?

Huh, what is Willow thinking? What am I thinking? What the freaking hell was she doing, arranging not one but two more interactions with Brody? She was a masochist.

"Well, that was fun." Chuck walked back to where she still stood, somehow incapable of moving. "So when are you and Brody going to—?"

"I will hit you if you say another word, Chuckles."

CHAPTER EIGHT

"So is it a date, or not?"

"Not."

Singo cocked an eyebrow before taking a mouthful of beer.

"Sounds like a date." Nate Young snagged a peanut from the complimentary bowl on the bar and tossed it into his mouth.

Brody crossed his arms and settled back on his stool. "Y'know, Youngie, for a veterinarian, you know bugger all about people."

"There's a reason I'm a vet, mate. Me and people don't gel."

"Youngie's right." Singo scooped some peanuts out of the bowl. "Sounds like a date."

Brody reached for his beer—a Crown Lager. It had been bloody tricky to find a pub in San Diego that served it—and shook his head. "I don't even know where we're going. And Will and Sash will be there, so not a date."

"Did Randi indicate the girls should be there?" Singo asked.

"Good question." Nate dug out another peanut. "Did she say you should bring the girls?"

A hot knot tightened in Brody's chest.

He'd spent way too many minutes over the last few days thinking about what *next Friday* was going to be. So many minutes he'd started to freak out. A forty-two-year-old bloke shouldn't be freaking out over catching up with a woman, whether it was a date or not.

Fuck a duck, what if it is a date?

"Hell." He downed a mouthful of beer.

Singo slapped him on the shoulder. "She's coming around to your place this arvo, right? For the tea party with Sasha?"

The words tea party sounded so strange spoken by a bloke so intimidating to look at. "She is."

"Ask her then."

"What? Just say, 'Hey Randi, are we going on a date sans kids next Friday night, or is it a platonic thing with the girls and Chuck included?'"

"Chuck's her son?"

"Nephew. Great kid. You'd like him, Singo. Smart, switched on. Sarcastic sense of humor. Got intelligent geek written all over him."

"I don't do kids."

Nate laughed. "Says the man who plays with Legos for a living."

"I don't play. I build. I design. I create."

Brody snorted. "What were you *creating* when I spoke to you on Monday?"

"A new *Star Wars* installation at Legoland. Luke, Artoo, and C-3P0 are trying to bake a cake in a cantina."

"You play."

Singo grinned. "Yeah, I play. It's a hard life, but someone's got to live it." He popped a peanut into his mouth.

Nate grunted and fixed Brody with a steady look. "Back to your situation, mate. Do you want it to be a date?"

"No."

Bullshit.

Both Singo and Nate raised their eyebrows.

His throat grew thick. "I don't."

Shit.

"It's okay if you do, Thorton," Nate said. "It's been two years since Bridget…"

"Died? Or since I killed her?"

Nate winced. "You didn't kill her, and you know it."

"She was pissed at me when she drove off, Youngie. Seriously pissed. Fifteen minutes later, she runs a stop sign and gets wiped out." His gut clenched. A cold, prickly tension crawled over him. It had been a long time since he'd been so blunt when it came to Bridget's death, either aloud or in his head. "If she hadn't been so angry with me, she might have paid more attention to the road."

"Don't do this to yourself, mate," Singo said. "It doesn't help anyone. You have no idea what caused Bridget to miss that stop sign, just as you had every right to tell her she was pushing Willow too much with training."

Brody let out a sigh and pushed his beer away. He wasn't thirsty anymore. "I found Willow looking at her medals and trophies last night."

It had been almost midnight. She'd been sitting in the middle of her bed, her room lit only by the glow from her smartphone's screen.

He'd been about to crawl into bed himself, exhausted after a busy week at work and a week of confusing thoughts about Randi, and had found Willow like that during his final check of the girls before hitting the hay. He'd stood in the dark hallway outside her room, a vise clamping around his heart, his pulse thumping in his ears.

It was the first time he'd witnessed her showing any interest in what had once been such an important part of her life.

Maybe he should encourage her to start competing again after all?

Or was he just trying to give himself a reason to see Randi more often?

Christ, he was already using one daughter to keep her in their lives, was he so fucking lame he'd use his other one?

"Mate?" Someone shook his shoulder.

"Huh? What?" He frowned at Singo and Nate.

Nate flicked Singo a look. "I said, do you think Willow's ready to start jumping again?"

He burst out a shaky breath and rubbed at the back of his neck. "I don't know. It was such a thing with her and her mum."

"And now it could be a thing for her and Randi," Nate said.

Brody's gut churned. "Why do you two keep bringing the bloody conversation back around to Randi?"

Another flicked look passed between them. Singo cleared his throat. "Mate, ever since you met her at the water park, you've…how should I put this?"

"Come to life?" Nate suggested. "You say Sasha's come to life whenever Randi's with her. Hell, Thorton, you've done the same just talking about her. I want to be in the same room as the pair of you one day so I can see what you're like when you're with her."

"Hey." Singo slapped his shoulder again. "Maybe Youngie and I can come 'round this arvo for the tea party? Or better yet, the date on Friday night?"

"It's not a date."

Singo grinned. "But you want it to be, right?"

"I'm out of here." Brody straightened from his stool. "You two are more than welcome to come around this arvo if you want." He slapped enough bills on the bar to cover all their beers plus a tip. "But I will smack the shit out of you if you behave like a pack of idiots. Got it?"

Singo laughed.

Nate smiled. "Go have fun, Thorton. Keep us posted on the not-a-date date."

"Ha-ha. Funny bastards, aren't you."

Nate dipped his head in silent acknowledgment. Singo shoved himself off his own stool and extended his right hand. "It's good to see you happy, mate. You might think you're not allowed to be happy, but we like seeing you this way."

A heavy weight on his chest, Brody shook Singo's hand. "Cheers, mate."

He took the Trolley to the station closest to home and then walked the rest of the way. His neighbor, Mrs. Herdan, had shooed him off just after lunch, telling him he needed some "man time to himself" and promising to teach Willow and Sasha how to make a clementine cake while he was out. Mrs. Herdan—a lovely old spinster in her seventies who doted on the girls—often offered him help since Bridget's passing, saving his sanity more than once.

Catching up with his fellow Aussies kept him sane. Well, it did normally. Today's effort, however…

Bloody hell, he needed his head read. Even thinking Randi had suggested a date told him he was walking a fine line. He'd shut down any notion of…well…romance with her in his kitchen, so why would he think she'd been suggesting a—

A car slowed to a halt beside him just as he was about to turn into his driveway. "Want a ride?"

Before he could stop himself, he grinned at the familiar female voice. Happiness burst in his chest, spread through him in a wave of heat. Trying to keep his expression casual, he gave Randi a smile. "I know it's a long way, but I'll walk." He patted his stomach. "I need to work on losing this middle-age spread."

She laughed. Crikey, he liked the sound of her laugh.

"Suit yourself. I'll see you there." She slid her sunglasses back onto her face, flashed him a devilish smirk, and then slowly turned into his driveway.

Be cool. There's nothing between us. Nothing at all.

She climbed out of her car, and he balled his hands into painful fists to stop the groan threatening to rumble in his chest.

A long white dress covered her body, draping off one smooth shoulder in a flowy curtain. The soft fabric seemed to be in love with her curves and dips, drawing his eye and making his pulse thump. Her hair hung over her bare shoulder, plaited into a loose braid that brushed against her right breast.

Breast. Hell, he shouldn't be looking at her right breast. Or her left one for that matter. He should be... Christ, her hips were sublime, especially how they swung when she walked toward him.

"I bought macaroons for the tea party."

His brain registered the white box in her hand just as he jerked his stare back up to her face. This close, he could see her eyeshadow was a smoky, stormy gray, the kind that had always done it for him back in the day. It made the light blue of her irises almost iridescent. Mesmerizing.

Was she trying to drive him crazy?

"Randi!" Sasha came barreling out of Mrs. Herdan's front door.

Thank bloody God for that. Who knows what the hell he would have said or done if she hadn't?

Kiss her. Like I wanted to at Phil's BBQ on Tuesday night.

He hadn't then, even though he had stepped toward her, and he wasn't going to now. It was off the table. No matter how...intrigued he was by her.

Intrigued. Is that what I'm calling it?

"Hi, Sasha." Randi held the white cardboard box out to her. "I hope you like macaroons."

"What are macaroons?"

Randi's lips curled. "Oh, just the most delicious little delights you've ever tasted."

"As good as Daddy's cupcakes?"

"I don't know." Randi smiled, first at Sasha and then at him. "I'll need to taste one to find out."

Cupcakes. Crap. Crap, crap, crap.

"Dad hasn't made cupcakes," Willow said, striding past

them all as she headed toward the front door. "And macaroons are full of artificial colors."

"Hi, Brody." Mrs. Herdan waved at him from her front porch. "Is this your new lady friend Sasha has been telling me all about? You look good together."

Brody scrunched up his face. Maybe it wasn't too late to turn around and go back to the pub?

They baked cupcakes. She, Brody, and Sasha. Brody wore his apron with the pink chef's hat wearing love hearts. Of course he looked so goddamn sexy she kept getting distracted. It was possible the batter had three eggs in it instead of two. Sasha laughed and smiled throughout the whole adventure, giving out random hugs to her and Brody whenever the mood seemed to take her.

Willow sat at the dining table, on her phone, ignoring them all.

Although every time Randi glanced her way, Willow was watching them. After the fifth time of Willow pulling the classic crap-I've-been-busted-look-away routine, Randi had to bite her tongue to stop herself from chuckling. She did not want Willow to get angry or offended. Seriously, it was easier dealing with moody teenagers when she had her teacher hat on.

What kind of hat did she have on now? Not a girlfriend hat, that was for sure. A friend-of-the-family hat? Not really, given she was pretty certain only Sasha and Brody considered her that. An acquaintance hat? What allowances did that give her?

Kissing one of the acquaintances had initially been on the list, but now it had been struck off.

Damn, she really needed some kind of definition of the situation so she could find the right hat.

"Ready to bake." Sasha skipped over to the oven and opened its door. "Put them in, Daddy."

While Brody slid the loaded cupcake tray into the oven, Randi offered Willow a smile. "Are you going to join Sasha and me for the tea party?"

"Hey, that's a good idea." Brody wiped his hands on his apron, straightening. "Careful closing the door, maniac."

"I need a new calculator for school, Dad," Willow said. "Can you take me to the mall?"

Brody frowned and flicked a glance at Randi. "Really?"

Willow nodded. "Miss Lockwood and Sasha will be okay. Miss Lockwood is here to play with Sash anyways, not us."

Brody's frown deepened. "Do you really need—?"

"It's okay." Randi touched his forearm. Probably shouldn't have, because the innocent contact detonated a delicious little tightness in the pit of her stomach. "If you're fine with Sasha and me partying alone, you and Willow can go. In fact, as a teacher, I insist." She pulled a melodramatic stern face. "School stuff always comes before fun stuff."

Sasha giggled.

"You sure?" Brody asked.

Willow smiled, but it seemed uncertain, as if she wasn't sure how to feel about what was going on.

"Sure. But be warned, we're not going to save you any cupcakes, are we, Sasha?"

"No, we are not." Sasha grinned.

Brody chuckled, slipping the adorable apron over his head. Had it always been his, or did it once belong to his wife?

"All right, we'll be back ASAP." He dumped the apron on the counter, dropped a quick kiss on Randi's cheek, and froze.

Randi blinked, incapable of moving.

Oh God. Oh God, oh God, oh God.

Willow gasped.

Sasha laughed. "Yay. Daddy kissed Randi."

"Shit." He jerked backward, eyes wide. "Shit, I mean, crap.

Sorry. I didn't mean…" He swiped a hand over his mouth, a mouth only a second ago that had pressed to her cheek. "I didn't…it was…"

Sweet and natural and…wonderful, all wrapped up in one quick, innocuous peck on the cheek.

Too wonderful. And most likely the action of a distracted mind. He'd probably already been in the car and on the way to the mall in his head, dealing with the crazy Saturday afternoon rush, and muscle memory had initiated the goodbye process—complete with a quick goodbye kiss—without any thought behind it.

Yeah, that was it.

"I'm sorry," he said again, Adam's apple jerking up and down.

"That's okay." She waved a dismissive hand and smiled. Everything inside her was far from smiling, however. Everything inside her was squeezing and thrumming.

He didn't move.

Neither did she.

Talk about awkward with a capital *awk*.

And sweet and wonderful and God, how amazing would it be to get a kiss like that every day? Just a simple, habitual kiss that spoke volumes about how special—

"Dad? Can we go?"

Brody flinched at Willow's question.

"Coming, Will."

He turned and hurried from the room.

Willow met Randi's gaze. For a thirteen-year-old, she had the poker face of a pro.

"Want to say something, Willow?" It was such a teacher question, but it was out before Randi could stop it.

Willow shook her head. "No." Something flickered across her face. Uncertainty again? And then she left, too.

Letting out a slow breath, Randi smiled at Sasha. "So, tea party time?"

Sasha regarded her, expression as unreadable as Willow's had been. "Do you like Daddy? A lot lot?"

Here we go. "He's very nice."

Whoa, talk about the understatement of the century.

"Do you like it when he kisses you?"

And here we really *go.* "Why?"

Sasha shrugged. "I think Willow gets angry about it, but I don't mind."

Should she be relieved or disappointed? She chewed on the inside of her mouth, processing the conversation. Sasha would have been four when her mother died. Did she remember her as much as Willow?

"I—" she began. God knows what she was going to say. There was a reason she was a middle-school teacher and not an elementary one. Little kids were hard.

"Let's have our tea party now while the cupcakes are still baking. Don't forget the macrons." Sasha bounded out of the kitchen, heading for the living room.

Macrons. This kid was adorable.

Bringing the box of macaroons with her, Randi crossed to the rug in the middle of the living room where the tea party was already set up and sat cross-legged opposite Sasha.

"Macrons." She passed the macaroons across the teapot, plates, cups, and saucers.

With a big grin, Sasha took the box and, after a few moments of oohing over the contents, selected a pink one for herself—strawberry—and a green one for Randi—chocolate mint.

"Would you like me to pour?" Randi indicated to the teapot. Was there anything in it? She'd never partaken in a tea party growing up. Playtime in her family had been strictly academic pursuits, piano lessons, or brain teasers. As a consequence, she could play the hell out of Beethoven's Piano Concerto No. 5 while reciting *pi* to four places.

"Yes, please," Sasha answered around a mouthful of macaroon in her best prim-and-proper British accent.

Oh, so there's water in the teapot? Excellent.

"Do you want to be Daddy's girlfriend?"

Randi missed her cup, pouring water on the rug. "W-why?"

"Do you already have a boyfriend?"

"No, no." Oh God, she wasn't ready for this conversation. "I had one. But then I didn't."

"Did you dump him?"

Randi blinked.

"Willow's friends talk about dumping boys all the time. Does it hurt?"

Having never been the dumper, Randi didn't have an answer. Speaking from personal experience, being the dumpee...yeah, that sucked.

"Do you like Daddy just 'cause Willow's good at jumping?"

Oh man.

Sasha frowned at the open box of macaroons, her strawberry one already devoured. "That's what Willow said last night. She said that you only want to be Daddy's girlfriend so she'll go back to long jumping again."

"That's not—"

"Do you want her to do long jumping again?"

Crap, how do I proceed here? "I've seen videos of her jumping. She's very good."

Sasha nodded. Clearly, that was an indisputable fact as far as she was concerned. "Aunty Alicia said Mommy said she was good enough to go to the Olympics one day."

"She is." That wasn't a lie. The footage Randi had watched of Willow competing at various meets was impressive.

"Willow said Mommy and Daddy used to fight about all the training Mommy made her do." Sasha plucked at the macaroon in her fingers. "She said they were fighting about it when Mommy got car-crashed and died."

Randi drew a slow breath. Oh God, where had all the heat in the room gone? She *couldn't* ask Willow to compete again. Not knowing this now. A promotion was one thing, but she wouldn't emotionally traumatize a child for the sake of professional advancement. She wouldn't.

"I'm sorry," she said, voice a scratchy whisper.

Sasha frowned at her macaroon. "I miss Mommy."

Randi swallowed.

"Hey, wanna see what I'm good at?" Sasha asked, the smile on her face so far removed from the intense conversation they'd just been having.

Throat thick, Randi nodded. "I would love to."

Sasha leaped to her feet and threw herself into a handstand-slash-cartwheel that ended with her crumpling into a giggling fit on the rug.

If only there were competitions for lopsided, wildly enthusiastic living-room gymnastics.

CHAPTER NINE

Singo and Nate met him at his driveway.

Climbing out of his Nissan, he closed the driver's door and grinned at them. "So you really are going to crash the tea party?"

Singo held up a bottle of pink lemonade wrapped in a candy-pink satin bow. "It's not crashing if you bring the hostess a bottle of her favorite beverage."

"Did you bring *my* favorite beverage?" Willow asked, rounding the front of the SUV.

"Don't worry, Will." Nate walked up to her. "I did."

He handed her a bottle of Bundaberg Ginger Beer, a soda made only in Australia.

Willow snatched it from Nate's hand with a laugh and hugged it to her chest. "You're the best, Mr. Young."

Nate dipped at the waist. "I am. Much better than Singo and your dad here, I reckon."

"Bloody oath," Willow responded in a passable Aussie accent. "Now I'm going to hide this."

She turned on her heel and scampered into the house.

"That wasn't as painful as I thought it would be." Singo

frowned at Brody. "I thought you said she's been giving you a hard time."

"Ah, wait until you're inside and see how she behaves with Randi about."

Nate raised his eyebrows. "Jealous?"

"I don't think so. Maybe...protective? She's mentioned her mother more times today than she has in the last month."

"Makes sense." Nate shrugged. "I made Mum's life a living hell when I was a kid and she started dating again after Dad shot through."

"Randi and I aren't dating."

Singo smirked. "Sure you're not."

"That's it. I'm uninviting you two to this tea party."

Singo laughed. "Too late, mate. We're here. Ready, Youngie?"

Nate nodded. "Ready."

They headed inside. Brody brought up the rear, chuckling even as a ball of nerves rolled in his gut. Nerves. The kind a bloke got when introducing his new girl to his family and friends.

"Singo!" Sasha's excited shout hit Brody before he stepped into the house. He walked into the living room just as Sasha launched herself at Singo.

"Heya, squirt." Singo spun her around, his smile as wide as hers. "How ya goin'?"

"I'm having a tea party with Daddy's maybe girlfriend, Randi. Hi, Nate. Did you see Randi?"

"She's not his girlfriend," Willow ground out from the kitchen.

Brody flicked an apologetic look Randi's way.

She was straightening to her feet from the floor, a half-eaten bright-green macaroon in her hand, an easy smile on her face.

Hell, he really, *really* liked that smile. It did things to him.

"Hi." She gave that smile first to Singo and then Nate.

Something cold and unfamiliar traced down Brody's spine. Jealousy? "I'm Randi. Sasha's friend."

Sasha's friend. Not his. There was a significance to the description, but he wasn't sure what.

"G'day." Nate extended his hand. "Nathanial Young. Most people call me Nate."

She took his hand in hers and shook it. "Nice to meet you, Nate."

"Nathanial sounds funny," Sasha protested. "Willow calls him Youngie."

"Y'know who else calls me Youngie?"

"Who?"

"My mum."

Sasha's eyebrows shot up. "Really?"

He nodded.

"I call him a pain in the butt." Singo chuckled, initiating a handshake with Randi. "Hi. I'm Adam, but most people in this room call me Singo."

"Hi." Randi smiled again.

Damn it, he really needed to find a way to make himself immune to that smile, otherwise he was—

"I tell you what, squirt." Singo tapped Sasha's cheek. "I like seeing this big grin on your face. Makes my heart feel good."

"Thanks, mate." She dropped him a cheeky curtsy, her Aussie accent flawless. "Wanna cuppa?"

The oven beeped. Her grin split wider. "They're ready. The cupcakes are ready. Willow, help me get the cupcakes out." She bolted into the kitchen.

Willow rolled her eyes, put the bottle of ginger beer Nate had given her into the fridge, and then slipped her hands into oven mitts.

Which left the four of them—the adults—standing beside the tea party, looking at one another.

"Gentlemen?" Randi waved her hand at the floor. "Help yourselves to a macaroon."

"Onya." Singo chuckled.

Nate studied her. "So, Brody tells us you're an art teacher at Willow's school."

"I am."

"And the pair of you are going on a date Friday night."

Singo coughed out a spray of macaroon crumbs.

Brody blinked. "Jesus, Youngie."

"What?"

"Pardon my tactless friend here." Brody whacked the back of his hand against Nate's chest. "He works with animals for a living."

"And I play with Lego." Singo wiped at his mouth. "So now that's out of the way, what are your intentions with our good friend here?"

"I'm going to kill you both," Brody groaned.

Randi laughed. "No, no, it's okay. I can answer this. First, I'm going to ensnare him with my wit and sinful curves. Then I'm slowly going to insinuate myself into every facet of his life, every thought he has, until he signs everything he owns over to me, *everything*. And then, when he's completely and utterly at my mercy, I'm going to reveal I'm actually a guy and he's just been part of a bet I made with a frat-boy friend of mine. What do you think?"

Singo chewed it all over. Nate narrowed his eyes and nodded. "Fair enough. Go for it."

Brody smacked his hand against Nate's chest again. "Oi. Aren't you meant to look out for your mates?"

"Nah, the exact same thing happened to me about six months ago. You'll be right."

Brody dragged a hand down his face. "And I thought this introduction was going to be hard."

Singo laughed. Randi grinned.

"Do we want hot cupcakes without frosting?" Sasha shouted from the kitchen. "Or colded down ones with frosting?"

"Both?" Nate suggested.

"Oh, I like him," Randi said.

"Too bad. You're going on a date with me Friday night."

Randi's gaze locked with his, lips twitching. "Am I now?"

Singo clapped him on the shoulder. "Guess that answers that. It's a date. Now, to the next question. Who is babysitting the girls? Me or the animal doctor?"

"Both," Sasha cried.

Date. Hell, he couldn't go on a date with Randi. He couldn't go on a date, period. He had to think of his girls, of their lives, and feelings. And yet...

His phone buzzed in his jeans' pocket, and he yanked it out.

Shit. Alicia. What the hell did his sister-in-law want?

"Give me a sec, guys," he said, connecting the call. "Hi, Alicia. What's up?"

At Alicia's name, Randi dropped her focus to her feet.

"Hi, Aunty Alicia," Sasha shouted from the kitchen. "We're having a party."

"Sasha," Willow groaned. Willow had never been close with Alicia, even before Bridget's death. Alicia had done her best to be everything Willow needed her to be after the funeral, but Willow always held her at arm's length. But Willow held most people that way. She was the introvert of the family, something Alicia—an events-organizer—struggled to comprehend.

"A party?" Disapproval filled Alicia's voice.

"Tea party. Singo and Youngie are here."

"Your Australian friends?"

"Yep. And Randi."

"The woman from the water park?"

"Yep."

"Is she now?"

"Yep."

"Why?"

"Why what?"

"Why is she there? You know, Brody, you only have to ask for help, and I will be there." There was no censure in her voice. "I don't mind at all."

"She and I are going out together Friday night."

Silence.

Why the hell did I tell her that?

Randi looked up at him, her expression unreadable.

He swallowed and then flicked a look at Willow and Sasha in the kitchen.

Sasha, God love her, was grinning, a half-eaten, frosting-free cupcake in her hand. Willow stood beside her, expression as impossible to decipher as Randi's.

"So that's happening," he continued, dropping Sasha a wink before he turned to Singo and Nate. What end result did he want out of the declaration? For Alicia to give him some room? To let her know he was ready to move on with his life?

It was like someone had put his mouth into drive and cut the brakes. Maybe his mates could do something to shut him up? "What's happening in your world?"

Singo shook his head. Nate snorted, abandoning him in his time of need for a macaroon.

"Well," Alicia said, "I *was* calling to suggest I come visit with you and the girls this weekend, but…"

"Yeah, nah." Hell, it was such an Aussie thing to say. He really *was* stressed. He rarely slipped into such colloquialisms these days. "We're good, aren't we girls?"

"We're good," Sasha called before frowning up at Willow. "What are we good about, Will?"

Willow met his gaze. Christ, Bridget used to get the same look on her face when she couldn't decide whether to hit him or hug him. "Daddy's happy. That's what we're good about."

His gut clenched. *What does that mean?*

"Is there anything else I can do you for, Alicia?" He didn't *not* like his sister-in-law. He just wasn't up for her level of

LOVE AND OTHER RESPONSIBILITIES | 111

drama today. It was almost like at some point she'd appointed herself the matriarch of his little family, and while he was grateful for everything she'd done for him, he just needed...space.

God, does that make me a selfish bastard?

Maybe. He was proving himself to be a shit in all facets of his life at the moment, it seemed.

She sniffed on the other end of the line. "I guess not today. Would you like me to pop around sometime this week? Sasha mentioned at Wet 'N' Wild she wants to learn how to braid her hair, and I thought I could perhaps teach you both."

"Yeah, nah, I'm good." It wasn't a lie. Was it *wrong* to feel so good? "We're good."

"Good," Sasha crowed.

Willow rolled her eyes.

He slid his gaze from Willow to Randi. She was looking up from her feet once more, a soft frown on her face. "I reckon I've got this plait thing covered," he said, running his gaze down the length of the thick braid of dark hair tumbling over Randi's shoulder.

"Brody..." Concern filled Alicia's voice. "Do you know what you're doing?"

He blinked. "About what?"

"You don't need to replace Bridget. And I'm—"

"I'm not replacing Bridget." The words left him on a low growl. Fuck, how could she think that was even a possibility?

The room went cold. Silent.

Shit.

Without looking at anyone, he turned. If he gripped the phone any tighter it'd probably crack.

Like I will?

"I don't mean to upset you," Alicia said. "But what do you really know about this woman?"

"I know enough."

Heat razed his back. From everyone staring at him, or from something else?

Anger? At himself? Or the situation?

Or at Bridget for not being there?

"It's probably better we chat later, Alicia." Once he'd finally got his own head around the situation. Not before. Who the bloody hell knows what he'd say next?

"Fine." Ah, the dreaded *fine*. Yeah, he was in the shit. "I will call you later."

She disconnected before he could say goodbye.

Well fuck.

Letting out a breath, he shoved his phone back into his pocket, and turned to face everyone.

Singo and Nate looked sympathetic, the typical my-mate's-up-the-creek look. Sasha was eating a macaroon, so she'd clearly moved on. Be buggered if he could read Willow's or Randi's expressions. He gave Randi a sheepish chuckle, rubbing at the back of his neck. "Were you prepared for this kind of insanity when you arrived today?"

She smiled. But it didn't light up her eyes, not like it normally did. "It's okay."

It wasn't okay. The afternoon had derailed. "I'm sorry."

"Honest, it's fine."

For a split second, it looked like she was going to say more. Her gaze locked on his, and then she cleared her throat and smiled—really smiled—at Sasha and Willow. "Those cupcakes smell delicious. Do you think they are ready for frosting?"

Six days without eating a cupcake. A tragedy of epic proportions, thanks to the Thortons.

Of course, Melanie Murrell *would* decide to make the subject of her in-class drawing task a cupcake, wouldn't she? And because Melanie's mother was a pastry chef, she always brought in freshly baked and decorated cupcakes for everyone in art class, as well as for Randi. The trouble was, Randi couldn't look at a cupcake now without thinking about last Saturday at Brody's house, and thinking about last Saturday at Brody's house only confused the crap out of her.

"Miss?"

Dammit, Melanie wanted help.

Maybe it was time for a career change? How stressful would a professional snake wrangler's job be? Or a flamingo breeder's?

"Miss?"

Yeah, breeding flamingoes was looking more and more appealing.

Being a flamingo breeder would not change the fact that it's Friday.

Her stomach fluttered.

She'd spent the last six days expecting a text or call from Brody canceling whatever tonight was.

That text or call never came.

She'd also spent the last six days replaying the conversation he'd had with his sister-in-law over and over in her mind. The side of the conversation she'd heard, that was.

And she and I are going out together this Friday night. That's what he'd said. *"I'm not replacing Bridget."*

Which basically meant tonight she was going out on a date with a guy who would forever be thinking about someone else.

Crap, why am I doing this to myself? He isn't that good-looking.

That was a lie. He was. He really was, but it had nothing to do with how good-looking he was, and everything to do with how goddamn nice and funny and caring and generous he was. How he loved his daughters, how he clearly loved his friends. How unpretentious he was, how genuine…

Oh crap, she was falling in love with him.

Falling? Don't you mean fallen?

"Miss? Are you okay?"

She blinked.

Every student in her class stared at her. Scott—her knight-protector from days ago when Brody had first come to the school to confront her about Willow and long jumping—was half off his stool, as if about to run to her.

"What's wrong?" she asked them.

"You just"—Melanie frowned—"like, groaned. Really loudly."

"I did?"

Everyone nodded, almost in unison. Scott slowly put his butt back on his stool, but he didn't look convinced he wasn't going to need to make a mad dash in her direction soon.

"Sorry." She moved the charcoal pencils strewn over her desk. "Was just thinking about all the grading I'm going to need to do when you all hand in your art history essays."

"What art history essays?" Scott asked.

She flashed him an evil grin even as her pulse pounded in her ears. "The one I'm going to give you next week."

Her class groaned.

She laughed just as the bell rang.

"Saved by the you-know-what," she muttered. "Okay, guys. You know where to put your works-in-progress. All supplies packed away. Remember, I'm grading your finished drawings this time next week."

To a chorus of farewells and weekend wishes, her class streamed out of her room.

Closing her eyes, she dropped her forehead to her desk with a thud.

In love with Brody Thorton. I'm in love with Brody Thorton. Good grief, what am I going to do?

"You are." Thud. "A masochist." Thud.

"Everything okay, Miranda?"

Excellent, her principal had arrived. Yay.

Lifting her head, she smiled. "Hi, Dave. How are you?"

"Have you convinced Willow Thorton to return to the track team?"

Geez, don't pussy-foot around, Dave. "I—"

"Because we need her on that team."

"I—"

"And I don't want excuses." He glowered. Yep, definitely a glower. "I know you can do it."

She didn't even get the chance to say anything before he continued.

"Someone ready to become a head of a department should surely be capable of achieving this."

Code: want your promotion? Get Willow jumping again.

He turned his glower onto the untouched cupcake Melanie had handed her at the beginning of the lesson. "Do you always eat cupcakes in front of your students, Miss Lockwood? Not very professional."

She almost offered it to him. Almost. It was too lovely to give to an irritating SOB. "It was a gift from a student."

He grunted. "Back in my day as a teacher, we didn't allow food in class. Nor did we encourage our students to attempt to offer bribes."

Don't roll your eyes. Don't say anything snarky.

"Let me know as soon as you can re Willow Thorton." He strode from her room.

She huffed out a breath. Those flamingoes were looking more and more appealing.

"Why are you still here?" Sydney Shelton walked through the door. "It's Friday. End of the day. And you're still sitting at your desk. Looking very frazzled, I might add."

"Don't you have science papers to grade?"

Sydney patted the satchel hanging over her shoulder. "This is my Friday night. The glamorous life of a teacher, eh? Want to come around to my place with your own papers to grade? I can drink cheap wine while you drink cheaper water, we can order in Italian and laugh at the dreams we once had back in our college days of how wonderful our future lives would be."

"I can't. I've got a d—" Randi snapped her mouth shut.

Sydney's eyes grew wide. "Girl, were you about to say date. You have a date tonight? With who?"

"Frank." Yeah, she totally didn't know any Franks.

"Frank who?"

Crap. "Frank…" *Think!* "Harrington."

"Frank Harrington?"

"Yes. Nice guy. Met him…at the beach. Last week."

"Harrington? Like the actor Kitt Harrington? The guy who's in that show you love so much with the dragons in it?"

Shit. That's what she got for going on and on about Jon Snow to Sydney throughout the last season of *Game of Thrones*, and for lying. But there was no way she'd tell Sydney she was going out with Brody Thorton. That would be—

"Oh, for Pete's sake, Randi." Sydney burst out laughing. "Colleen saw you and Brody Thorton and his daughters at Phil's BBQ on Tuesday last week. Just fess up. That's who you're going on a date with, isn't it?"

Randi's stomach divorced her. "Sydney." She leaped to her feet and waved her hand frantically. "Shush."

Swiping at her hand, Sydney laughed again. "Why?"

"You know what Dave's like. He does not approve of any kind of teacher/parent social interaction at all, and I'm still trying to convince him I'm perfect for the head of the arts faculty."

"He just needs to goddamn give that promotion to you and quit with the carrot-stick routine."

"I wish. If he knew I was…was…" Going on a date with Brody Thorton. She couldn't say it aloud. It was too surreal.

Sydney perched on the edge of her desk. "You know, every single female teacher here is in lust with him. Probably quite a few of the non-single ones as well. And a few of the male teachers, I bet."

"With Dave Pascoe?"

"What?" Sydney screwed up her face. "Ew. No. With Brody Thorton. I already told you he's one of those parents we teachers fantasize about. I mean, you should've heard some of the things being said about him when he volunteered for the Dunk Tank at the school's Spring Fair during Willow's first year here. Sitting in that booth in a wet white T-shirt and Australian flag board shorts." She sighed. "I can still see that white shirt clinging to his body…"

"Sydney." Randi groaned.

Sydney wriggled her eyebrows. "What? Once you see it, you can't *unsee* it, and baby, I saw it. I made sure I saw it. Don't think I saw much of anything else at the fair. The Dunk Tank made more money that year than any other booth. I think I spent almost a hundred bucks trying to drop Brody Thorton into the water. He's not just swoon-worthy, he's lust-worthy. The stuff of debauched sexual fantasies. You should be crowing about this date, not lying about it."

"It's not a date." Which is why she'd dropped half her week's salary on that new dress she saw in the window of the Fabulous Rag Boutique only yesterday. "I'm just seeing him—"

Sydney made a *woo-hoo* sound that promptly dissolved into giggles.

"What are we, five?" Randi scowled.

Sydney grinned. "What are you going to wear? Have you kissed yet? How many times have you been out?"

"Can you be quiet?"

"No. Now answer my questions."

"I'm helping him with his youngest daughter," she ground out. "She's been sad since her mother died, and for some reason I cheer her up."

"So the daughter's going out with you tonight?" Sydney pouted. "Well, that's no fun."

Rolling her eyes, Randi dropped back into her seat. There

was no way she was going to correct Sydney about Sasha not being a part of the night's dinner.

"I'm not seeing him for fun," she said.

Ah, but seeing him is fun. Why else are you going tonight? If not to enjoy yourself?

"So he's still out there? On the market, I mean?" Sydney wriggled her eyebrows again. "I've still got a shot?"

No, you freaking don't have a—

"I have no idea what Brody Thorton's dating relationship status currently is." She dragged in a slow breath. Jealousy was not a part of her repertoire, especially over a guy she had no right being jealous over. "I'll let you know when I do."

Sydney studied her, chewing at her thumbnail. "Hmmm, I'm not convinced." She grinned wider. "Can I remind you of this conversation when you and Brody get back from your honeymoon?"

"Out." Randi pointed at the door, fighting with her own need to smile. It was too damn hard being angry with Sydney, even if she was being ridiculous.

Sydney laughed. "Of course, can't hold you up getting ready for your date. Send me a selfie of what you're wearing before you go. Oh, and wear your hair down. If I had hair like yours, I'd wear it down all the time. Men go crazy for long hair."

"Get out."

Sydney's laughter trailed behind her as she hurried from Randi's room.

Letting out a sigh, Randi smoothed her hand over her head and down the long length of her traditional at-school ponytail. Goddamn it, how many people knew about her and the Thortons? Colleen McDonough—the middle school's resident nurse —wasn't one for gossip, but she *had* told Sydney. Had Sydney told anyone else? Was that why Dave had stomped in here adamant she get Willow back on the team pronto? Did the principal suspect she was sort of but not really seeing Willow's father?

Is that how we're classifying it? "Sort of but not really?" Good to know.

"Goddamn it," she muttered, shoving herself to her feet. She had a date—or not—to get ready for.

Chuck was already at home when she arrived, stare locked on his laptop. "Hi, Aunty R," he called without looking from the screen as she walked into the living room. "How was school?"

"Good, good." She dumped her keys and satchel on the sofa. "How goes the homework?"

"Good, good." He tapped at the keyboard. "Have I mentioned before how annoying calculus is?"

"Ah, you love it, you weirdo."

He grinned without tearing his focus from his laptop. "I do. You going out tonight? Can I order in pizza?"

"You can. Just don't tell your mom if she calls. You know what she's like with non-brain-feeding food."

He flipped her a thumbs-up.

She hurried for her bedroom. Showered for way longer than she normally did. Washed her hair twice. Conditioned it. Shaved her legs and under her arms. Should she shave elsewhere?

Oh, who was she kidding? No one was seeing down there anytime soon except her lady doctor for her yearly checkup.

A few minutes later, hair dried and slicked smooth with her straightener, and makeup applied in the closest she could get to smoldering but no-we're-just-friends sensuality, she slipped on the most expensive dress she'd ever bought.

Soft and flowy, it seemed to almost float and swish around her legs like mist. Far more feminine than anything she'd worn before, the vibrant blues and purples of the abstract print brought out the blue in her eyes and made her skin somehow look creamy.

She swallowed, the reflection in the mirror someone she was completely unfamiliar with. Bare shoulders, a scooped neckline, an asymmetric hem and strappy heels added to the look.

"Whoa," she whispered with a tiny half twirl. "I actually look pretty."

So this is what she looked like when she made an effort? Huh. Who knew?

But why the effort, hmm?

She glowered at her reflection. Tonight was about enjoying herself. That was it. No deluded expectations, no unrealistic fantasies, not even a hope of a one-night stand. It was about interacting with a guy she enjoyed spending time with, and that was it.

What about Dave's demand of getting Willow jumping?

"Oh, shut up." She strode into the living room. Seriously, the butterflies in her stomach could go take a hike.

"Holy crap, Aunty R. You look gorgeous."

She arched an eyebrow. "And you sound surprised."

"Hell yeah. I've never seen you look like that before. Mr. Thorton is going to blow his l…blow his mind."

"Chuck, I don't even know what to say to that."

He grinned. "Say thank you for the compliment, awesome nephew."

"Thank you for the compliment, awesome nephew."

He laughed. "Have fun on your date."

"It's not a—"

Her phone rang.

"If that's Mom, I'm not here." Chuck ran from the room.

"Why aren't you here?" Yep, it was Stacey. "What have you done, Chuck?"

Wherever he'd fled to in the house, he didn't answer.

"Good grief," she muttered, connecting the call. "Hi, sis."

"May I speak to Charles, please?"

"And a *how are you oh I'm okay* to you, too." She let out a sigh. "You have heard of this thing called sibling affection, correct? Where you actually take the time to be congenial to your sister?"

"Hello, Miranda," Stacey drawled in her ear. "How are you? I'm doing well. Busy. Very busy. Now that we've wasted time, may I speak to Charles please?"

Oh man, what would it have been like to have a normal family? "He's not here."

"But his phone tells me he is. Please put him on."

"His phone?"

"Of course his phone. You don't think I'd fly to the other side of the world without activating location services on his phone, do you? How would I know what he is doing? What if something happened to him? How would I know?"

Randi blinked. "Um, your sister, his aunt, would call you? You know, the person you asked to care for him? I am quite capable of looking after your son, Stacey."

The beat of silence said loud and clear that Stacey doubted it.

"Ouch," Randi said. "Guess I know how much stock you put in my abilities."

"You're being silly now, Miranda."

"Yeah, that's me. The silly one of the family." A bitter taste filled her mouth. "Just out of curiosity, you do know what I do for a living? How do you think I manage a classroom full of students if I can't be responsible for one fifteen-year-old?"

"But those students aren't my children." Okay, Stacey had her on that. If *she* had a child, she'd probably be overprotective as well.

Like the way you're throwing away a promotion to save Willow from feeling more grief and sorrow?

"Besides," Stacey went on, "I can't imagine any of them will ever have the potential to succeed like Charles—"

"Oh for Pete's sake, Stace, put a sock in it, will you."

A sigh came through the phone. "May I please speak to

Charles, Miranda? His father and I have something to discuss with him."

"He's honestly not here." *Lying to your sister. Way to go.* "He must have left his phone behind when he went to the beach."

"The beach? He should be studying."

"It's Friday."

"So?"

Randi laughed. How that answer brought back so many memories. Fridays spent longing to play some kind of fun, imaginative game with Stacey and Aaron after school. Waiting for her older brother and sister to finish their homework so she could ask them to draw with her, color with her...do *anything* but chess or sudoku or math quizzes with her. It took her way too many years to realize Fridays were no different to other days in the Lockwood house. Work hard, study hard, achieve, achieve, achieve, succeed, succeed, succeed, and then repeat.

It had been a Friday when Randi had brought home her first B+ on a test. A percentage and fractions test. She'd been eleven years old. That was the Friday her dad called her first tutor. B+ was not acceptable for a Lockwood. There came many tutors after that. All of them had looked at her parents liked they'd lost their minds when they'd explained her grades needed to be improved. She was, after all, an A-student. One tutor went so far as to suggest her parents needed to see a shrink.

Fridays weren't fun in the Lockwood house. *Fun* wasn't fun in the Lockwood house.

"Please tell me Charles is studying, Miranda. Revising his school work."

"Stacey, Chuck *is* studying at the beach." God, she was so good at lying to her sister. One thing she didn't fail at, it seemed. "There's a group of his fellow honors students down there quizzing each other on Julius Caesar as we speak."

"Oh, that's good. Thank you." A relieved breath, a polite laugh. "I left him in your care I know, but I *am* assuming you are instilling in him a better work ethic..." She trailed off. It seemed even Stacey recognized when she'd perhaps crossed a line.

"Don't fret, sis." Randi ground her teeth. "I assure you Chuck is doing well under my less-than-exemplary supervision."

"That's not what I mean, Miranda."

"Yes, it is. But that's okay. I'm not rubbing off on him. Although he *did* say a sentence the other day with a dangling modifier, so..."

"Miranda."

"*Staaaacey.*" If anything was going to bring the conversation to an end it was Randi dragging out Stacey's name. Protracted vowels were one of Stacey's pet peeves.

Another sigh came through the phone. "I have to go. Please tell Charles I called and that we wished to talk with him. Oh, and remind him he needs to email his father his revision notes for this month's chemistry and physics studies."

"On it." Maybe. Or maybe she'd take Chuck to Universal Studios and they'd see who threw up first after going on the Revenge of the Mummy ride immediately after drinking a monster slushy. That'd teach her sister.

"Perhaps if you took things a little more seriously, Miranda, you wouldn't be just an art teacher. Perhaps—"

"Perhaps you should have stopped talking after you said 'I have to go.'" Her stomach churned. Being the black-sheep failure of the family hurt, no matter how often she convinced herself it didn't. "Say hello to Bradley for me. Don't eat too many croissants."

"Croissants? Miranda, you know I'm gluten—"

Randi hung up.

"That sounded like fun."

She arched an eyebrow at Chuck, slowly inching back into the living room. "Oh, and now you come back?"

He flashed a sheepish grin at her. "Yes."

Shaking her head, she laughed. "I don't blame you. I love your mother, Chuckles, but she makes my teeth hurt."

"Thanks for telling her I wasn't here."

"That's okay. Why did I do that again?"

He toed the floor and shrugged. "I don't know. Mom keeps talking about when I move to France and..." He shrugged again.

Another knot twisted in her stomach. She wasn't looking forward to the day he left. She'd miss him. Who else would she talk to at—?

Her phone vibrated in her hand, Brody's name and number appearing on its screen.

Her breath caught in her throat.

He's cancelling.

She connected the call. "Hi. Everything okay?"

"Absolutely." God, she really needed to somehow stop her body reacting the way it did at the sound of his voice. "Just letting you know I'll be picking you up in ten minutes."

She blinked. "Picking me up? I thought I was meeting you there."

Chuck laughed. "And you thought it *wasn't* a date, Aunty R."

CHAPTER TEN

He was rusty. And nervous. Bloody hell, he was nervous.

Did he open her car door for her? Hold out her chair for her? Did he offer to select the wine? No, no wine. She was a teetotaler. She'd told him that on their first date. No, not date. They'd never been on a date. The first time she'd come to his house. Tonight was their first date. Wasn't it?

Fuck.

It had been too many years, decades, since he'd been in this kind of situation.

This kind of situation.

He flicked Randi—sitting silently in the passenger seat beside him—a glance.

She was gorgeous.

A cold tension coiled through him, one he had no trouble recognizing.

Guilt.

Yeah, he was in the kind of situation he'd never anticipated being in again. He was going out for dinner with a beautiful woman who made his chest tight and his breath quicken and stirred in him a longing he'd thought he'd never experience again.

Christ, what would Bridget make of this *situation*?

She'd probably laugh and say "Go hard or go home, big guy."

"Thank you for picking me up." Randi smiled at him. Was he crazy, or was she nervous as well?

"I was ready early and thought I'd come get you."

Ready early. Huh, that was an understatement. He'd been checking his bloody watch since around eleven a.m. for the time he could walk out of work. Anyone would think he was keen.

When Singo had walked into the house at five—being the victor of the who-can-bribe-Sasha-the-most contest to decide who would babysit her and Willow—Brody had needed to pour his mate a drink just to stop himself from bolting out the door. He'd already been showered and dressed by five. Dressed, reconsidering his chinos and white linen shirt, wondering if he should shave, checking his armpits for unwanted BO despite the fact he'd damn near emptied a can of deodorant there.

He'd hoped the succession of deep, slow breaths he'd taken on Singo's arrival would banish the nerves. Of course, he also knew that hope was prone to plant a feather wanting to grow a chook.

The impromptu meditation hadn't banished his nerves.

Nor had Willow helped. Unlike Sasha, who was over the moon about his adventure out with Randi, Willow could only glare at him, bottom lip set in a pout, arms crossed over her chest. She hadn't even said goodbye when he left. She *had* pointed out he was leaving really early for an eight o'clock reservation. Even now, he couldn't work out if it had been anger or betrayal in her eyes as he'd left.

"Where are we going?"

He swallowed. For some reason, it felt like someone had upended a bloody truck full of sand in his mouth.

"I've been told to try Truluck's Seafood, Steak, and Crab House." Nate had insisted it was the place to eat. "So I figured we could give it a shot. Have you eaten there?"

She shook her head, causing her hair to slip and slide around her bare shoulders.

He bit back a groan. He wanted to snag a fistful of her hair, wanted to feel the cool, silken strands comb through his fingers. Wanted to draw her head to his and press his face—

"We can blame Youngie if it's no good."

He'd TripAdvisored the restaurant three times since making the reservation last Saturday, just in case someone posted a bad review.

"I rarely go to restaurants to eat." She laughed. "I'm a ramen-noodles-on-a-budget girl. Exorbitant student debt, remember? So I plan to use and abuse you tonight."

He choked.

"Oh God." She slapped a hand to her mouth. "I don't mean it that way. Not that I don't... I'm shutting up now."

"No, no, keep going." He laughed. Couldn't help himself.

Groaning, she buried her face in her hands. Her hair tumbled over her shoulder, hiding her behind its curtain. "And here I was thinking I could do this."

"Do what?" If he reached out and tucked her hair behind her ear, what would she do?

She lifted her head and let out a shaky laugh. "Not make a fool of myself."

"You haven't."

Throwing him an askew glance, she snorted. "You're sure about that?"

"Hey, do you know how many times I checked my armpits since getting dressed this arvo?"

"How many?"

"Ten."

She burst out laughing.

"At least."

She covered her mouth with her hand, muffling her giggles.

"Wait, wait." He raised his right arm a little and took a loud sniff. "Make that eleven."

She laughed again.

He grinned. Yeah, he wanted to hear that laugh every day for the rest of his life.

The rest of his life…

Cold guilt knotted itself around his happiness. Fuck, what was he—

"Can I ask a question?" Hesitancy laced her voice.

"Sure."

"Is this really a…a date?"

His gut clenched.

"Because I honestly don't know," she went on. "And if it *is*, then how does that line up with your declaration last week that there can't be anything between us, and if it *isn't*, why the hell did I go out and buy this dress to impress you?"

His gut clenched some more. The dress was beautiful. And she'd bought it for this night. He wasn't too much of a bloke to miss the significance of that.

"I mean"—she fiddled with her seatbelt—"there's a part of me that so desperately wants it to be a date because you're amazing and incredible, and let's face it, hot. But there's another part—a more rational part—that's all too aware you come with some serious baggage. None the least being the fact you're the father to a teenage daughter who, I think, would rather see me ejected off the planet than be in any way connected to you. Does that make sense?"

It made perfect sense. He got it. He really did. So why the bloody hell couldn't he answer?

Because he didn't like the answer?

If he said it *was* a date, he was finally admitting aloud he was thinking of a future beyond Bridget, and self-condemnation would likely tear him apart.

And if he said it wasn't a date, that they were just two new friends spending time together—the justification he'd been giving himself since last Saturday—he'd have to accept he was fucking lying, not only to himself but to Randi as well.

He liked her.

He wanted her.

But he had no clue what to do with that truth.

He opened his mouth to say…something.

"You know what?" She let out a sigh. "That was unfair of me. I'm sorry. Let's just enjoy dinner. No questions or expectations. Just dinner and conversation. Okay?"

He nodded, even as every molecule in his body screamed at him to pull over to the curb, cup her face in his hands, and kiss her.

"So," she said with a wobbly laugh. "Read any good books lately?"

They finished their discussion on books just as he pulled into Truluck's Seafood, Steak, and Crab House's valet parking. Discovering she read thrillers didn't help his mental state. It made *not* kissing her harder knowing she, too, was a Jack Reacher fan.

Heart thumping faster than it should, he smiled at her as the valet approached. "Ready?"

"Ready."

He had to give it to her, she didn't seem to fluster. Was it a teacher thing, or just her? Whatever it was, he liked it.

Crap, he had to stop thinking about how much he liked her. At least until he sorted out in his own mind what they were. Or were going to be. Or could potentially be.

Ah shit.

He scrambled from behind the wheel, tossed his keys to the valet, and then hurried around to the passenger side. Just as Randi opened her door.

"Beat you." She straightened from her seat, eyes twinkling.

"I need to lift my game."

She smiled. "I know a good track and field coach who can whip you into shape."

"Can you give me her number?"

"Hmm, I'll think about it."

Fuck, there was no denying it. He liked her a lot.

No matter how much he tried, he couldn't stop himself from smoothing his palm over the small of her back as they walked into the restaurant. It felt right being there. The warmth of her body radiated into his palm, sending tingling heat up his arm and through his chest. And lower.

Thank bloody God, they were seated at their table almost immediately. Not that he'd be at risk of embarrassing himself, but his chinos wouldn't hide any...movement down south if it were to occur.

A waiter appeared. Brody ordered his favorite appetizer—salt and pepper calamari—followed by steak, salad, and chips. No matter how long he lived in this country, he'd never get used to calling chips "fries."

Randi cast him a look over her menu. "Remember when I said I was going to use and abuse you tonight?"

Of course, his mind went straight to the gutter. "I do."

She lowered her menu and smiled up at the waiter. "I'll have the crab claws to start, then the prime ribeye, extra bloody, with mashed potatoes and the chef's topping."

He swallowed. If he wasn't careful, he'd fall in love with her, and where would he be then?

Up the proverbial creek without the proverbial paddle.

She studied him, chewing on her lip. "Too much?"

"Hell, no. Just wondering how I'm going to steal some of the crab claws without you seeing."

She laughed and tucked a strand of hair behind her ear. At the sight of her neck—so smooth and creamy and there—he swallowed again. What would it feel like beneath his lips? Would she moan if he nibbled at it?

His phone buzzed in his pocket.

"Sorry." He dug it out, jerking his stare from her neck, his heart a thudding cannon. "Singo said he'd call if there were any problems with..." His chest tightened. Willow. It was Willow calling him.

Willow, who hadn't wanted him to come out with Randi tonight. Who'd been even more surly and moody than normal these last few days.

Willow, who he half suspected, was threatened by Randi's presence in their lives.

Connecting the call, he put his phone to his ear. "Heya, Will. What's up?"

"Daddy, you need to come home."

Where was she calling from? Her voice sounded like she was in a tunnel.

"What's going on, Will?" She'd been giving him hell lately. Would she really go so far as to bring his night out to an end just because she wanted to? "Where are you?"

Randi frowned, worry in her eyes. "Is she okay?" she mouthed.

"Please come home, Daddy," Willow said. "I need you to come home." The last word broke into a sob.

Something cold sliced through him. "What's going on, honey? Why are you—?"

"I'm in the bathroom. I got my first period. There's blood all over the sofa and Sasha is trying to stop Singo from seeing it."

He blinked. "You got your what?"

On the other end of the connection, Willow burst into tears.

Fuck a duck.

Randi frowned, watching him drag his hands through his hair for the umpteenth time. They'd made it to the sidewalk. That was a start. "Do you have sanitary pads at home?" she asked.

If ever there was a definition for the word "blank," Brody's face was it. He looked at her like a deer in the headlights. "What?"

Randi bit back a soft chuckle. Oh boy, the poor guy.

She plucked the parking stub from his hand and handed it to the valet.

The second Brody had uttered the word *period* during his conversation with Willow, his face running white, Randi had known their night was done. She'd waved over their waiter, explained they had an emergency situation and that they had to leave, apologizing for the inconvenience. Thankfully, the kitchen hadn't started making their meals.

"Pads," she repeated. "Or tampons?"

Brody shook his head. "I don't... I... Bridget may have..." He stopped, scrunching up his face. "Hell, I don't have a clue."

She placed her hand on his arm. "It's okay. I'll help, if you and Willow want me to."

She pictured Willow at home with the hulking great big Singo. Did the other Australian know what was going on? How to deal with it?

She remembered her first period. Remembered the embarrassment of it coming while she was at school. At least she'd had a big sister to go to, although Stacey had just shoved a tampon at her and told her to figure it out. "Oh, and tie your jacket around your waist," Stacey had whispered. "You've got blood on your skirt."

Randi had helped more than one student at school cope with the inescapable and always inconvenient arrival of her first menstruation. As a consequence, she had a little emergency kit in the bottom drawer of her desk in her room, with enough supplies for the student to make it through until the home bell rang. She also had a tampon in her purse. One. Her backup tampon in case her period sprung itself on her while she was out and about.

Willow would need more than one tampon. At thirteen, tampons were scary things anyway.

"I saw a Walgreens on our way here," she said to Brody. "We can get everything we need there on the way home."

He nodded and frowned. "I should have been prepared."

She laughed. "Oh, Brody, no one is prepared the first time. Trust me. Even those who think they are. It's going to be okay. Willow is going to be fine. I promise."

His SUV arrived, and he promptly climbed in and slammed the door shut.

The valet looked at him, and then at Randi.

"He's Australian," she said, giving the young man an apologetic smile and a tip.

Chuckling to herself, she hurried to the passenger side and climbed in herself. "Let's—"

Brody pulled away from the curb. A few seconds later, he let out a groan. "Shit, I forgot to tip the valet."

"Brody. Do me a favor; take a deep breath."

He did as she instructed.

"And another one."

Again, he complied.

"It's going to be okay," she said, keeping her voice calm. "Willow's going to be okay. It's a natural part of growing up, and she is going to handle it better than you can imagine."

"I should have been there," he growled.

"Worry about that later." Her heart twisted. There was no missing the anguish, the guilt in his voice. "What you need to do now is get home to help Willow feel safe and happy and loved, okay?"

Shoulders bunched, he nodded even as his grip tightened on the wheel.

She touched his arm, all too aware how corded the muscles under her fingers were. "It's probably better you don't break the steering wheel before getting home though, right?"

He burst out a breath before shaking his head. "Struth, I'm a mess."

She held up her hand, thumb and fingers almost touching. "Little bit. But hey, if it helps, my father had a complete mental breakdown when my sister got her period. He stood up from the dinner table on the first night and informed us all there was to be no such nonsense going on in his house, and she had to stop it immediately."

Brody's eyebrows shot up.

She laughed. "Not overly smart for a Rhodes scholar. But to be fair, he was an only child of only-children parents."

"And how did it go? Your sister *stopping it* immediately?"

"Suffice to say, my sister is a master at passive-aggressive comebacks. She told him—in French—she was sorry she'd failed him, and she would ensure to continue her transition into being asexual as soon as he learned to put the toilet seat down."

"Ouch. Your family is scary."

"You have no idea."

He laughed. Laughter was good. Now, if only she could keep him like this during the purchasing of Willow's sanitary supplies. "There's the Walgreens."

His phone buzzed as they were entering the store.

"Willow," he told her, reading the text message on his screen. "It says to hurry up. With about twenty exclamation marks."

He tapped something back and sent it off.

Randi led him to the appropriate aisle. He stood back, staring at the wall of sanitary pads, tampons, and other feminine supplies.

"No idea." He rubbed at the back of his neck and threw her a sheepish grin. "Bridget was pretty private about this kind of thing."

"Do you mind if I just…" She took a step toward the shelves.

He laughed. "Go for it."

She selected a variety of items, explaining why she'd picked the ones she had. He was an attentive student. By the time he paid for the basket full of pads and tampons, he seemed relaxed.

But he was still moving at a quicker pace than normal. Clearly, the need to get home to Willow ate at him. She understood. Admired it. If her father had been so willing to be involved in such facets of her life, would she want to talk to him more?

Doubtful. He'd probably tell her she was menstruating all wrong, not up to the high Lockwood standards.

Brody's phone kept buzzing during the drive back to his place. All Willow. All wondering when he was getting there. Finally, he passed it to her. "Can you let her know we're almost there."

Randi tapped out a message. *Your dad's coming ASAP, Willow. We'll be there soon.*

A few seconds later, Willow replied. *Are you coming with him, Miss Lockwood?*

I'm in the car, she texted back. *Would you like me to come in when we get there?*

She waited for the reply-being-written indicator to appear. It didn't.

She waited some more and yelped in shock when the phone burst into life in her hand, the unmistakable Australian song "Down Under" filling the SUV.

"Shit, that's Singo." Brody hit the connect button on his steering wheel. "Mate, talk to me. What's going on? How's Willow?"

"She won't come out of the loo," Singo answered. "I have no idea what's going on, but Sasha won't get up from the sofa and won't tell me why no matter how much ice cream I bribe her with."

"Willow's got her—"

Randi whacked his arm and glared at him.

Brody glared back, rubbing at his bicep.

She raised her eyebrows at him. She had no idea if Willow was going to be okay with her father's friend knowing her personal situation. If it had been her, she would have died of embarrassment if her father blurted it out to everyone.

"Will's having a moment," Brody said. *Better?* He mouthed at her.

She nodded.

"And Sasha…" He rubbed at his mouth. "Y'know what, Singo. Don't stress. We'll be there soon."

"If you say so, mate." Singo didn't sound convinced. "Hurry the hell up, will you. Otherwise *I'll* eat all the ice cream."

"Hi, Adam," she said. "Can you tell Will her dad's about five minutes away? And tell Sash she's an amazing little sister."

"Can do. Sorry your night got stuffed up on my watch."

"It's all good, mate." Brody chuckled. "No worries. Might tap you for another night sometime soon, though."

Another night?

A wave of something very close to delight rolled through her. Damn it, she really needed to check her hopes and dreams at the door. There couldn't be another night, no matter how much she'd enjoyed this surreal one. She couldn't do it to herself. Or Brody. Neither of them were ready for wherever this thing might be headed, that was painfully clear to her now. Nor would she do it to Willow, who had made it very clear what she thought of the situation.

"Thank you."

She frowned at him. "For what?"

"Being with me during this." He slid her a quick look as he turned the corner. "I know neither of us really knew what tonight was meant to be, but I'm pretty certain this wasn't how we saw it finishing."

She laughed. It was that or ask him how *he'd* seen it finish-ing. From the second she'd slipped into the sexiest underwear she owned when she was getting ready, she'd refused to fanta-size about the night's conclusion. She suspected exactly where her brain, her body, would see the night ending, and it was foolish and dangerous to go there.

"I'm glad I could help. I really like Willow and Sasha."

"And me?"

Her breath caught in her throat. "You?"

"Do you really like me?"

She swallowed. "You're passable company. A five out of ten, maybe. The weird accent takes off a point or two."

He laughed, a shaky, strained sound.

They turned into his driveway and came to a halt in front of the closed garage door. "Randi…" he began.

"Go in and be with your family, Brody."

"You're not coming in? I think I *need* you in there with me."

She smiled and shook her head. "I asked Willow while I was texting with her if she wanted me to come in. She didn't answer. I don't want to upset her any more than she already is tonight. All she needs right now is her dad." She let out a low chuckle and tapped the bag of pads and tampons on her lap. "And these. But please, tell her I'm more than happy to help her with anything she needs anytime she wants."

She opened the passenger door and climbed out.

Walk away. Walk away. Quickly. Quickly.

She was almost at the end of the driveway when Brody's call stopped her.

"Oi, Randi."

Heart thumping, mouth dry, she turned to face him. "Yes?"

He walked toward her, the SUV's lights reflecting on the garage door turning him into a silhouette. "Two things," he said as he drew closer.

"What are they?" She tried not to fidget. Tried not to lick her lips.

"One, I picked you up from your place, remember? How are you getting home?"

Well, crap.

"And two," he stepped closer. So close she could feel his heat reaching out for her, teasing her. "I need to do this."

He feathered his fingertip up the side of her face, cupped her cheeks in his palms, and brushed his lips over hers.

CHAPTER ELEVEN

K issing her was stupid.

But he did it anyway. Because he couldn't *not* kiss her.

One short, soft kiss. That was all. Just one, and then he'd bring it to an end. Get inside to Willow.

Just one.

Ah hell, her lips are incredible.

She pulled away.

Ah hell. Again.

"Go inside to your daughter," she whispered, her palms on his chest. Could she feel his heart smashing against his chest? Could she feel how much he wanted to draw her to his body and kiss her again? "She needs you."

"Come inside with me."

Why couldn't he step back? Why couldn't he do what she said? Christ, what kind of father was he if he was more hung up on kissing a woman than tending to his daughter?

She shook her head. "I'll grab an Uber."

"At least come and wait for it inside?" He swallowed. "Please?"

His phone buzzed before she could respond. He stepped back and pulled it from his pocket.

Daddy? Where are you?

"Go inside," Randi instructed, her voice soft.

"Is this it?" He swiped at his mouth. "Is this... us...are we..."

She pulled a shaky breath and let it go. "Let's give it a few days and see what happens."

He damn near said no. The thought of not seeing her for a few days, of not talking to her, hearing her laugh, for any amount of time was a cold punch in the gut.

"Thank you," he said instead. "For coming into our lives."

She nodded. "You okay if I just wait on your porch for my Uber?"

"I am."

She smiled. "Go inside."

He did. It was one of the hardest thing he'd done, though, walking away, leaving her standing in his driveway.

He jumped back into his car, opened the garage door, and parked inside.

When he climbed out, he couldn't see her.

With a choppy sigh, he hurried inside.

"Daddy!" Sasha cried, excitement launching her off the sofa.

"Jesus." Singo jolted to his feet, stare locked on the seat cushion. "Where'd all that blood come from?"

"Daddy?" Willow's voice—high and full of anguish— sounded from the direction of the main bathroom.

"Singo," Brody squeezed his friend's shoulder, "I'll bring you up to speed in a moment, but first..."

He ran down the hallway, the plastic bag containing the items he'd bought with Randi banging against his knee, Sasha in hot pursuit.

"Is Willow going to be okay?" Sasha whispered, taking his free hand when he stopped at the closed bathroom door. "She said girl things had started happening to her. Am I going to get girl blood down there as well? Where's Randi? Is Randi coming in? I heard you call her name outside. Where is she? Is Willow okay?"

"Will? Honey?" Brody gently tapped on the door.

It opened. A crack. Tear-reddened eyes peered at him through the narrow gap. "I'm sorry for ruining your night, Daddy."

The words were barely more than a rasp.

He shook his head and smiled, curling his arm around Sasha as he did so. "You didn't ruin my night, honey. Not at all."

Willow sniffed. A fat tear escaped her eye and trickled down her cheek. She suddenly looked so much younger than her thirteen years.

"Randi took me to Walgreens and showed me what to buy you." He held the plastic bag up. "It's all in here."

Another sniff, this time followed by a wipe of the nose with the back of her hand. "Is Ran... Is Miss Lockwood still here?"

"She's outside on the porch."

"Can I go get her?" Sasha begged, tugging on his shirt.

"Can you get her, please?" Willow asked. "I don't... I want to talk to someone about this, and as much as I love you, I..." she petered off.

He let out a gentle chuckle even as his throat thickened. "I understand, hon. It's a girl thing."

She nodded, another tear running down her cheek. "I wish Mom was here," she whispered.

His heart cracked. "Oh, baby, I know."

Sasha tugged on his shirt again. "Can I go get Randi now? To help Will?"

"Go get Randi."

She bolted. "I'm getting Randi, Singo," she shouted, no doubt running through the living room for the front door.

"Is Singo okay?" Willow asked through the crack. "I think I freaked him out. Does he know what's going on?"

"He's a tough bloke. A little blood won't stress him out."

"Dad." She rolled her eyes. But her lips twitched, and laughter tinged her protest. That was good. Better than the tears, especially when he couldn't hug her. As much as he wanted to, he wouldn't push the door open unless she invited him in. And the fact she'd asked for Randi told him she wasn't going to do that. "Please go check on him."

"Okay, hon. You going to be—"

A warm hand pressed his arm. "Hi, Willow, it's Miss Lockwood."

Was it so wrong to feel so good at such a simple touch?

"Hi, Miss Lockwood." Willow frowned through the crack. "I'm sorry for being a nuisance."

Randi smiled. "You're not being a nuisance. Not at all."

Willow flicked him a look. "You can go now, Dad."

"You sure?"

Willow nodded.

He turned to Randi and mouthed *thank you.*

Her smile sent his pulse pounding. Or maybe it was the adrenaline rush of the moment?

Handing her the plastic bag full of sanitary supplies, he nodded. "I'll go check on Singo and Sash."

Singo and Sash looked up at him as he entered the living room. Someone had placed a whole lot of toilet paper on the sofa where Willow must have been sitting. Probably Sasha.

"Is Will okay?" Sasha bounded to her feet.

He smoothed his hand over her head and dropped a kiss onto her forehead. "She is. Wanna go get dressed for bed?"

"Aww, do I have to?"

"Get thee to thy bedroom, child," he admonished with a playful grumble.

She rolled her eyes—could she mimic Willow any better— and stomped away.

"Beer?" Brody asked Singo, heading toward the kitchen.

Singo nodded. "Willow okay?"

"Yeah" He and Singo were close mates, but how much did his daughter want Singo to know? "She is. She will be. It's a…"

"Girl thing?"

Pulling two bottles of Bud from the fridge, he raised his eyebrows.

Singo shrugged. "Figured as much. Two older sisters meant I knew all about that world by the time I was ten."

"I freaking froze, mate." He held out a beer to Singo. "Like a deer in the headlights. It was woeful. Thank God for Randi."

"I noticed Willow asked for her." Singo took a slug. "That's good. She wasn't overly fond of her while you were out. Told me Randi was interested in you only because she wants her to jump again."

"She what?"

Singo tapped the bottom of his bottle to Brody's. "Cheers, mate. The life of a single dad to a teenage daughter."

Rubbing at his face, Brody let out a groan. "Fuck a duck, what am I going to do about *that*?"

"Does it help that Sasha stuck up for Randi? Told Willow Randi liked you even back in the water park. Said something about you two kissing."

Brody groaned again.

Singo chuckled. "Babysitting your girls is definitely an experience. Before the situation occurred, I was learning all sorts of stuff about you. Example, you're lactose intolerant and get the shits big time if you eat ice cream."

Brody gaped at him. "Who thought you needed to know that?"

"My life wasn't complete until I found that out. Or that you cried at the end of that Pixar movie, the one about the old guy and his house."

"Sasha told you that, didn't she?"

"Nope. Willow. Sasha told me you cried at the end of *Toy Story 3*."

"Who *doesn't* cry at the end of *Toy Story 3*?"

"Good point. Cheers."

They both took a mouthful of beer.

"Okay, I better get to cleaning the sofa."

A while later, sofa cleaned and beer consumed, Brody shot a look toward the bathroom. "Reckon everything's okay in there?"

Singo propped his feet on the coffee table. "Yeah. I suspect Randi's got it all covered. You've got a good one there, Thorton. Don't let her go."

Don't let her go. Hadn't that been almost *exactly* what he'd been doing out in the driveway after their kiss? He'd been about to let her walk *out* of their lives when he was just bloody well getting around to the fact that he wanted her *in* their lives.

He swiped at his mouth and then jolted to his feet as Willow and Randi walked into the living room.

Willow walked straight up to Singo and hugged him. "Sorry if I freaked you out."

Singo chuckled and gave her a hug in return. "It's all good, Will. I've got sisters."

She pulled away, cheeks pink.

"Can I hug you, Will?" Sasha approached her like she would shatter at the slightest touch.

Willow snagged her in a bear hug. "No hugging allowed." She laughed, lips pressed to the top of Sasha's head. Sasha giggled in her arms and squeezed her back.

Brody smiled. "You okay, hon?"

Willow nodded, not letting go of Sasha. "Yes. But I think I'd like to go to bed. Is that okay?"

"Sure."

She hoisted Sasha up onto her hip. "Want me to read you a book, Sash?"

"Hell, yeah!"

Willow smiled at Randi. "Thank you for helping, Miss Lockwood."

"Anytime, Willow."

Anytime. Brody swallowed. Why did the answer make him want to take Randi in his arms and kiss her senseless?

Jiggling Sasha about on her hip, Willow laughed. "Say goodnight, maniac."

"Goodnight, maniac."

They left.

Singo cleared his throat. "I'll just bugger off then."

"No, no." Randi shook her head. "My Uber is only a few minutes away."

Singo frowned. "Uber? You're not staying?"

"I'll let you two guys dissect the night." Mischief danced in her eyes, even as uncertainty flicked across her face. "Besides, I've got schoolwork to grade."

Christ, he didn't want her to go. Not at all. But the way they'd left things before Willow asked for her help... It was clear Randi *was* going. And that was for the better. It really was. He had to remember that. His true-love story had already been told, complete with an ending.

Randi wasn't that ending. Raising his girls, dedicating his life to them, that was his ending.

It had to be. Any other option was selfish on his behalf.

———————

"I'll walk you to the door," Brody said.

Randi collected her purse from the table, her chest tight. "Goodbye, Adam." She smiled at Brody's friend. "It was nice to see you again."

"Singo. Seriously, no one I like calls me Adam."

She dipped her head at the compliment. "Bye, Singo."

The walk to the front door was quiet. Every time she tried to say something, the goddamn words deserted her.

Thank you for dinner. They were words. *Is it wrong I'm glad Willow asked for my help?* They were also words. *God, I think I'm falling in love with you.* Also words. But could she say any of them?

Nope.

"Thanks for helping Will out." Brody pulled the door open, and they stepped through it. He touched her lower back for a fleeting second, and her stupid heart rocketed into space.

"More than happy to help."

He closed the door behind them, and her heart hit the stratosphere. They were alone. On his front porch.

Say something profound.

Say something.

"Tonight is your trash night as well?" *Holy crap, what the hell?*

He chuckled, scanning the trash cans already placed out by his neighbors. "It is."

She ducked her head. *God, I'm an idiot.*

Her phone beeped in her purse, an alert message from Uber. "I suspect my Uber will be here soon," she mumbled. "You don't have to wait outside with me if you don't—"

"Randi."

She lifted her head.

"I really want to kiss y—"

She rose up on tiptoe, curled her fingers into the front of his shirt, and kissed him.

Really kissed him.

No holding back.

And with a raw, animalistic growl, he kissed her back. He slid his tongue into her mouth and over her teeth. He captured her hips with firm hands and yanked her closer to his body, the heat of his arousal impossible to deny. So hard. So there.

She moaned, hungry for everything.

He dragged one hand up her waist, over her ribs, tauntingly close to the underswell of her breast before moving it back down to her hip…and lower.

His fingers skimmed the curve of her ass cheek, and her knees trembled, even as she deepened their kiss.

She couldn't get enough of him. It was as if she'd been starved of his taste, his touch. She cupped his face, reveling in the rasp of his bristles against her palms before tangling her fingers in the hair at his nape.

In return, he squeezed her ass with both hands, drawing her closer still to his hips. Closer. Hah. Could they get any closer? Maybe without their clothes…

He dragged his lips from hers, nipping at her chin before exploring the side of her throat. Exploring—more like ravishing. Holy hell, was it possible to orgasm from just a kiss on the neck?

Although there was nothing *just* about the way his lips moved over the side of her throat. He took utter possession of her, his hands on her ass, her hips, holding her close as he nipped and nuzzled.

A hitching whimper fell from her, and he captured it with his mouth. She was undone by the wave of intense pleasure rushing through her.

So much pleasure, and at the same time, not even close to enough. She wanted him touching her. Needed it like air. Raking one hand down his back, she snared his wrist and covered her breast with his hand.

He froze—for a split second—and then squeezed what she'd given him, thumb working her hard nipple through her dress as he spun her around and pressed her to the wall beside the door, pinning her there with his hips and hands.

So good. So goddamn good.

She moaned into his mouth and rolled her hips, aching for the rigid length trapped between them to grind against the curve of her sex.

He kneaded her breast more, his palm driving her to a

sexual urgency no hand should be capable of achieving. A hungry fire swept through her. She arched against him, lifting her leg and wrapping it around his hip.

His hard length rubbed against her sex, a torture of delicious pressure and proximity. How good would it feel to experience the same contact without their clothes separating their skin, their bodies?

With another growl, this one lower and so carnal it sent a shiver up her spine, he tore his lips from hers, every muscle in his body becoming still.

"Randi…" Her name was barely a breath.

She swallowed.

He pressed his forehead to hers. "Cancel your Uber," he whispered, his hand slowly beginning to knead her breast again. "Let me take you—"

The door opened, and Willow stepped out.

"Dad, has Miss— Oh my God, what are you *doing*?"

Fuck.

She moved. Fast. One second she was in Brody's arms, his hand on her boob, her leg wrapped around his hip, the next, she stared at Willow from damn near on the other side of the porch, her face burning.

Willow stood staring at them, eyes wide, mouth open.

And then it wasn't open. Then it was twisted in anger.

"Will—" Brody stepped toward Willow, his hand out.

She shrank back from him. "I thought…" She shook her head and glared at Randi. "So you're not just being friendly with Dad and Sasha to get me to start jumping again. You're being friendly because you want to get in Dad's pants."

"Willow," Brody snapped.

"It's okay, Brody," Randi said, holding Willow's glare.

"I actually started to think you were nice." Willow hugged herself. Her voice cracked, like a wall of grief choked her. "But you're just a slut."

"That's enough, Willow," Brody said.

Tears spilled from Willow's eyes, and she turned her glare on him. "What about Mom? How can you do this to Mom? How can you—"

A car horn blasted from the street.

Randi's Uber.

"Willow," she said, flicking Brody a look. Did he want her to step up? Say anything? What *could* she say? Nothing Willow had said was true, but Willow wouldn't believe her, not at the moment. Maybe later, when she'd calmed down.

Yeah, after she's recovered from catching her father copping a feel, right?

Her Uber hit the horn again.

"Don't talk to me," Willow snarled.

Brody stepped closer to Willow, reaching for her arm. "Will, you're being ridiculous."

Randi winced. Bad choice of words. No girl wanted to be told they were being ridiculous by their father, no matter what was going on.

"It's not what you think, Willow." She had to try. For Willow's sake. For Brody's. "I'm not..." She stopped. She *did* want to get into Brody's pants. And if she denied it...

"Please go away." Willow glared.

"Willow." The anger was leaching from Brody's voice, his face. In its place...

Guilt. And haunted grief.

"I think it's best I leave." The words tore at Randi's throat.

Willow hitched in a choppy breath, wiping at her tears with the back of her hand as she continued to watch her.

Brody began to shake his head and then stopped, wrapping an arm around Willow. His gaze met hers above Willow's head. A frown pulled at his eyebrows.

The Uber driver honked again.

Randi smiled. Hell, it hurt to do so. "If you ever need anything, Willow, you know where my art room is."

Willow sniffed, looking at her through wet, spiky lashes and then dropping her stare to the floor.

"Randi," Brody said, but she stopped him with a shake of her own head. "Thank you for dinner."

She turned and hurried down the stairs to the waiting car. It wasn't until she was in the back seat, the Thortons' place a block behind her, that it dawned on her she'd thanked Brody for a meal they'd never had.

Biting her bottom lip, she slumped back in her seat and closed her eyes. Thankfully, her driver wasn't chatty. She didn't have it in her to keep up jovial conversation right now.

Hopefully, when she got home, Chuck would be so absorbed either in studying or in one of those computer games he played, she wouldn't need to explain why she was back early.

In her purse, her phone beeped.

Throat tight, she pulled it out and stared at the text message from Brody on the screen.

"I'm sorry everything went to hell tonight. I'm not sorry for kissing you, though. Clearly the situation is complicated."

She snorted. Complicated.

"It's okay," she typed back. *"I understand where Willow is coming from. I would freak out if I busted my dad kissing another woman. She's allowed to have a meltdown."*

She hit send. Better to address only the Willow component of the complicated situation. Responding to the him-not-being-sorry-for-kissing-her component would mess with her head.

Her phone buzzed. *"She shouldn't have called you what she did, though."*

She smiled—a little—at the fact he didn't write the word "slut." It was gentlemanly.

She rolled her eyes. Goddamn it, she needed to get a grip on her emotions.

"I've worked with teenagers long enough to know that when

they are hurt they are prone to lashing out. And she is hurting, Brody. She's not being ridiculous."

Hovering her thumb over the send button, she chewed on her bottom lip. Would he get angry at her gentle rebuke of his word choice? She wasn't his wife, nor was she his girlfriend, or Willow's mother. She didn't have the right to reprimand him on how he fathered his daughters from any of those positions. But she *was* a teacher, and she did know teenagers.

"Speaking from a teacher's POV," she added. And then hit send.

Perhaps it was better to keep reminding him of her role in Willow's life. Perhaps it was better she kept reminding *herself.*

She was already in a tenuous position with Dave regarding Willow's place on the track and field team. She was only asking for trouble if the prudish principal got wind of her...interactions with Brody outside of school.

Interactions. Ha. That was right up there with *complicated* for understatement of the day.

She waited for a response.

And waited.

By the time her Uber pulled into her driveway, she'd given up on Brody replying. Yep, she'd stepped over a line.

"And that's that," she muttered.

"What?" her driver asked, twisting in his seat to look over his shoulder at her.

"Nothing. Thanks for the ride. Definitely a five-star trip."

"Don't forget to take a mint and some water if you want."

She snagged a mint from the little container located in the middle of the back seat. "Got one."

Of course, if she ate the mint, she'd remove all lingering taste of Brody's kisses.

Shaking her head, she climbed out of the car. "Good grief, Miranda."

Halfway to her door, her phone buzzed.

She stopped. Pulled it from her purse.

Brody had finally replied. *"If I called you tomorrow morning, asked you to breakfast, would you say yes?"*

Would she? Every selfish fiber of her being wanted to. But every fiber of her that remembered the hurt and pain in Willow's eyes said *no*. Yelled *no*, in fact. Bellowed *no* so damn loud it was a wonder her head didn't explode.

Chest tight, she moved her thumb over her screen.

CHAPTER TWELVE

Brody reread Randi's text for the fifth time. No, make that the sixth time.

Tomorrow? No.

What the hell did *that* mean?

He paced his living room, the flickering lights from the game of football Singo was watching on the television as chaotic as his state of mind.

Did she want him to call her now? Or in a few days? Or not at all?

He dropped into the closest chair and clawed a hand through his hair.

"Want my advice?"

He cast Singo a sideways glance. "Hit me with it."

Singo reached for the remote, muted the game, and settled back into the sofa. "You go to Randi's house and sweep her off her feet."

"Really?"

"Yep. But not until *after* you fix the situation with Willow."

"How do I fix the situation with Willow? What *is* the situation with Willow?"

"Willow doesn't want you replacing her mum. And she just

busted you snogging a woman who seems to be in line to do just that."

Brody rubbed at his face, launched himself from the chair, and paced some more.

"Plus, there's the whole Alicia thing."

He stopped and blinked at his best mate. "The what?"

"Alicia stepped in when Bridget died, right?" Singo scratched at the bristles on his jaw. "She became as close to a replacement mum as the girls could get. And now, Alicia is being usurped by Randi—who is far more laid-back than Alicia could ever be, so I have no problem with that at all. But it's probably hard for the girls. Although Sash is already in love with Randi, it may be a little harder for Will."

"Will's never been close with Alicia."

Singo let out a dry snort. "I get that. But let's be honest, it's probably really hard for Alicia as well, given she kinda put her life on hold to help you out with yours."

He swallowed. Alicia *had* put her life on hold. In the months straight after the funeral, she'd slept on the very sofa Singo was sitting on so often Brody had grown to expect to see her in the kitchen every morning when he stumbled out of his bedroom, hollow and aching. Even now, two years after Bridget's death, Alicia still called every week. Still dropped around at least once a fortnight, bringing with her a casserole or a cake, sometimes both.

She hadn't expected anything of him, he was sure of that. But she'd sacrificed so much of her time for him and the girls… And she'd lost her only sister. Her only sibling…

A cold lump rolled in the pit of his gut. "So I've got to fix the Willow thing, and the Alicia thing?"

"Yeah, I think you should."

"Before I can do the Randi thing?"

What was the Randi thing? Just sex? Sex and something else? Or something even more…

Nope. He wasn't going there. He had to shut that thought

down. "Something even more" couldn't even be a possibility. That part of his life, romantic entanglements, was done and dusted. Had to be. Close friendship he could do. Since Randi had come on the scene, he was beginning to suspect close friendship and sex were maybe a possibility, but something even *more* than that?

Guilt slicked through him, like tainted oil on the surface of water.

Thinking about sex with Randi was dangerous.

And if they hadn't been interrupted by Willow, sex on the porch likely would have bloody well been a reality.

"Christ." He swiped at his mouth.

"Did I help?"

He snorted at Singo's chuckled question. "Everything's as clear as a bloody bell, mate. Onya."

Singo reached for the remote. "No worries. Anytime."

Raking his hands through his hair again, Brody let out a breath. "Okay, I'm going to go have a convo with Will."

"I'll wait right here." Singo unmuted the television, and the living room filled with the sounds of the game again.

The noise faded as Brody approached Willow's bedroom.

She'd retreated there as soon as they'd walked in from the porch, throwing over her shoulder that she was going to bed and didn't want to talk to him.

He'd almost followed her but remembered how Bridget had reacted to him doing just that when they had any argument—which were few and far between.

Hell, he hoped he'd given her enough time.

The low glow from under her door told him her bedside lamp was on. Maybe she was reading? Or drawing. Both activities were on her go-to list when she was angry, although lately, she'd retreated to headphones and her phone instead.

Right now, her phone was in the kitchen—rules of the house were all iDevices stayed out of the bedrooms after six p.m., including his own.

Stopping just outside her door, he cocked his head.

Silence.

Not only from her room, but also Sasha's across the hall. In fact, Sasha's room was dark; not even her night-light was on.

With a gentle knock on Willow's doorframe, he stepped into her room.

Ah man.

Both Willow and Sasha were asleep on the bed, Willow hugging Sasha as Sasha hugged Skips, the floppy soft-toy kangaroo given to her by Great-Uncle Rob back in Australia for her first birthday.

Asleep.

A hot lump filled his throat. He hadn't said goodnight to either of them, let alone gone through Sasha's normal bedtime routine—the singing of a silly song, a joint reading of whatever picture book she selected from her bookshelf, and a whole lot of hugs and kisses.

Shit. Willow had fallen asleep pissed at him, and Sasha had missed out on something she held dear.

Walking on silent feet to the bed, he dropped a soft kiss on Sasha's cheek, and then Willow's. Neither moved nor woke.

Disappointment warred with guilt.

He left. By the time he made it back to the living room, guilt won the war.

He was doing a bloody piss-poor job of being a good father, and an even crappier one of being faithful to Bridget's memory.

Singo raised questioning eyebrows as he entered the room.

"Asleep." He dropped onto the sofa and checked his watch. 9:07 p.m.

Early for Willow. She must be out of sorts.

Yeah, he was definitely in the running for Dad of the Year.

"Want me to grab you a beer?" Singo half stood.

"Nah. Actually…" His heart thumped into his throat. "I think I should probably call Alicia."

LOVE AND OTHER RESPONSIBILITIES | 157

"Now?"

"Now." He strode into the kitchen and picked his phone up from the charging station. As he did, a message flashed on Willow's. From Chuck. *Want me to help you get through that tricky bit on* HZ *we were talking about yesterday?*

Chuck?

Well, if nothing else, Willow had made a new friend out of all this. That had to be something.

Alicia answered just as he returned to the sofa. "Brody? Is everything okay?"

"Everything is fine, Al." Hell, guilt really was ripping him apart. He hadn't called Alicia Al since...well, since he'd first met her and she corrected him. He clawed at the back of his neck. Beside him, Singo raised his eyebrows. "I was just thinking we should..."

Talk? Chat?

"Catch up."

"Are the girls okay? I miss talking to them."

Nope, seemed he could feel more guilt, after all.

"The girls are fine. We're all good. Honest." Once again, Singo raised his eyebrows.

"I thought you were out tonight? With the woman from the water park?" Was she angry at him? Disappointed? He couldn't tell.

"We...got home earlier than planned."

"Didn't work out? Such a shame. She seemed such a nice woman, what with the whole skimpy bikini and kissing complete strangers in a public place and all."

Ah, Alicia. Don't do that.

"That's not—"

"But I'm glad you've got that out of your system," she went on. "I guess it had to happen at some point."

"Alicia, you need to stop."

"Stop what? Caring about my nieces? About what my brother-in-law is subjecting them to?"

Scrunching up his face, he pinched the bridge of his nose. "Y'know what, Alicia. This was a bad idea. Clearly, we're not on the right page to have this kind of chat. How 'bout I catch up with you later?"

"Brody, wait."

The panic in her voice stopped him ending the call. Alicia was never panicked. She was poised and controlled at all times.

Biting back his sigh and swallowing the ball of anguish making its way up his throat, he slumped back in the sofa. "I don't want to argue with you. You are an important part of my girls' lives, but I'm not going to argue with you over this."

"What is this, though?" Her voice shook. "Is it serious?"

Hell, if only he knew. "If it is?"

"I gave up so much of my life for you, for the girls, Brody. And now..." A soft sob filled the connection. "Now I feel like I'm just being tossed aside."

"That's not what's happening here." His gut churned. "I just..." *What?* "I just..."

"You just need to get on with your own life?" She was calm again. "I understand that, Brody. I really do. But the more you get on with your own life, the more my old life slips away."

He frowned. "How am I—?"

"I lost my sister when you lost your wife. And my best friend. Bridget was the one person I always knew would be there for me when I called her. When she died, I lost the one person I could rely on to laugh at my lame sense of humor, who tolerated my OCD tendencies. I lost..." Her voice cracked. "I lost Bridget just as much as you did. And every minute I spend with Willow and Sasha, I'm spending it with Bridget. Whenever I see Willow smile, I'm smiling with Bridget. Any time I hear Sasha laugh, I hear Bridget laugh. And I will never deny you moving on with your life. I have no claim on you, no expectations, but...I just wasn't prepared for it happening so...so soon."

Holy fuck. Fuck. I'm a bastard.

Mouth dry, he scrubbed at his face with a shaky hand. "Al…" There goes the nickname again. "I never meant you to feel like this. I'm sorry."

She sniffed, the sound followed immediately by a wobbly laugh. "I know I come across as a cold bitch most of the time. And I guess I am. I'm sitting in my living room all alone right now, and all I can think about is how much I miss my sister and how unfair it is that you're moving on and I c-can't."

Ah shit. Shit.

"Alicia, I'm coming over." He shoved himself out of the sofa. "Give me fifteen, and I'll be there."

"No, no, no." The denial tripped over itself. "I don't want that. I don't know why your date with the woman from the water park didn't work—"

Randi. Her name is Randi.

"—but I don't want you coming here." Another shaky laugh. "Not because I hate you, I don't. I promise. But because I hate the idea of you seeing me like this. Of anyone seeing me like this."

"Alicia…"

She laughed again; a weak laugh lost in a sob. "I promise, if you turn up at my door tonight, I won't let you in. I'll call neighborhood security and tell them I have a peeping tom at my window."

He let out his own laugh. It was as weak as hers. "Okay. I'm not coming around."

"Good. Make sure you don't. But is it okay if I come and visit sometime soon?"

"Of course you can. How's breakfast tomorrow sound? Is it okay if I am actually here, though? I owe you a hug."

"I'll take the hug. As long as you don't force me to eat any of that vile Vegemite while I'm there." She laughed before he could respond. "I'm kidding. Not about it being vile, though."

"A toasted cheese and Vegemite sanga is definitely on the menu."

"I have no idea what you just said, Brody Thorton."

He chuckled. "All part of the plan, Al."

She laughed. It wasn't as wobbly or sad this time. "Please never call me Al again."

"Deal."

"Good. Now, would you like to tell me all about this woman you're…dating? Or has it really not worked out?"

———————

"So it didn't work out?"

The question for the ages.

Randi let out a sigh. With a quick glance at Chuck at the dining table—immersed in his homework on his laptop—she clutched her phone tighter and walked out onto her back patio, into the hot morning sun.

"Well?" Sydney prompted, curiosity threaded through her voice. "Did it?"

"It… I don't know." Which was a lie. Kind of. Their kiss had been the very definition of *working out*. Their lips and bodies and hips and hands all perfectly fit together.

"I don't know? What does 'I don't know' mean?"

"The night was interrupted, and we ended up not eating dinner."

"Why? How?"

Life. It was the only answer Randi came up with as she lay sleepless in bed the entire night after their failed dinner, staring at her dark ceiling and trying not to constantly touch every part of her body Brody had touched.

Life was both the why *and* the how.

Goddamn life.

"His…" No, she wasn't going to violate Willow's privacy. "It just wasn't meant to be."

Good grief, how clichéd.

"Well, that sucks."

It did. But maybe it was for the best. She couldn't let a few kisses make her forget Brody was a baggage-heavy complication she didn't need.

So that's how things are now? If it's too hard, don't try? Guess that's one way to never fail.

"Did you have any success convincing Willow to return to the track and field team?"

"I'm not pursuing that anymore." Another fail.

"So there goes the promotion?"

"I guess so." And a third fail. Her parents would be so proud.

"Aunty R?" Chuck's call floated out to her from inside the house.

"I have to go, Sydney. If Carol, or anyone at school, wants to gossip about—"

"I'll shut it down, girl. Promise."

"Thanks. See you at school tomorrow."

Ending the call, she turned to head back inside and almost collided with Chuck.

"Whoa, Chuckles." She snagged his arm to steady herself. "Practicing your ninja skills?"

He grinned. "No ninja skills here. You're just old and need a hearing aid."

"Ha-ha. Tell me again why I agree to let you live under my roof?"

"Because you love me?"

"Hmmm, jury's still out on that. What's up?"

"I want to ask you to drive me somewhere, but I don't want you making a big deal about it, because it's not a big deal. It's just a thing, okay?"

She blinked. "Well, now I'm totally going to make a big deal about it."

"Aunty R."

"Kidding. Where do you want me to drive you? If it's a bar or a crack house, I may be inclined to say no."

"Oh well, in that case…" He grinned.

God, I'm going to miss him when he leaves.

"Seriously, where do you want me to take you?"

He regarded her for a few moments before his hand crept up to the back of his neck and an uncertain frown creased his forehead. "Umm…"

"Are you in trouble, Charles?" Oh God, she didn't have it in her to cope if he was. "Where do you need to go? Please don't tell me it's the cops. Or a doctor. I don't need to take you to the doctors, do I?" All the sex-ed classes she'd been a part of in her teaching career flashed through her mind. "You haven't got a girl… Or caught…"

She couldn't finish either question. Good grief, Stacey was going to kill her.

Chuck's eyes widened. "*Damn*, Aunty R. Eww. No, no. All I want you to do is drive me to Willow Thorton's place."

"What?"

He smiled, although it wasn't for her. "She's stuck on a hard spot in *Horizon Zero Dawn*, and I said I'd help her get through it."

"You want me to take you to Willow's place?"

"Yeah."

"Brody Thorton's daughter?"

"Yeah."

"Where Brody is?"

"Where Mr. Thorton is." Chuck frowned. Of course he did. He had no clue how Friday night had gone. He'd been studying when she'd arrived home, and she hadn't told him. What aunt would tell her teenage nephew she'd spent the night maybe or maybe not flirting, then shopping for pads, before damn near getting to second base, and then fleeing in an Uber? "Did you guys have a fight or something?"

"No. No." If she shook her head any faster, she'd shatter a disc. "Why do you say that? No. Not at all. Sure, I can take you to *Willow's* place. We can go now. Want to go now?" She did not want to go now. Not so soon after the bone-melting, mind-shattering kiss.

It's been over a day. Almost two.

Exactly. Too soon.

"Er…sure. Now would be good."

Crap. "Let me just get my keys."

He looked at her like she was slowly turning into an iguana. "Okay."

"Meet you in the car."

He continued to look at her that way for the entire drive to Brody's place. Maybe because she babbled about the most ridiculous things—chocolate chips to cookie dough ratio in Subway cookies, the last time she saw an alligator, the best way to remove bird poo from a shirt. Ridiculous things. By the time she pulled into the Thortons' driveway, she was talking a mile a minute about God only knew what.

She sat behind the wheel, gripping it like a life preserver, refusing to look at the front porch.

"Are you coming in?"

"What?"

Chuck's eyebrows shot up. Oh boy, she must really look freaked out.

"Are you coming in? To see Mr. Thorton and Sasha and Will—"

Sasha. I can go in and say hello to Sasha.

"Yes." She opened her door, tried to climb out, got stopped by her seat belt, freed herself, and climbed out. "Sasha."

"Are you okay, Aunty R?" Chuck frowned at her over the roof of her Toyota. "For real?"

She sucked in a slow breath and let it out. "I am." She would be. By the time she got back into her car and drove away again.

He didn't look convinced.

Still didn't look convinced as he knocked on the Thortons' front door.

Please don't let Brody answer it. Please don't let Brody answer—

The door opened and Brody stood on the other side of the threshold.

Damn it.

His stare locked on hers. His chest heaved. The whole ground shook, from his ragged breath, or from her thumping heart, she didn't know.

"Hi, Mr. Thorton," Chuck said. "Willow asked if I could come over and help her with a bit on *Horizon Zero.* The computer game we were talking about at dinner the other night."

"Sure, Chuck." Brody smiled at him. Oh God, why did her stomach have to cramp at how gorgeous that smile was? "Willow's in the living room."

Chuck gave Randi's arm a playful slap. "Aunty R came to see Sasha."

Great, she'd needed her teenage nephew to explain why she was there. Because clearly, she couldn't string two words together herself. Cheeks burning, she shuffled her feet. "I just...just thought..."

"Sasha's at a friend's place having a playdate."

Brody's calm statement cut right through her. "Oh, okay. I'll just... Chuck, let me know when you want me to come get you. Bye."

She spun on her heel and hurried for her car. No visit to the gym required today; she was doing a hundred-yard dash right now. Well, a twenty-yard dash. In Olympic-record time.

Thank God for keyless entry. Flinging herself behind the wheel, she buckled in, started the engine, and reversed out onto the street. Sure, she was probably abandoning Chuck. Sure, she was probably the biggest coward in the world, but she was okay with that. Better that than stand in front of Brody and look at his lips, which was exactly where she'd wanted to look the second he opened the door.

She needed some kind of intervention. Maybe she could call her ex. A one-on-one with Professor Jerk-wad would definitely cure her of her *desire-itis.*

She also needed a triple-chocolate shake from Wendy's. *Drive-thru, here I come.*

The house was crypt-like when she got home. Too quiet.

Half-consumed shake deposited on the kitchen counter, she dug her phone out of her bag. Music. She really needed music. Loud music.

Connecting her phone to the room's Bluetooth speaker, she hit play on her favorite playlist.

Fallout Boy blasted through the house.

"Ahh, that's better."

So much better. American punk rock was the perfect soundtrack to go with the shame gnawing at her thanks to her undignified flight. What better way to spend a Sunday alone than to chew over every foolish thing she'd said and done since Brody Thorton crashed into her life—although technically, she'd crashed into his.

"Let's start this misery fest with cookies." She walked into the kitchen. "Lots of—"

Her phone buzzed with an incoming message. So damn loud, thanks to the Bluetooth connection, that she let out a startled yelp.

She snatched it from the counter, and her heart smashed into her throat at Brody's name on her screen. And at the message he'd sent. *"Knock knock."*

Oh God. Oh God…

"Who's there?" She sent back. Maybe Sasha had come home early from her playdate and was playing with Brody's phone? What other reason could there—

"I'm at your front door, Randi. You probably couldn't hear it over all the Fallout Boy."

Front door? He's here?

"Good choice in music, btw. Any chance you'll let me in?"

Let him in? Was he kidding? How could she let him in? If she did, she'd only embarrass herself.

Her phone buzzed. *"Please?"*

Mouth dry, she licked her lips. Okay, she was going to open the door. She was going to stare him down and tell him whatever was going on with them *wasn't* going on anymore. She was going to say hello and then goodbye. That's what she was going to do.

And she was going to do it now. While Fallout Boy screamed about their songs knowing what she did in the dark. Poor songs. They were bound to be traumatized by now.

She strode to the door and opened it.

She pointed at Brody, who stood with his hands pressed to both sides of the doorframe, stare already locked on her face. "Listen, buster, I—"

"I know I shouldn't be here." He shook his head. "Trust me, I tried like fucking hell to stay away. I'm eaten up by guilt and clearly lugging around more baggage than even I knew I had, but the thought of letting you walk away from me, from us? Fair dinkum, I just can't. I'm sorry, Randi, but I want you too fucking—"

She shut him up. With her mouth.

What else was a woman to do?

CHAPTER THIRTEEN

He hauled her to his body. And then off her feet. Carried her into her home, her legs wrapped around his hips.

He kissed her the whole way. No fucking way was he going to stop kissing her. To hell with guilt and self-loathing and doubt. When it came to Randi, there were no doubts. He'd figure the rest out later, but for now…

Kicking the door shut with his foot, he deepened the kiss. It was everything he needed, everything he wanted. Hot and wild and hungry and demanding. She kissed him like she meant it. It blew his mind. Almost blew other things. At this rate, with the way his body was responding, he was in danger of embarrassing himself.

But be buggered if that was going to stop him kissing her.

He couldn't. Physically impossible.

Her tongue stroked his. Her fingers raked over his scalp. Pain and pleasure sheared through him and, with a growl, he pinned her back to the wall and rolled his hips.

His trapped erection ground against her soft warmth, and she whimpered into his mouth, squeezing her legs tighter around him as she pulled her lips from his. "Brody…"

Christ, had anyone ever moaned his name like that before?

Thick and husky and full of desire? Anyone ever *looked* at him like that before?

A hot urgency throbbed through his groin.

"I want to f—make love to you," he rasped, forehead pressed to hers. Hell, if he didn't bury himself inside her soon, he'd go insane. "So bloody much it hurts."

She shifted in his arms, enough so she could lift his gaze to hers with a touch of her finger to his chin. "*Fuck* me first, Brody." A devilish light danced in her eyes, and he was lost to her. Utterly lost. "We can *make love* after that, okay?"

He crushed her mouth with his and gave himself over to everything she was and everything she was doing to him.

For this moment, there were only two adults surrendering to their ravenous desire for each other.

She unlocked her legs from behind his back and planted one on the floor, keeping her other one wrapped around his hip. He snagged the back of her thigh, drawing it higher up her side as he dragged his other hand up over her hip, her rib cage, her breast.

She moaned, encircling his wrist in a tight grip, keeping his hand on her boob when he tried to move it up to her throat.

He chuckled at her silent but undeniable demand he keep his hand right where it was. Sure. He could do that. No worries at all. Everything about her boob beneath his palm was fucking perfect.

Rolling his hips again, he dragged his thumb over the hardened pebble of her nipple.

She tore her mouth free of his, her nails once again clawing at his scalp. "Suck it. Please?"

"Done," he growled, sliding his hand beneath the hem of her shirt and shoving it upward. His cock jerked at the exquisite sight of her full breast encased in royal-blue lace a heartbeat before he captured her nipple and sucked.

The lace of her bra scratched his tongue. The warmth of

her flesh seared his control. The pleasure in her gasp drove him closer to the edge.

"Holy crap…" She raked her nails across his shoulders, driving her groin harder to his.

He lifted his head and, without hesitation, pulled the edge of her bra aside to uncover her breast—creamy-smooth and round with the most perfect nipple he'd ever seen. Dusky-pink and glistening with the moisture from his mouth.

"Fuck me," he groaned, captivated.

She arched, thrusting the newly exposed perfection closer to him. "Please, Brody."

Hell, he loved the way she said his name. It made him horny.

Bending a little, he flicked the tip of his tongue over her nipple.

She hissed and fisted her hand in his hair. "Again."

No worries there. Getting him to stop might be the trouble. He tongued her nipple again, slower this time.

She moaned, once again hugging his hip with her leg, drawing their groins harder together. "Tease."

The way she breathed words when aroused was another thing he loved. He could get addicted to the sound.

Cupping her breast with one hand, he swirled his tongue around her distended nipple and then drew it into his mouth once, twice, with a gentle sucking motion.

"Holy…crap…" The words dissolved into a breathy moan, and she tightened her fist in his hair. "That's good. Do it again."

He did.

"Again."

He chuckled and complied.

"Oh God…again."

He sealed his lips around her nipple and sucked deeply, flicking his tongue as he did.

"Oh yeah." She arched, her moan loud, ragged.

He lost himself in the moment, feasting on her breast—sucking, nipping, teasing—reveling in her unabashed responses. Growing hotter, hungrier with each whimper and moan and begging insistence for more.

Releasing her nipple with a sucking pop, he explored her throat, her jaw, her lips—would he *ever* get enough of her lips? Doubtful. Who knew he would get addicted so quickly?

And not just to kissing her, but to touching her, feeling her soft body pressed to his, having her moans of pleasure in his ears.

As if attuned to his very thoughts, Randi whimpered and broke their kiss. "I want to be naked with you. Now."

Before he could move, she hooked her fingers under her shirt hem, yanked it up over her head, and threw it aside.

She smiled at him, her hair a mess, one boob exposed, one still imprisoned by the lacy cup of her bra, the tiny gold circle of her belly ring glinting in the room's morning light.

His wild, horny woman.

His.

Yes, his. From the second he'd seen her at the water park, from the second he'd noticed her climbing the steps behind him and Sasha, she'd been his. He hadn't known it then, *she* hadn't known it then, but their bodies had. Their souls and hearts. And gravity and an incompetent pool attendant had helped it all come together.

His woman. And he was—

"Hurry up and get naked with me, Thorton."

"On it," he chuckled, taking a step backward and stripping his shirt from his body.

"So I didn't remember it wrong."

He frowned at her whispered statement. "Remember what wrong?"

"How fucking hot your bare chest is." She skimmed her fingertips over his stomach, up his chest, skirting his right nipple. Every one of his nerve endings went on high alert. *Touch it. Please, touch…*

She didn't. Not with her fingers, at least.

"I just need…" she whispered, a second before closing the tiny distance between them and closing her lips around his nipple.

Fuck. Fuck, yeah.

He fisted his hand in her hair, a raw groan tearing at the back of his throat.

With a soft pop, she pulled her mouth free. Suddenly, she looked shy. Her cheeks turned pink. "I'm sorry. Was that too forward? I've never done that to anyone before… I mean, I just—"

Cupping the back of her head, he chuckled. "Randi, never ever apologize for wanting to do that to me. Ever. Got it?"

"Got it."

"Good. Now let's get the rest of these clothes off and—"

She unzipped her shorts and wriggled out of them, undies and all. Kicked them away.

He couldn't bite back his groan, nor stop himself pulling her to him.

But she laughed and shook her head. "Wait."

"What for?"

Reaching behind her back, she unclipped her bra. It fell to her feet, and she kicked it away. At least, he thought she did. He couldn't stop looking at what she'd revealed to him.

Randi Lockwood. Entirely naked. In front of him.

"This."

He dragged his stare up to her face, his heart smashing into his throat. "Ahh, you see this?" he said. "This was worth the wait."

Her cheeks grew pink again. "Thank you. Now, your—"

He shook his head. "I don't mean just…just what we're about to do. I don't just mean the sex, Randi. Or you being naked. I mean you. *All* of you, everything about you. You."

She *was* worth the wait. He didn't know what that meant, it meant something, something big, but he'd figure it out later.

Bullshit. You know. Just open your bloody mouth and say it.

"Randi. I think I—"

She destroyed the distance between them and kissed him until his knees shook. Made love to his mouth as she unzipped his fly and shoved her hand down his open jeans.

She gripped him and squeezed him until nothing existed except her hand on his cock and her body pressed to his.

At some point, he'd extracted himself from his jeans and boxers. No idea when. Maybe around the time they both moved from near the door to the living room. They got there somehow, but however they did, it didn't involve not kissing or touching each other.

The backs of his thighs bumped the back of the sofa, halting their progress.

He took advantage of the moment, spinning her around to press her arse against the leather, scooping one of her glorious breasts into his hand and feasting on her nipple.

She clawed at his shoulders, his name a low groan of approval.

Hell, he loved how uninhibited she was. How open.

He moved his mouth to her other breast, worshipped it. Adored it. So full and heavy. And then he moved lower, needing to taste her. Needing to have her on his tongue.

Tight black curls tickled his lips as he sought out the tiny button of her clit.

She spread her thighs. So lush and warm beneath his palms. "I should warn...warn you it's a bit...untrimmed down—"

He plunged his tongue into her heat to show her he didn't give a rat's arse about whether it was trimmed or not.

"G-guess"—she raked at his shoulders, his scalp—"you don't care..."

Not one iota.

He licked and flicked and nibbled and explored, her gasps and demands he keep going pushing him closer to his own edge. It wouldn't take long for him to lose control completely. He'd need to start singing the Australian National Anthem in his head the second she even looked in the general direction of his groin, let alone when she actually... Nope, couldn't think about her touching him. He'd embarrass himself.

He smoothed his hands over her exquisite body and back to her thighs. She moaned, the horny sound growing shallow, faster as he continued to move his tongue.

"Holy...holy crap, Brody." She bucked, her voice shocked. "I'm going to..."

She did. It was incredible. She cried out his name, found religion, cursed just as loudly.

He didn't stop until she begged him to, and then only slowly, lavishing her body with long kisses and playful nips.

"Goddamn, you know how to make a girl come."

Joy and pride rushed through his male ego, and he grinned up at her. "What? You think a bloke from Down Under is going to suck at going down?"

She rolled her eyes even as she shoved her hair—damp with perspiration—from her face. "Should I tell you now I haven't fallen for you for your sense of humor?"

His heart tripped. He straightened to his feet, sliding his body against hers before nibbling a path up the side of her throat to her temple. "But you have fallen for me?"

"Ask me later."

He inched back a little, searching her eyes for...what? That she felt for him the way he felt for her?

And what way is that?

She grinned and trailed her fingers down his chest, over his abs, to claim his engorged dick in her warm hand. "After we take care of this."

He sucked in a ragged breath, the pleasure of her holding him almost too much to bear.

Australians all, let us rejoice… "Deal," he croaked, singing in his head.

She squeezed his length, gave it an almost ungentle tug. "Now, let's talk condom."

He scrunched his eyes shut and ground his teeth. *Shit. Shit, fuck, shit.* He didn't have a bloody condom.

Shit.

"There's got to be one in here."

Swinging open Chuck's bedroom door, Randi scanned the anarchy. She hadn't stepped a foot inside this room for over a month. Not since Chuck had come down with the flu and she'd brought him soup in bed while he was recovering.

In the month since she'd been in here, the pile of school textbooks had grown almost as high as the pile of laundry. Some of the clothes on the pile she recognized as those she'd washed only a few days ago. Some… God, when was the last time she'd even *seen* Chuck wear that shirt?

"I'm sorry."

She threw Brody, standing behind her and as naked as she was, a smile. "No need. We'll find one." She flicked his erection a quick look. Yep, still impressive, still rigid. Still waiting.

A flurry of excitement whirled through her stomach and settled between her thighs. Condom. They needed a freaking condom fast. Before Brody realized he was about to have sex with her. Seriously, when he looked like that, and she looked the way she did—too many curves, probably too many stretch marks, no thigh gap to speak of, thirty-five years of gravity doing what thirty-five years of gravity did, plus a roll or two where fashion mags said rolls shouldn't be.

"C'mon, Chuck," she muttered, entering his room. "I *need* a condom."

She searched. In drawers. Under the mattress. One day

she'd tell him about this, and they'd both laugh, and then she'd offer to pay for his therapy.

Not today, though. Today, she was getting—

Brody chuckled behind her. "You have the hottest, sexiest arse I've ever seen."

Dropping Chuck's pillow back onto the bed, she grinned and wriggled her ass. "Thank you. On a side note, I think I almost come every time you say *ahhrrss*."

"The accent does it for you?"

"Oh, it does it for me."

"Crikey, that's good for a bloke to know."

She scowled at him even as the junction of her thighs grew damp. "You did that on purpose."

He winked at her. "Bloody oath, love."

"I have no comeback for that." She shoved Chuck's sock drawer closed—she really needed to talk to him about the state of his room—and shoved her hands on her hips. "And no condom."

She had a contraception implant. Getting pregnant wasn't an issue.

So what is?

She trusted Brody. Insane as that may be, she trusted him. In all honesty, she probably knew him better than she'd known any of her previous relationships. Despite being in a serious relationship with Professor Jerk-wad for over eight months, she'd never had sex with him without one.

She'd have sex with Brody in a heartbeat without a condom, but did Brody feel the same about her? Did he trust her the way she—

"I have a contraceptive implant." Well, blurting it out was one way of finding out. "The kind that goes under my arm and keeps working for five years." She met Brody's steady, unreadable gaze. "I don't know if that means anything to you or... Hey!" She burst into surprised laughter as he damn near ran into Chuck's room and scooped her off her feet.

"Answer your question?"

"You could say that." She clung to him. How freaking strong was he?

"What's up?" He frowned. "You look panicked."

"You should put me down. What if you hurt your back before we can—?"

"I'm forty-two, not sixty-two."

"And I'm not a waif."

"Just tell me where your bedroom is, woman."

God, he's amazing. "Second door on the right."

"On it." He strode from Chuck's room, carrying her. If she wasn't already in love with him…

Oh no.

Oh no, no, no.

She *was* in love with him. Totally and utterly in love with him. She couldn't deny it. And if he told her he had feelings for her, she'd just blurt it out, like she did about her implant.

What did she do? What the ever-loving hell did she do?

Have amazing sex. And then figure it out.

"Okay, amazing sex it is."

Brody laughed. "We are so on the same page."

Were they? God, what if they were? Was she ready to be a…a…

Nope. She wasn't going there. The word *mother* was off the table. Amazing sex, *that* was where she was going—to her bedroom, carried by the hottest man in the world, to have amazing sex.

Crap, she hadn't had sex for so long. What if she did it wrong? What if he didn't like her jiggling bits? What if—

He dumped her on her bed, followed her onto it, covered her with his body, and kissed her.

And then he kissed her collarbone, her shoulders, her neck, her breasts. Holy hell, he knew how to kiss her breasts. He moved lower, spending an inordinate amount of time exploring her stomach and hips and inner thighs with his lips and

LOVE AND OTHER RESPONSIBILITIES | 177

tongue. He spent a lifetime down there. It was incredible. And yet…

"Brody…" She hitched in a shaky laugh. "I'm not complaining at all, but if I don't feel you inside me soon, I'm—"

He slid up her body, the tip of his erection nudging her folds. Supporting his weight with his elbows, he feathered his fingers along her jawline. "Hush. I'm worshipping you, woman. Idolizing the perfection of your body. Allow me this moment."

Liquid heat pool in her very center. "Well, in that case…"

He began his exploration of her body with his mouth again, lingering longer this time on the curve of her neck, the hypersensitive spot where her leg became her groin…

Goddamn it, he was going to be the death of her. Death by pleasure. What a way to go.

"Have I mentioned," he murmured against her inner thigh who knows how many minutes later, "how fucking hot and sexy you are?"

"N-no." It was hard to talk when his tongue flicked over her clit the way it did. "I d-don't think…"

He lifted his head and locked his gaze on her. "Miranda Lockwood, you are so fucking hot and sexy I can't think straight when you're near me."

The feeling's mutual, bud.

"Sorry?" she offered on a shaky laugh. "Want me to stay away from—"

He covered her body with his and kissed her, nudging her folds open with the head of his hard cock.

Oh yes…

She tangled her hands in his hair, giving herself over to it all. Sure, she was probably going to walk away from this with a broken heart and a shattered soul, but it was worth it for this, right now…

His lips grew slower, more intense on hers. He shifted his

body, smoothing one hand down the length of her side to draw her knee upward. Her sex opened more to him, took a little of his distended crown deeper.

Waves of pleasure washed through her, drowning the dark fear of what would happen after. It didn't matter. Not right now. All that mattered now was her and Brody.

He shifted again, aligning his hips more with hers, penetrating her more.

Stretching her wider. Filling her.

Oh God, it was incredible.

His low groan vibrated through his chest into hers. His grip on the back of her thigh grew fierce. He moved his mouth to the side of her neck, kissing and sucking even as he snagged her wrist and pinned her arm to the mattress. She arched beneath him, wrapped her leg around his back, craving all of him.

"In...inside me, Brody..." Her plea fell from her in a shallow breath. "I need...you inside me now. All the way. As... as deep as you..."

He raised his head, gazed down into her face, his eyes ablaze with pleasure, and buried himself inside her with one fluid stroke.

Yep, death by pleasure. The only way to go.

Perfect, exquisite pleasure.

They moved as one, their rhythm in harmony. He held her wrist, the back of her thigh, and stroked in and out of her, his stare holding hers. She moaned, a lot. Couldn't help it. His name, the name of God, the word "yes" over and over. She made sounds of desire and surrender.

And when their rhythm grew faster, when his strokes grew wild, she reached the pinnacle and cried out, squeezing his length inside her, gripping him in powerful pulses as she tumbled over the edge. As one orgasm and then another shattered her into a million pieces.

And then Brody joined her, burying his face into the side

of her neck, her name nothing but a groan, a plea against her flesh, as his release erupted inside her.

Filling her.

Minutes—or maybe hours—later, they slowly drew still. The pulses of her orgasms faded, each one as wonderful as the first. He released her thigh, her wrist and, with gentle pressure, rolled to his side until she lay stretched atop him, his length still embedded in her.

She let out a shaky laugh, nestling her head beneath his chin. "Wow."

The understatement to end all understatements. It was that or tell him she loved him, and she couldn't do that. She wouldn't do that to him, or herself.

"Yeah, wow is right." He chuckled, trailing his fingertips up and down her back.

"Thank you." Yep, another understatement. Closing her eyes, she tightened her inner muscles around his spent length. Was it wrong to not want him to withdraw?

"You're welcome. Give me a few minutes to get my strength back, and we'll do it again."

Raising her head, she studied him. *Don't say "I love you." Don't say "I love you."* "Do it again? I don't know if I can survive that a second time. It was too good."

He grinned. "That was just the fuck-me part. Remember, you said after that we'd get to the make-love part."

"I did say that, didn't I?" Of course, that was before she'd discovered the second he penetrated her she would be lost forever. *God help me.*

"You did." He reached up and brushed a strand of her hair from her cheek. "That still okay with you?"

Beyond okay. *Beyond* beyond okay. Nothing was more okay. The only thing that would be more okay was spending the rest of their lives making love together.

Oh girl, you are in so much trouble.

"Still totally okay with me." Could she sound any huskier?

He smiled, his gaze dropping to her lips. "I'm a fan of long, slow foreplay. How 'bout you?"

Her heart thumped faster. Her stomach fluttered. "Very much a fan."

"Like, really long. You okay with me bringing you to the edge of orgasm over and over for an hour or so before finally making you come so hard you almost pass out?" He flicked her a devilish smile.

Yeah, so, so much trouble. "I think I can endure. For you."

He chuckled. Inside her, his embedded cock pulsed with his laugh. "God, you are amazing. I'm so glad we met. So glad…" He touched his thumb to her bottom lip. Grew motionless. "Randi…"

His nostrils flared. His Adam's apple jerked up and down, and he licked his lips.

Her heart smashed faster into her throat.

Oh no.

"Randi, I know it's insane," he whispered, his eyes searching hers, "but I think…I think maybe I'm…"

No. Stop him. Stop him saying something you can't cope with right now. Stop him.

She cupped the back of his head and drew his lips to hers, kissing him before he could say what she feared he would say. Used every part of her body to stop him. Gave new definition to the words *long foreplay.*

Blew his mind. Stole his words.

It was better that way. Safer.

So why the fuck did it hurt so much?

CHAPTER FOURTEEN

They'd made love with such hungry passion he doubted he'd be able to walk tomorrow.

It was amazing—and a distant part of his mind was pretty impressed with the fact that for a bloke in his forties, he still had serious staying power. *Incredible* staying power.

Except for the fact that every time he tried to talk to Randi about the possibility he might be feeling something more for her than just friendship—huh, friendship—she would deflect in some way. Yeah, right. Deflect. That was one way of saying she'd shut him up with the most intense pleasure he'd ever experienced. He'd received the best blow job of his life when he'd started a sentence with "I think I."

Was she scared? Of what he was maybe feeling? Or was it what she was feeling?

He was fucking petrified, but no matter how much he'd tried to talk himself out of it, he was definitely in deep.

The entire drive to her place this morning had been one long internal monologue about why he should turn around and go back home.

Clearly, he hadn't listened.

And now, here he was, naked in her bed, her cheek on his

chest, her bare thigh draped over his leg, his lips still cool with the moisture of their last kiss, and his heart still pounding from their last mutual orgasms.

A part of him had no fucking clue where to go from here. The rest of him couldn't be happier he hadn't listened to himself.

Turning his head slightly, he pressed his lips to the top of her head, closing his eyes as he breathed in deeply. Her hair smelled like watermelon.

"Will you have dinner with me tonight?"

She stopped tracing lazy circles with her fingertips on his chest. Her hand grew still. *She* grew still. "What would Willow think of that?"

He didn't know. Willow had refused to talk to him about what she'd seen on the porch Friday night. She'd avoided him like the plague all Saturday, even when Alicia came for breakfast. She'd spent Saturday night on her phone or talking to Sasha. If Sasha hadn't been there, he doubted she would have uttered a word.

The silent treatment had continued this morning, Willow interacting only with Sasha. After Sasha left for her playdate, Willow had retreated to her room and hadn't left it until Chuck arrived.

And what did I do the moment *that happened? Raced to Randi's place. Took off, and rushed to…to…get laid. Father of the Year award goes to Brody Thorton.*

He'd sent Willow a text an hour ago, asking how she and Chuck were doing, and all he'd got back was a short *good*.

It was better than the silent treatment, and the fact Chuck had sent Randi a text with a little more detail around the same time had helped. *"All good if I don't come home for lunch? We're having too much fun. Will's kicking HZ butt."*

He swallowed, face pressed to Randi's hair, breathing in the scent of watermelon again. Why was life so bloody complicated? It hadn't been when he was younger. He'd listened to his gut back then. His gut had given him an incredible life here in the States, an amazing life with Bridget.

So why wouldn't he listen to his gut now? His gut was bloody well screaming at him to press Randi to her back, pin her there with his body, and confess just how fucking much he liked her, wanted her.

Loved her.

Hell, there was the word.

And that was exactly the reason why he wasn't listening to his gut. *The* word.

Love.

Because he loved his daughters more than life, and he had no clue what loving a woman who wasn't their mother would do to them. Mess them up?

Tear them apart?

And yet, despite all that, despite the guilt and torment, he wanted to be with Randi more than he could comprehend or articulate. Wanted to date her, cherish her.

"I'm pretty bloody certain I'm in love with you, Randi." The confession fell from him on a low breath.

Her fingers curled on his chest. She stiffened. "Don't say that." She sat up, swung her legs over the side of the bed, and turned away from him. "Take it back."

A cold pressure pushed at his temples. "Take it... I'm not going to take it back."

"You don't mean it. You might think you do, but you..." She shook her head. She didn't look at him. "And even if you do mean it, I don't...don't... Oh God, Brody, why did you have to say that?"

She pushed herself off the bed and almost sprinted from her room.

He swallowed, cold. Okay, so this wasn't how he thought things would go.

Thought? Yeah, what thought? There'd been no thought.

Not about telling her how he felt. He'd acted on gut instinct. He loved her, and he'd bet his left nut she loved him back.

And now she'd left the room, left him, alone in her bed.

Maybe his gut had grown senile?

"Fuck this." He scrambled from the bed, scanned the floor for his jeans. Nope. He'd taken them off in the living room. Righto then.

Snatching a pillow from the bed, he pressed it to his groin and hurried from the room. "Randi?"

He found her in the kitchen, her back to him, her palms flattened on the counter.

She'd wrapped a soft throw blanket around herself. He wanted nothing more than to pull it from her body and show her just how he felt about her demand that he "take it back."

Swallowing, he leaned his hip on the counter's edge and studied her profile. "What's going on?"

Her frown deepened. She didn't look at him. "I think we need to establish the fact that this, you and me, is purely a sexual thing. That's all it is. We hardly know each other, so we can't be throwing the…the L-word around. And even if we *do* feel, I mean, even if *you* do—" She scrunched up her face and let out a ragged breath before shaking her head. "Let's be serious here; you come with an instant family, and I am not mother material."

"Bullshit."

She raised her eyebrows at him.

He shook his own head. "That's all bullshit. I don't want to be with you just so the girls can have a mother figure in their life, but bloody hell, saying you're not mother material? You don't give yourself enough credit. You're amazing. I think Sasha loves you more than I do. And Will…she's prickly, I know, but she asked for you last night. When she needed help, she asked for you. Doesn't that tell you something?"

She turned away from him again. Why? So he couldn't see her face? Couldn't see the emotion on it? Because she knew he'd see the truth she was so desperately trying to deny?

He squeezed the pillow in his hands. A conversation of this magnitude shouldn't take place like this, with him covering his dick with a pillow, but it was. He couldn't stop it. "We know each other better than you think we do, Randi. Hell, I know more about you than I did Bridget when I married her. And this isn't just one-sided. You feel the same way about me. I know it in my gut."

Puffing out a sigh, she rubbed at her face. "See? That right there? That's part of the problem. You've been married. You're a widower. A father. I told you before, you come with too much baggage. I'm not good with baggage. I don't want it."

He gritted his teeth, eyes hot. "Here's some baggage for you. I haven't slept with anyone since Bridget died. Anyone. I didn't want to. Had no desire to. My sex life was done and dusted when she died. And I was okay with that. But the second I saw you at Wet 'N' Wild, the *very* second, you woke a part of me I'd buried with my wife. That means something. It means something big and important. You know it as well as I do."

Her shoulders stiffened, and she looked at him. His heart clenched. "It's...it's better I stick with just being a...a...I don't know, friend for Sash and teacher for Willow. A coach, if she wants to return to jumping."

"And us?" Fuck, could he feel any colder? Emptier? He'd felt like this once before. He'd sworn back then he'd never feel this way again.

She let out another sigh and gave him a wry smile. "Friends?"

Friends.

He'd been friend-zoned by the woman he'd just shared the most amazing sex with. The person who'd somehow made him realize he was ready to give his heart to someone else again.

The woman who made his life feel better. Complete.

Friends.

"Okay." It wasn't okay. Not at all. "Friends."

She closed her eyes, but not before he saw the tears welling in them.

They could be friends. That's how they'd started, after all. When he'd refused to entertain the notion of ever replacing Bridget, he'd thought of her as a new friend. Even though every inch of his soul told him this wonderful woman suddenly thrust into his life was more, he'd told himself she was just a friend. But they were more. He knew it, and she knew it.

Hopefully, she'd accept that one day. Until then…

"Randi," he murmured, cupping the side of her face with one hand.

She looked up at him.

"Can friends do this?" He lowered his head and brushed his lips over hers.

She moaned, a soft sound of surrender, and pulled away. "No."

He dragged in a ragged breath, and nodded. "'K."

So that was it. Friends. Why the hell did "friends" feel so hollow?

He pushed himself away from the counter.

It's better this way. Me and my girls, that's what it's about. Me, Willow, and Sash, beating the world.

She touched his shoulder. "Brody? Are you…do you really think you're…"

His heart smashed into his throat. "In love with you?"

"Yes."

"Yeah. I do. I love you. More than I thought was possible."

She caught her bottom lip with her teeth. "You're going to break my heart, aren't you?" she whispered.

He shook his head. "No. I won't."

"Promise?"

For an answer, he kissed her, lifted her onto the counter, and unwrapped the throw blanket from her body.

"Brody…" she whispered his name, eyes closing as he feathered his hands over what he'd revealed. She trembled, her nipples growing hard beneath his thumbs when he cupped her breasts in his hands.

"I love hearing you say my name." He moved his hands down her rib cage, to her hips. She parted her thighs wider, and he nestled deeper into the *V*. His erection nudged her folds open, as if coming home.

"Brody…"

His cock pulsed at the raw hunger in her voice, at the warm wetness kissing its crown. "Tell me you want me inside you, babe. Tell me…"

He wouldn't move until she allowed. Until she said so. He wanted her more than fucking breath, but he needed to know she wanted it as much.

She moaned, wrapped her legs around his hips, and—her hands burying in his hair—drew him closer. Closer. "I want you inside me. Now."

His world burned. Golden fire.

He penetrated her, inch by inch, until he couldn't go any deeper. Until there was nothing between their bodies at all.

Shaking, he cupped the side of her face with one hand, brushed his thumb over her lips, and kissed her.

Kissed her and made love to her and gave her everything he was.

———⋆———

She was deluded. It was all going to end in pain, of course. In disappointment. But the one thing she was an expert at was coping with disappointment. It didn't matter how badly she'd ached for her parents to be proud of her for paying her way through college with the money she made selling her art, for getting a teaching job straight out of college, she'd been disillusioned every time.

When you failed to live up to expectations over and over, when you failed to make your parents smile at your achievements, you learned to deal with despondency.

She'd deal with the sorrow of Brody breaking her heart. She would. She'd put on her coping face and deal. But until that happened...

"Penny for your thoughts?"

She rolled her head and smiled at Brody stretched out beside her on the floor watching her. "I was wondering when we actually moved from the kitchen bench to the living room."

He adjusted his head in his hand, grinning. "That was somewhere around the time I got a cramp in my right calf."

She laughed. He hadn't gotten a cramp. She'd almost fallen off the kitchen counter mid-orgasm. It seemed sex in your late thirties was fraught with physical danger.

He'd caught her no matter how awkward their new position was until she finished coming, and then he'd carried her into the living room, laid her on the floor, and brought her to orgasm again, this time joining her in release deep inside her body.

And then he'd kissed her until he was hard again, and they came together once more.

"I should thank you for the excellent rug choice."

She frowned. God, he was gorgeous. All naked and sexy and messed-up hair and sculpted muscles and stubbly five o'clock shadow. How good did that stubble feel against her inner thighs? Fucking amazingly good. "Rug choice?"

He nodded. "It's soft and fluffy. No carpet burn on my knees."

She laughed again. There was no point in fighting how she felt about him. It was an exercise in futility. She'd just surrender to it all, knowing that eventually it would come to an end. And then she'd deal with the pain and get on with her life. Like she always did.

Yep. Totally deluded. That's me.

"Carpet burn is definitely a mood killer," she said. Goddamn it, why hadn't she kept him in the friend zone like any sane woman who knew her heart was on the line would have done?

"It is." He rose up onto his knees, smoothing his hands over her hips. "What about you? No carpet burn on your butt?" He rolled her toward him with a playful tug.

Laughing, she showed him her ass. "No carpet burn."

"Bloody sexy arse, though."

Oh, there was that hot Aussie accent coming into—

Holy crap, he kissed her ass cheek. And the other one. Oh, and now he was kissing her hip. Her waist, the base of her spine, the back of her thigh…

The world grew hot and heady, and she forget how to breathe for a while as Brody spent an extravagant amount of time exploring her body below her waist with his mouth. Oh, not just below her waist. Now he was…

"Goddamn it, that feels good." She fisted her hand in his hair as he suckled deeply on her nipple.

He groaned around her flesh and slipped a finger into her wet heat.

Oh boy. Pleasure radiated through her, delicious ribbons of tight sensations unfurling from the point his finger—no, make that his two fingers—inched deep inside her.

Oh boy, oh God, oh yes.

Releasing her nipple with a gentle nip, he raised his head and gazed down at her. "I can't get enough of you, Randi."

She had to remember these words, the look in his face, the desire in his eyes when he was gone. When the Thortons were just a memory.

"You've made me insatiable," he murmured, moving his fingers to the swollen nub of her clit.

She hitched in a breath. So much pleasure. So intense. So wonderful.

He lowered his mouth to the side of her neck and, slowly

sinking his fingers back inside her, nibbled his way down to her breast once more.

Was it possible to orgasm so many times in one day?

He scissored his fingers, sucked on her breast, and moaned her name, told her how beautiful she was, how perfect, and yep, apparently it *was* possible.

And was it possible to make an Australian come so hard with her mouth he roared her name?

"Brody?" She trailed her fingers over his chest as—with a gentle pressure—she pushed him down onto his back. "I just need to find something out."

"What?" Curiosity and delight twinkled in his eyes. Another thing she would need to commit to memory—the way he looked when horny and playful.

"This," she whispered, smoothing her hand down over his sublime six-pack to wrap her fingers around the base of his engorged penis.

"What are you—fuck me," he groaned as she closed her lips around his erection.

A few long, wild moments later, she lifted her head from his groin, flicked her tongue over the tip of his pulsing erection, and smiled. Yes, apparently it was possible to make an Australian come so hard he roared her name.

"Remember how you said you like hearing me say your name?" She arched an eyebrow at him.

"I do."

She grinned and traced the areola of his right nipple with her fingernail. "I like hearing you roar mine."

His nostrils flared, and he snagged her around the waist and hauled her down to him and kissed her senseless.

He was still kissing her senseless, and she was kissing him back, when Imagine Dragons started singing about being on top of the world from somewhere nearby.

Tearing his lips from hers, he swore. "That's my phone."

She rolled off him, far more reluctantly than someone who

knew this was all going to end in tears should, and watched him scan the room.

"Where are my...ah, there they are." He crawled across the floor to where his jeans lay in a crumpled pile near the sofa.

A third thing to brand into her memory; the sight of a naked Brody moving on hands and knees across her living room, muscles coiling and flexing with a natural strength, skin glistening with perspiration from all the fucking they'd been doing.

Not just fucking. It's been so much more than that.

But calling it what it was... That would only make it all hurt even more when he was no longer in her—

"G'day, Brody Thorton speaking." A frown pulled at his eyebrows. "When?" He swiped at his mouth, gaze jumping around the room. "Why didn't Annette—she did? When? Okay, okay, I'm coming home. I'll be there soon." He removed the phone from his ear and frowned harder at its screen. Tapped it with his thumb a few times. Scowled. "Shit."

Something cold curled around Randi's chest. "Everything okay?"

"Yeah, yeah." He raked a hand through his hair and then snatched up his jeans again. "Sasha's been dropped back home. She got homesick and wanted to talk to me, but I didn't answer when her friend's mum rang."

"When was that?" The cold thing curled tighter.

He straightened to his feet and shoved his right leg and then his left into the jeans. "I guess when we were in the bedroom earlier."

When they were making love. How long ago was that? Two? Three hours? Oh no.

"I have to go." He yanked up his fly and clawed his hands through his hair again. "When she couldn't talk to me, she got upset. Annette had to bring her home, and when they got there Willow had no clue where I was."

Randi folded herself onto her knees, covering her breasts

with her arms. Her pulse pounded in her ears. "Is she okay? Are you okay?"

Another clawing of his scalp, this time as he scanned the floor. His jaw bunched. His Adam's apple jerked up and down. "The mother of my daughter's friend just returned my crying child home to find my other daughter alone with a fifteen-year-old boy, with no clue at all of my whereabouts. Because I was too busy fucking." He scrunched up his face. "Too busy to be there for my daughters."

All the heat vanished from the room. Or was it from her? Her very soul? "Is that what you think?"

Even her throat felt cold. The air in her lungs could be ice.

"I have to go." He strode across the living room, not looking at her. Agitation and disgust radiated from him in silent screams.

"Brody, don't do this."

"Do what?" His voice was emotionless. She flinched, cut by it. "Love my daughters? Or throw them aside for—" His jaw bunched.

"For?" A shard of anger stabbed the cold enveloping her. "Go on. Finish it. Throw them aside for me. That's what you were going to say, isn't it?"

He didn't answer. Instead, he snatched his shirt from the floor and yanked it over his head.

She sighed, hugging herself tighter. To think her heart was being ripped out while she sat naked in her home. Not how she'd thought the day would go, that was for certain. "You know, I *knew* you were going to hurt me eventually. I tried to warn myself over and over. *He's got baggage, Miranda. Don't fall in love with him, Miranda.* It was like a mantra, but I didn't listen. I *did* fall in love with you. I fell hard even though I tried not to. God help me, I tried. Because I *knew* you were going to hurt me. I just didn't think you were going to do it so soon after promising you wouldn't."

He studied her, his expression unreadable. Whatever he

was thinking or feeling about her confession, he'd closed it off to her. "I have to go," he said again.

She watched him cross to the front door. Didn't stop him. What was the point? Once again, as with so many things in her life, she'd failed.

He paused at the door, fingers gripping it so tight his knuckles were white. His stare found hers. His Adam's apple jerked up and down. "I…"

He stopped. Closed his mouth.

She didn't move. "I'll text Chuck soon and tell him I'm coming to get him." After she'd salvaged her pride and courage and buried her heartache.

His chest shook with a deep breath, and—with a single dip of his head—he turned, opened the door, and left.

CHAPTER FIFTEEN

"Where's Randi?" Sasha frowned at the empty space behind him as he hurried into his home. "Will said you were at her place."

A cold finger of guilt drilled into his chest. He hadn't told Willow where he was when she'd called, but clearly she'd guessed. So his thirteen-year-old had known exactly where he was, and probably had a fair idea of what he was doing while he was AWOL.

Fuck, could I get any lower?

Squatting down, he wrapped Sasha in a tight hug. "Heya, maniac. You okay? Sorry I didn't answer Annette's call. I didn't hear my phone ringing."

She squirmed out of his arms. "That's okay, Daddy. I was just missing you. Where's Randi?"

He swiped at his lips. Who'd dumped half the Simpson Desert in his mouth? "Randi's not…not going to be hanging out with us anymore."

Sasha's frown darkened. "Why not?"

How did he answer this?

With the truth?

The truth. Ha. What was the truth? He'd told a woman he

loved her, promised he wouldn't hurt her, and then did exactly that?

Cupping his hands over Sasha's shoulders, he gave her a smile. Christ, could she tell how fake it was? "I think we need more Thorton time. Just you, me, and Will, right? Us Thortons versus the world. The way it used to be."

"But I want Randi to verse the world with us."

He had no response to that. Slipping his hands from her shoulders, he straightened. "Where's your sister?"

"Why can't Randi hang out with us more? Is she mad at us? Did we do something wrong? Is she cranky 'cause we broke your date? Willow didn't mean to break your date. She didn't."

An invisible weight crushed his chest. "It's all good, Sash. Honest."

And that's the biggest lie I've ever told her.

"Is she still going to come here on Tuesday after school? She promised we would do a painting together on Tuesday."

"I don't... Where's your sister?"

"She's playing *Horizon Zero* with Chuck. Can I call Randi and ask her if we can still do painting on—"

"No."

She flinched. He hadn't shouted. He hadn't. But he'd... A fist twisted in his gut. Or maybe it was a knife. *Fuck.*

"O-okay," she whispered. She dropped her head. Her shoulders slumped. She slumped. "Sorry for making you mad, Daddy."

He crouched, squeezing her hands. "I'm not mad. You didn't make me mad. Sometimes grown-ups... Well, we just... Things get more complicated. Besides, the most important thing in my life is you. Seeing you happy. You're my world, maniac. You and your sister. Okay?"

She nodded. But didn't squeeze his hands back.

"I love you, Sash."

"I love you, too." No eye contact. No hugs. Just that shoulder slump. "I have to go to the loo."

Throat tight, he let her hands go. "Sure." Escaping to the toilet when she was upset or stressed. Something she hadn't done since the months after Bridget's funeral.

She ran up the stairs. Yeah, she was angry with him. He didn't blame her. He'd taken away something she adored.

That's the second time. First Bridget, now Randi.

The icy knife in his gut twisted deeper.

Dragging his hands through his hair, he straightened to his feet and headed for the living room. The sounds of Willow's favorite computer game floated on the air, ominous and moody. The perfect soundtrack to his afternoon.

"I'm home, Will." He paused at the living room's entry, taking in Willow and Chuck sitting side by side on the sofa, their stares locked on the television. "G'day, Chuck."

Chuck smiled at him. "Hi, Mr. Thorton."

Willow flicked him a glance and then went back to the game.

So, one daughter so furious with him she was hiding out in the toilet, one refusing to talk to him.

He continued through the living room to the kitchen. "How goes the game? Either of you want a Coke? A soda?"

"I'm not thirsty," Willow said.

"Yes, please," Chuck answered. "Water is cool, or a Coke. The game is going well. Will smashed through the *Into the Borderlands* quest, which is really tricky, and she's kicking ass, er, butt now."

Reaching into the fridge, Brody grabbed two bottles of Coke. He really liked this kid. "We have a rule in our house, Charles. You can say the A word, but it must be pronounced the Aussie way."

"Dad." Willow rolled her eyes and let out a sigh. "Stop it." She smiled at Chuck—a true smile. "I'm sorry. You don't have to say *arse.*"

Twisting the lids off the sodas, he made his way back into the living room. He hadn't seen Willow smile for a while. Definitely not at him. In fact, when *was* the last time? When she'd thanked Randi for helping her with her period?

Crap, he shouldn't have thought about Randi.

"Here ya go, Chuck." He handed Chuck a bottle.

"Thanks, Mr. Thorton."

"You can go now, Dad." Willow kept her stare on the television. "It's not like we need you here. I know you've got *other* things to do."

"Hey." The knife in his gut changed into a pounding hammer. "That's enough."

Chuck shifted on the sofa. "Do you want me to—?"

"The second Chuck got here, you took off, Dad." Willow narrowed her eyes, stare still locked on the screen. "Did you need to get in Miss Lockwood's pants that desperately? That you just…left? Got in your car and drove away."

Got in your car and drove away.

Guilt flayed him. He'd said those very words to Bridget five minutes after their fight over Willow's long-jump training regime. He'd called her on the phone, she'd answered, and he'd said, "So that's it? You just got in your car and drove away. No effort to talk about it like adults? No willingness to see things from my side? You're overtraining her. Pushing her too hard."

She'd told him he was being ridiculous, overprotective, and that she didn't want to talk to him until he started being reasonable. She'd ended the call before he could say another word, leaving him standing alone in their living room. A few minutes later, she was dead.

"I think I should…" Chuck straightened from the sofa. "Aunty R…"

Aunty R.

Another chill swept through Brody. The nice, smart boy who made Willow smile, who had played the most unsubtle game of matchmaking on the waterslide a lifetime ago, had just heard Willow state loudly and venomously clear that Brody was having sex with his aunt.

Christ, did life come with a reset button?

Nope, it doesn't.

Jaw tight, he looked at Chuck and then at Willow. "Will, you need to apologize to Charles."

"Why?"

"It's okay, Mr. Thorton. Honest."

Willow frowned. "Why do I need to apologize for what you've been... Oh shit." Her face went pale. She stared up at Chuck. "Oh God, I forgot. Miss Lockwood is your—"

"It's okay." Chuck shuffled his feet. Could the poor kid look any more embarrassed? "Honest. I just think I should probably call—"

Willow burst into tears, threw herself off the sofa, and ran from the room.

A nervous laugh hiccupped from Chuck. "Ahh...okay. That...umm..."

"Bloody hell," Brody muttered. He squeezed Chuck's shoulder. "I'm sorry, Chuck. I don't know... Will shouldn't have..." Crap, how did he finish this?

Chuck shrugged. And then frowned at him. "Are you and my aunt...? I mean, I know I shouldn't ask, it's just I've never seen her so happy, but then today she was acting all weird about coming over here, and now Will..." He stopped, shuffled his feet, dropped his head, and stared at the ground.

"Your aunt and I..." What? What possible conclusion to the sentence would make any sense? Bonked like rabbits today, confessed to being in love with each other, but now we can't see each other again because I can't do that to Willow and Sasha? It sounded absurd. It *was* absurd. But it was also the way it was. The way it had to be. "It's a..."

Chuck lifted his head and fixed Brody in a level gaze. "Don't say a grown-up thing."

Brody closed his mouth.

"I love my aunt, Mr. Thorton. And I won't let *anyone* hurt

her. She's too nice, too wonderful. So maybe it's better you don't come around or call her anymore, okay?"

And there we have it. Told off by a fifteen-year-old. "Charles, it's not…" He swallowed. Forty-two years of testosterone and male pride wanted to put the fifteen-year-old in his place, but Chuck was correct. It was better he stay away from Randi.

For everyone concerned.

Everyone? Really?

Chuck didn't move or speak. Hell, he was going to be an intimidating adult one day. Even now, his gaze was flinty.

He's protecting someone he loves, just like I'm *protecting those I love.*

"Sure." He gave Chuck a simple nod. "I understand."

"Good. Do you mind if I go find Will? I don't want her to think I'm pissed—angry with her."

And now the fifteen-year-old is being a better man than—

"Randi's here!" Sasha barreled down the stairs and ran for the front door, face split into a massive grin. "Randi's here."

Brody's gut clenched.

Sasha flung open the door. "Daddy, Randi's here."

Chuck regarded Brody, silent.

Sasha bounded into the living room. "She came. She came."

"She's come to get Chuck, Sash."

"No, no." Sasha grabbed his hand and tugged. "I sent her a text from your computer saying you were sorry." She tugged harder. "And now she's here!"

"You what?"

"Oh boy." Chuck shook his head. "This is—"

"C'mon, Daddy." Sasha yanked his hand with such force he stumbled forward a step. "Let's go talk to Randi. Can she stay for dinner? Can she have a sleepover? Can she—?"

"Sasha." He extracted his hand. Hell, she had a grip. "Stop."

"Hello?" Randi's voice, unsure and hesitant, floated in from the open door.

Brody's breath caught, and Chuck scowled. Just as Sasha let out an excited, "Come in, Randi!"

No. She wasn't stepping foot inside. She couldn't. Her sanity wouldn't survive. Neither would her dignity.

Footsteps pounded through the house, rivaling her thumping pulse, and Sasha ran up to the door. Through it.

"Randi." She jumped. Randi only just managed to grab her in time.

"How are you doing now?" she asked, giving her a gentle hug. "Feeling better?"

Sasha nodded. "Did you like what Daddy said in his text?"

"What text?"

"The one where he said sorry for being a poo head."

"A poo—"

Brody stepped up to the open door, expression as closed as it had been at her place. "Hi."

Goddamn it, she'd never get over the sound of his voice. She attempted a smile, lowering Sasha back to the porch. "Hi. I'm just here to collect Chuck."

Sasha grabbed her hand. "Come inside, Randi."

Randi met Brody's gaze. Go inside? To the place she'd so quickly felt at home?

Brody's jaw bunched, and he shook his head. "Miss Lockwood's just here to collect Charles, Sash."

Miss Lockwood. Well, at least she knew the status of their relationship now. Teacher and student's parent.

"Really?" Sasha dropped her hand. "Really? But the text..."

Brody's jaw knotted again. "I'm sorry about the text. I didn't write it."

Randi shook her head. "I haven't read it, but I'll ignore whatever it says."

He nodded. Didn't move. Did he know how much he was tearing out her heart? "I'll go get Chuck," he said, turning away.

Sasha tugged on her hand again. "Are you and Daddy not in love anymore?"

And there goes the rest of my heart.

Squatting down, she pressed her palm to Sasha's cheek. "Your daddy and I...are friends."

Now there was a word with teeth.

Sasha frowned. "So you still like Daddy, and Daddy still likes you?"

"Yes." It wasn't a lie, but how could she explain the complexities of it all to a six-year-old?

Sasha's frown deepened. "Is it me and Willow you don't like?"

"Hey, Aunty R." Chuck appeared in the doorway. "Let's go."

Stomach churning, Randi held Sasha's gaze. Tears shone in Sasha's eyes. Randi got that. She was battling her own. "I think you and Willow are the most incredible, wonderful people I've ever known." She tried a playful smile. "Even better than Chuckles."

"Hey," Chuck protested with a laugh. God, she loved him.

Sasha looked up at Chuck and back to her. "Are you sure you can't come in?"

Movement behind her drew Randi's focus. Brody. And Willow. Both watched her. Both wore expressions a professional poker player would envy.

"I'm sure," she whispered. Leaning forward, she dropped a kiss on Sasha's cheek. "Be awesome, little one."

Straightening, she smiled at Willow. "Don't forget, the unveiling of your mascot logo happens this week."

Willow nodded.

"Talk to you later, Will," Chuck said, slinging an arm around Randi's shoulder. "C'mon, Aunty R."

He turned her around and walked her down the path.

Unlocking the car, she gave him a sideways glance. "You didn't say goodbye to Brody?"

He shrugged. "Didn't feel like it."

"Hey?"

He paused, passenger door half opened. "What? Don't lecture me on disrespecting my elders, Aunty R, because I—"

She kissed his cheek. "You are the best nephew ever, Charles. I'm so glad you're mine."

He rolled his eyes, face on fire. "Yeah, yeah. I know. Now get in the car. I think we both need copious amounts of curly fries, and we need them now."

She bought them the biggest serving of curly fries from Arby's she could, and they spent the rest of the drive home battling each one for the best curl. She didn't ask Chuck why he seemed angry with Brody, and he didn't explain. By the time she pulled to a halt in her driveway, she actually felt okay.

Not awesome. Not happy. But...okay. And okay was, well, okay. Did she really want anything more? At least she had her nephew and her job. Maybe not her promotion, given her attempt to get Willow back on the track and field team had never really gotten off the ground, but she still had her teaching position. And regardless of what her family thought of her being a teacher, it was enough for her.

"Aunty R?"

"Chuck?"

He fidgeted in his seat, one hand on the passenger door latch. "If you really like someone, but circumstances make it difficult to be with them, what do you think you should do?"

She bit back a sigh. What indeed? "You really like Willow, huh?"

He didn't answer. Instead, he opened the door. "I've got

homework. Let me know when you want me to help get dinner ready."

He hurried inside. She plucked a cold curly fry from one of the containers. "Do you think he was talking about Willow?"

The curly fry didn't answer.

She grimaced. "This is the problem with having a super-smart nephew. I have no clue when he's being a normal teenager and when he's being an insightful pain in the ass."

The second she said the word ass, she heard Brody, and then Sasha, and then Willow say *arse* in her head.

"Goddamn it, the Thortons have ruined ass for me."

Arse.

She flung open her door, stomped inside, and stopped at the sight of Chuck on his phone in the middle of the kitchen, shaking his head. "No. I don't want to, Mom."

Mom. Oh boy, Stacey had called him.

Frowning, he turned and thrust his phone out to Randi. "I don't want to talk to her. She's not listening to me."

Stacey was still talking as Randi brought the phone up to her ear. "Hi, sis. What's going on?"

"I take it you didn't tell Charles I called two days ago?"

"Must have slipped my mind. What's up?"

"Of course, why am I surprised you didn't follow through? It's very typical behavior, isn't it?"

"Stacey, did you call to insult me, or was there another reason?"

An uptight sniff came through the phone. Stacey was not happy. "I told Charles his father has found a job for him here in France for his summer break. We bought his plane ticket an hour ago. For whatever reason, he hasn't been answering my calls for the last few hours. Or days, for that matter. Or replying to his father's emails. What has he been doing? Studying, I hope."

France. Summer break. Only a matter of weeks away…

Randi swallowed. Cold. Goddamn it, why did she feel so cold?

Because Chuck is leaving.

"Chuck's been having fun," she said.

"What does 'having fun' mean? He should be studying. His father emailed him a strict study timetable last month."

Throat tight, she looked to Chuck. He stood head down, palms pressed to the refrigerator, thumping the toe of his foot against it over and over.

"He's been playing a computer game."

The answer would infuriate Stacey.

So why poke the bear?

"With a girl."

Chuck raised his head and grinned at her.

She grinned back.

"A girl?" Disbelief crackled through the connection. "He knows we don't approve of computer games *or* girlfriends. His grades will—"

"Sis, just shut up about grades for a moment and think about something for me, will you?"

Silence.

Chuck stared at her.

"Fine," Stacey finally snapped. "Tell me, *sister*, what I must think about?"

"How happy is your son?"

"What do you mean, 'how happy is my son'?"

"How happy is he? Do you know? I mean, I know you know how well he's doing at school, but do you know how happy he is?"

"Why would I...I don't understand what you are asking, Randi."

Randi sighed. "When we were kids, did Mom and Dad ever ask us how we were feeling? If we were happy?"

Another beat of silence. "They asked us how well we were doing at school."

"But never how we were doing in our hearts, right?"

"Our hearts? My God, Miranda, have you become a... a...Buddhist?"

Letting out a chuckle, Randi shook her head. "No. I think I've just come to realize I'm okay with being the failure of the family, is all. Because, apart from the fact I just had my heart ripped out, I'm actually happy."

"Your heart... I am so confused by this conversation. Now put Charles back on so I can tell him when his flight is and what will be expected of him in his summer job."

"Chuck?"

Chuck looked at her. She smiled. "Do you want to go to France for the summer?"

"No."

She nodded. "Actually, sis, you can cancel the flight. You put your son's well-being in my care when you left for France, and I take that responsibility very seriously. And one of the most important things Chuck needs is to be happy. He doesn't want to go to France for the summer. He wants to stay here. And maybe I'm being selfish, but I don't think so. I think I'm thinking of Chuck, because he's going to be happy here, hanging out with his friends, making new ones, playing computer games, and maybe even getting a girlfriend. Okay?"

"What is going *on* with you, Miranda?"

She laughed at Stacey's stunned confusion. "There are more important things in life than success, sis. When you under-stand that, give me a call."

She ended the call, pressed her phone to her forehead, and burst into tears.

"Aunty R?" Chuck was at her side before she could pull herself together. "Are you... Fuck, I mean, freak, are you..."

She waved a hand—the one holding his phone—and shook her head. "I'm okay. Hormones. Just hormones."

"You're thirty-five, Aunty R, not fifty-three."

A wet, wobbly laugh fell from her. Wiping at her eyes, she gave him a sheepish smile. "I hope that was okay?"

"Are you kidding? I don't want to go to France for the summer. I want to… Well, everything you just told Mom. Although the girlfriend thing might be a bit hard with you and her dad playing some kind of weird not-talking-to-each-other game."

She shook her head again. "Well, that one I can't help you with. Sorry about that."

He frowned. "Are you really…not going to, y'know, see each other?"

"I think so."

"Well, that sucks."

"You said it, Chuckles."

"Aunty R?"

"Yes?"

"Thank you. When I'm a zoologist, I'll make sure you get a family discount to the zoo."

She grinned. "And that makes the hell your mom is going to make our next Thanksgiving all the more worth it."

He laughed. "You okay?"

"I am."

"Mind if I go do my homework now?"

She waved her hand in the direction of their bedrooms. "Be my guest. I have work to do myself before tomorrow."

Opening her laptop a few minutes later, she stared at the email from Dave Pascoe sent only an hour ago.

Subject: Promotion. Track and Field coach expectations. Willow Thorton.

A cold lump rolled in her stomach as she clicked on the mail from her principal.

Well, it looked like it really *was* time to embrace her failures.

CHAPTER SIXTEEN

"Sasha says she's not talking to you."

Brody lifted his head out of his hands as Willow dropped into the armchair next to the sofa.

So, one daughter decides to start talking to me, and the other stops.

"She says until you stop being a poo head—her word, not mine—she's pretending you're not here."

"Fair enough." Really, what was he meant to say to that? He cast Willow an askew look. "What about you? Think I'm a poo head?"

She regarded him, so like Bridget his heart ached. "Yes."

He let out a ragged sigh and combed his fingers through his hair. "Fair enough," he repeated.

Silence stretched between them. He swallowed, wanting to say…something.

"Have you and Miss Lockwood broken up?"

"We weren't—"

"Yes you were, Dad."

Another shaky breath escaped him. "Okay, let's talk about this. Seriously. I think we need to."

She slumped back in the armchair, gaze locked on him. "Okay."

"Tell me what's eating you. Lay it all out. No bullshit, no sugarcoating it. What's in your head?"

A frown pulled at her forehead, and she slid her stare to her knees.

"It's okay, Will. I'm not going to get angry."

She scowled more at her knees. "The thought of you and Miss Lockwood making out was gross."

"And that was it? You just didn't like the idea of your father and a teacher…making out? Or was it the idea of your father and someone not Mum making out that was gross?"

"Did you fall in love with her?"

He swallowed again.

"You said no bullshit, Dad. Did you fall in love with Miss Lockwood? *Are* you in love with Miss Lockwood? Or did you just want to f—get in her pants?"

No bullshit.

"Yes. I fell in love with Randi." Hell, had spoken words ever ripped apart a man so much?

Willow scrunched up her face and, shaking her head, twisted away from him in the chair.

Swiping at his mouth, he leaned forward and rested his elbows on his knees. "Does that make you angry? Or hurt? Both?"

"Both." The mumbled reply tore at him some more. She curled into a ball in the armchair.

"Okay. I get that. Because of Mum?"

She nodded, face pressed to her folded knees. "You're not supposed to love anyone else. Only Mom."

"But I love you. And Sasha."

Her shoulders shook, and she buried her face deeper into her knees.

"And I will never stop loving your mum, Will. Not ever.

No matter what happens in my life, no matter *who* is in my life, I will never—"

"So why were you fighting with her then?" Willow rounded on him. Tears swam in her eyes. Anguish twisted her face. "She died because you were fighting with her. Over long jump. And you weren't listening to each other!"

An invisible hammer smashed into his gut.

"I heard it," she went on. "Every word you were shouting at each other."

Rage and grief. It was all there. In her voice, her face.

"Will…" Fuck, he was numb.

"You thought I was outside with Sash, but I wasn't. I'd come back in because we both wanted a cookie. I heard you fighting. I heard you telling Mom she was making me train too much, that she was pushing me too much. I heard Mom telling you she was sick of your Australian laid-back attitude to life, that you were never as successful as you could be because you were too relaxed about things."

Numb? No. He wasn't numb. He was ice-cold. And slowly shattering to pieces.

He'd kept the fight from Willow; she'd been only eleven when Bridget had died. Too young to know what had caused her mother to leave the house. Too young to know his part in the death of the most important person in her life. He'd never mentioned it to anyone until it had spilled from him during a conversation with Singo and Nate last year. He'd held it inside until one too many beers had loosened his tongue and unleashed his guilt.

But he'd kept it from everyone else, including the two people whose lives were the most impacted by it all.

And now…

His gut rolled. "Will…why didn't you—"

"And then Mom left. She grabbed her bag off the table, and she left." The words were emotionless, just empty sounds and syllables. "And I went back outside to Sasha and she asked where the cookies were, and I told her you and Mom were having a fight, and she got upset so I told her I was kidding. And then a little bit later Mrs. Herdan came over and told us she was going to look after us for a while, and *she* fed us cookies until I felt sick, and we didn't know where you'd gone. Then hours later, when it was dark, you came home and told us Mom was dead."

Jesus, he'd fucked everything up. Everything.

"And that's why I don't eat cookies anymore," she whispered, dropping back into the chair. Like she'd lost all strength. "And that's why I don't jump anymore."

Everything. And then some.

He pushed himself from the sofa and squatted down in front of her, gripping the arms of the chair. "I'm sorry, honey. I can't… I wish…"

Tear-red eyes slid to him. "That you could take it back? Stop the fight so Mom didn't go away? You took it *all* away, Daddy. You took Mom away, you took my sport away… You took it all. And now you're trying to replace it, replace M-Mom with Miss Lockwood, and I hate you for doing that. I hate that you're ready to forget Mom. I hate that I miss training and competing, but every time I think of it, I think of Mom and you fighting, and I *hate* that. I hate…"

She crumbled into sobs. Heart-tearing sobs that flayed what remained of the pieces of pain and guilt he'd become.

He wrapped her in his arms and held her. She struggled for a heartbeat, and then hugged him so tightly he couldn't breathe. But that was okay, that was fair. He didn't deserve to breathe. Not at that moment.

He hugged her and cried with her. And whispered he loved her over and over. Whispered how sorry he was. So sorry. God, he was sorry.

"I hate…" She pulled away from him, face wet, eyes puffy.

"Me?" He touched her cheek. Brushed a tear away with his thumb. "You're allowed to, honey."

She sniffed and shook her head. "I hate that I am angry with you, Daddy. I *don't* hate you. I hate the hole we have in our hearts. I hate that so much. But I don't hate you."

He bit back a choked sob. "I'm glad. You're kinda the whole reason I breathe, you know that, right? You and your sister?"

She nodded.

He brushed another tear from her cheek. Hell if he could feel any part of his body. This was what numb really felt like.

"Daddy?"

His heart thumped.

She swiped at her nose with the back of her hand, a little girl lost in the brutal journey of growing up. "Do... Are you and Miss Lockwood...?"

He shook his head. "No, no. You don't need to worry."

She frowned. "You love her, right? And you want her to... to...be with you? With us?"

He gave another shake of his head. His gut had long abandoned him, replaced with a twisted knot. "Our family? It's you, me and Sasha, okay?"

Willow frowned again. "But..."

"Daddy?"

They both turned at Sasha's soft, hesitant voice.

She stood in the entrance to the living room, eyes puffy with tears, bottom lip wobbling. In her arms, squeezed tightly against her chest, was Skips, her soft-toy kangaroo.

Brody drew a deep breath. Skips—Sasha's knight in acrylic fur—had been holding up the fort in her bedroom since Randi entered their lives, but now here he was, out of the bedroom. "Heya, maniac."

She sniffed, glistening eyes sliding from him to Willow and back to him. "I'm sorry. You're not a poo head."

He offered her a wan smile and waved her to him. "Well, I have been a bit of a poo head lately. But I won't be anymore, promise."

His future had to be lived for his girls, not himself. And seeing them happy would make *him* happy.

Sasha shuffled over to where he crouched down in front of Willow. She climbed onto one of his bent knees and wrapped her arms around his neck. "I love you, Daddy."

"Love you back, little one."

She pulled away and studied him, eyes solemn. "Are you finished being angry with Randi now?"

He swallowed. Willow didn't say a word. Waited, just like Sasha, for his answer. "You know what I think?"

Sasha shook her head. "What?"

He tapped her nose. "I think we should go to Disneyland. Right now."

Blue eyes opened wide. "Now? Now now?" Sasha gaped at him. "Can we go now?"

He grinned, even as a cold rope coiled through his insides. Deflection, thy name is Brody Thorton. "Right now. We'll get there for dinner, and stay in a motel tonight, and be a little late for school tomorrow. No biggie, right? We've got season tickets, after all. Let's make use of them."

"Yay. Yay, yay, yay! Willow, did you hear that? We're going to Disneyland! Let's go. Let's—" She scrambled off his leg and bolted from the room, calling to Willow to follow. To hurry. To get moving.

Letting out a shaky laugh, he smiled at Willow. "Why not, 'eh?"

She studied him, the inscrutable, enigmatic stare Bridget had mastered. "Sure." She pushed herself out of the armchair and headed for her room. "Why not."

He dropped his face into a hand. So it had happened. He'd become one of *those* dad's using bribery to avoid tears.

Great. Bloody great.

She ignored all the phone calls and text messages. Childish, yes? Satisfying, definitely.

It made for an interesting Monday. *And* Tuesday. Between every lesson, she'd check her phone and yep, there they were, text after text, message after message from Stacey. Ignoring them also gave her something to think about that wasn't Brody Thorton.

Every time she ignored a message or a text, she prided herself on how she was spending her energies elsewhere rather than dwelling on how much she missed him.

Forty-eight hours, plus change, of adamantly *not* missing him. *Go me.*

Of course, every time she congratulated herself on how much she was *not* missing him she had to accept the fact that it was all a goddamn lie. Every time she praised how well she wasn't missing Sasha and Willow—who she hadn't seen at school for the last two days—she accepted she was missing them all, including Brody, like hell. Anytime she thought she was being so focused on forgetting them she'd almost burst into tears. Oh God, how much longer before her heart stopped feeling like it had been ripped out of her chest?

Of course, the best way to shove all that pain and misery down was to focus on every text message and missed call from Stacey. Irking Stacey had become her favorite pastime.

Maybe she should call their parents and inform them she'd finally found something to excel at? Would they be proud?

Probably not. They wouldn't consider her successful until she irritated Stacey into murdering her. Which, based on the last text Stacey had sent—"*Am I to assume you have decided to abduct my son, Miranda? If you don't return my calls, I will contact the authorities, and believe me I HAVE CONTACTS!!!*"—might not be that far off. Good thing Stacey lived in France.

Still, if nothing else, Chuck was on her side cheering her on and doing everything he could to keep her mind off Brody.

Yeah, there was no way she was giving him back.

Not until her heart recovered.

"What are your thoughts on living with me until you're about sixty, Chuckles?"

He shot her a look from the kitchen where he was retrieving the ketchup for their dinner—homemade burgers and fries. Her hips were never going to forgive her. "Rent free?"

She pretended to ponder the question. "Only if you agree to stop me adopting a million cats, and maybe vacuum the house every now and then."

He closed the cupboard door. "Deal."

She laughed and then scrunched up her face when her phone burst into life with the *Doctor Who* theme music.

Oh yay. Dr. Lockwood calling. Repeat, Dr. Lockwood calling.

Chuck picked her phone up from its charging dock and showed it to her. "It's Uncle Aaron. Did you want me to answer?"

Chuck and Aaron had an interesting relationship. Aaron was the highest of achievers of the Lockwood siblings and a confirmed bachelor. He regularly announced Chuck was the son he'd never have. Stacey, who viewed her big brother as competition when it came to accolades, always responded to such claims with a sharp reminder Aaron had still been only a freshman at fifteen whereas Chuck was already a sophomore.

Chuck—who as far as Randi could tell had somehow gotten *her* sense of sarcasm and humor—would tell both of them during these conversations that he always considered Dwayne The Rock Johnson the father he'd never have because of The Rock's impressive biceps and ability to eat thirty pancakes in one sitting.

"I'm answering it," he said with a smirk before Randi could say anything.

Oh boy, this is going to be interesting.

"Hi, Uncle A." Chuck flipped the ketchup bottle in one

hand and pressed Randi's phone to his ear with the other. "Are you calling Aunty R on Mom's behalf?"

There were a few beats of silence as he listened to whatever Aaron said. "Wow. She really said that?"

"Said what?" Randi straightened to her feet and hurried into the kitchen. *Hmmm, maybe all this family drama isn't worth me forgetting about Brody.*

Forgetting about Brody. Yeah, right.

Chuck pressed her phone to his shoulder, lips twitching. "Apparently, Mom told Uncle A you've brainwashed me in some way. Compelled me to stay with you when I really want to go to France. That's some awesome powers you've got there, Aunty R."

"Phone." She wriggled her fingers at him. "Phone."

He shook his head, grinned, and returned her phone to his ear. "Aunty R is waving a fob watch in my face, Uncle A. Should I be worried? She's been doing it daily since Mom and Dad—"

Randi snagged her phone from his grip and, glaring at him, pressed it to her ear. "Hi, Aaron."

Laughing, Chuck flipped the ketchup bottle again. "Help me, Uncle A," he mock cried.

"Why is Stacey calling me at three in the morning insisting you are corrupting Charles?" Aaron asked. As always with Aaron, every word he uttered sounded like he was bored.

"Because I am?" Yes, this was much better than pining for Brody. Totally the best way to forget having her heart broken.

Aaron grunted. "I know you and Stacey don't always see eye to eye, Randi, but is she correct? Have you convinced our nephew to defy his parents' wishes?"

Leaning against the kitchen counter, she let out a sigh. Aaron was the only member of her family who called her Randi. It was a small thing, but it always made her feel closer to him. God, her family was messed up. "I asked Chuck if he wanted to go to France for his summer break. He doesn't. I told Stacey that."

"And if Stacey wants him to?"

"Remember when you were sixteen, and Dad told you you were going to Washington for the White House's school leadership summer program that he'd enrolled you in without your knowledge?"

"I do." There was an edge to Aaron's answer. He knew exactly where Randi was going with this.

"Remember what you did in response to that?"

"I do." He'd moved out. Spent the summer living with their grandparents—aging hippies who earned a living via a jarring combination of playing the stock market with cutthroat success and mural commissions mostly paid in cash…or sometimes other forms of trade Randi's parents discussed only in whispers when they didn't think their children were listening. Randi had inherited her artistic talent from her grandfather. Apparently, it had skipped a generation, because *her* father didn't have an artistic bone in his body.

"Do you remember how angry Dad was when you defied him?" she asked.

"He threatened to cut me off from the family for good."

"And did you relent?"

Ha. When did a Lockwood ever relent when they were doing something they wanted to do?

"I did not."

"Were you happy?"

Silence. Yep, there really was something about the notion of happiness that made her family so unsettled.

"Aaron?"

He sighed. His conflict echoed all the way from London. "I was happy with Grandpa and Grandma."

She let out her own sigh. "We were raised to never wonder or question the happiness levels in our lives. Do you realize that? It was never a consideration. Only our grades and our achievements. Why is that, do you think?"

Silence.

"I get Stacey is angry with me, but perhaps before she starts ranting about me and declaring me a bad influence, she should take the time to actually *listen* to her son about what he wants. He's an insanely intelligent young man, and she will lose him if she doesn't start thinking about his happiness. About what he wants in his life. The same way Mom and Dad almost lost you. In the same way—when it comes down to it—they lost me. Because let's face it, they *did* lose me a long time ago."

More silence.

She swallowed. *And there goes any chance I have of still being welcomed at a Lockwood family gathering.*

"We've been incredibly unfair to you, haven't we, Randi?"

She blinked at Aaron's question. "What?"

He laughed, the sound short and sharp. "We've mocked you for your life choices, your journey for so many years, but when it comes down to it, I'm beginning to suspect you're the most successful of us all."

She blinked again. Hell, she wasn't going to cry. She wasn't. "Not at the important things in life," she said. "I've failed at those."

Being in love. Being with the ones she loved. Yeah, big failure there.

"Have you?"

Chuck nudged her arm, and she smiled at him. He shook his head. "You haven't failed anyone," he whispered.

"Don't worry about Stacey," Aaron said. "I'll fly over to Paris tomorrow and settle her down."

"I'm not..." She dragged in a slow breath. "I'm not trying to drive a wedge between Stacey and Chuck. I promise. I'm just... I know what it's like to be pushed so hard by your parents that eventually you decide the only way to avoid hating them is to disconnect from them. I don't want that for Chuck. Or for Stacey."

Chuck studied her. On the other end of the line, Aaron let out another shaky sigh. "We definitely didn't treat you fairly, sis." His voice cracked. "For that, I am truly sorry."

He ended the call. Which was probably lucky because she was about to do something really lame like tell him she loved him.

Sliding her phone across the kitchen counter, she raised her eyebrows at Chuck. "Well, that was unexpected."

Chuck frowned at her. "Y'know, Aunty R, I've often wondered how you and my mom could be sisters. You're so different. But I see it now."

"You do?" Truth be known, she'd wondered the same thing more than once. She still considered it a distinct possibility she'd been swapped at birth in the hospital.

He nodded. "Yeah. One of the things I love the most about Mom is how focused she is. Her determination is amazing. Fierce, almost."

"And this is like me how?"

He laughed. "You have always been determined to give me the best childhood I could possibly have. From as far back as I can remember, you were fun. You taught me how to have fun, how to be silly and weird. You'll do anything you must to make certain I get the best from my teenage years. And you'll even fight your family to do so. You're fierce, Aunty R. You're caring and nurturing, and that's why you are such a good teacher, but whoa, you can be fierce as well. It's cool. One day, you'll make an amazing mom yourself."

Chest tight, she laughed. "X-nay on the Om-nay, Chuckles."

He shook his head. "Nah. You will make an *amazing* mother. And if Brody Thorton couldn't see that, well, he doesn't deserve you."

"Oh Chuck…" She bit her lip. First her brother, and now

her nephew? What was it with members of her family trying to make her cry today?

He shrugged. "Just calling it like I see it."

"Don't you have homework to do?"

Laughing, he grabbed her in a tight bear hug. "You are the worst person in the world at receiving compliments, Aunty R."

She closed her eyes and accepted the hug. It was too nice. "Thank you."

He let her go with a grin. "Now, let's eat dinner. The fries are probably cold and soggy by now."

Shooting the dining table a look, she snorted. "Let's go out for dinner instead. What do you say about Phil—The Cheesecake Factory?"

"Hell, yeah. I'll go put shoes on."

He ran from the room. If he'd caught the fact she'd started to say Phil's BBQ, he didn't show it.

Now all she had to do was not show just how hard that one little almost-slipup had hit her.

"Well," she muttered, walking to the table. "At least that's one restaurant I'll never have to worry about eating at again." No way she'd be able to walk into Phil's BBQ ever again without thinking of Brody.

Oh, who was she kidding? She'd never be able to breathe without thinking of Brody.

"Good grief, I'm so screwed."

CHAPTER SEVENTEEN

S taring at the screen in front of him, Brody shook his head. "All right, this is getting ridiculous."

Three days. Three days of throwing himself into his work in an attempt to forget all about Randi, and what had it gotten him?

Sure, he was so far ahead of his deadline on the poster for the next Sebastian Hart/Chris Huntley movie, he'd started to mock up a design for the nonexistent sequel during his lunch break. Okay, he'd spent the minutes in the car after dropping the girls at school and before collecting them again talking to new clients, touching base with existing clients, and basically drumming up so many new jobs his small team was about ready to mutiny.

And, yeah, he'd decided it was time for a complete rebranding of his business, which meant he'd spent the last three nights—starting Sunday night at eleven forty-eight—working, researching, sketching thumbnails, planning color schemes…

All those things, and the bloody second he allowed himself a moment to pause, to breathe, what happened?

Randi bloody Lockwood popped into his head.

Dropping his face into his hands, he let out a ragged sigh. *What the hell am I going to do?*

"Boss?"

Jolting upright, he raked a hand through his hair and smiled at his assistant. "Jen. What's up? Is that coffee I smell?"

"It is. The intern's brought afternoon coffee and snacks in for all of us. You want something?" She frowned. "You *have* been burning the candle at both ends lately."

He hesitated.

Jen narrowed her eyes. "I'm not bringing it in to you, boss. If you want it, you've got to come out and get it."

"What is it?" Maybe some social interaction with his team would be what he needed.

"Macaroons."

Fuck a bloody duck. He stood, snagged his satchel from the floor, and slung it over his shoulder. "Y'know what? I just remembered I gotta meeting at Will's school."

Jen blinked. "Oh. Okay."

"I'll be back later." *When all the macaroons are gone.* "Don't forget to send those logo mock-ups to the BBQ chook job."

"Chook?"

"Crap. Sorry. Aussie term. Chicken. Don't forget to get the logo mock-ups for the Happy Chicken House to the owners before six. See you later."

He hurried from the room, waving goodbye at the rest of his team without looking their way.

If he saw a macaroon…

Bloody Randi Lockwood.

His phone rang as he climbed into his car.

"Singo." He closed the door and let his head drop back against the headrest. This was good. He needed the distraction. "G'day, mate. How's it going?"

"Yeah, good. You?"

Swallowing, Brody pinched the bridge of his nose. Neither

Singo nor Nate knew how pear-shaped things had gone in his life. "Excellent. Perfect. Couldn't be better."

"Ahh." Singo cleared his throat. "Is that why I just got a call from Sash at her school asking if I will buy her a tub of triple-chocolate fudge ice cream and bring it around tonight?"

"She what?" Bloody hell. He dragged his hand down his face, over his mouth, and rubbed at the back of his neck. "Why did she do that?"

"Well, when I asked her why she was calling me, she said it was because you were sad, and seeing ice cream would make you sadder."

"She... Jesus, Singo." He swiped at his mouth again. "I'm sorry, mate. I'll have a word with her."

"No, no. Not at all. It's all good." He paused. "But I gotta ask, what's going on? Why are you sad?"

Why are you sad? For two years, no one had had the need to ask that question. If any of his friends or acquaintances saw him when he was down, they knew why. When you became a widower at forty, people knew why you were sad. It was a given.

But Singo—who'd been a pallbearer with Bridget's cousins at her funeral and who'd let him get so drunk in his living room a week after Bridget's death it was a wonder he hadn't slipped into a coma—was asking now. Singo, a man who played with kids' toys for a living even though he was one of the most insightful people Brody had ever met.

Why are you sad?

"Remember when you told me not to let Randi get away?" he asked. Had that really been only a few days ago? Felt like a different life.

"I do." Uncertainty filled Singo's voice. In the background, the sounds of kids laughing mocked Brody's state of mind. "Why? What did you...ah, what the bloody hell have you done, mate?"

A dry laugh tore at the back of Brody's throat. "I didn't let her get away. I *sent* her away. I made her go."

"Why the hell did you do that? She's amazing, perfect for you. For you *and* your girls."

"*Because* of my girls." His gut clenched. "Because what kind of father am I if I toss aside eleven years of love and life for some great sex?"

"And that's all Randi is? Great sex?"

"Yeah." The lie tasted bitter on his tongue.

"Bullshit. She's more than that, and that scares the shit out of you. She's the chance for a new life, a new future. She's what you and your girls need, and you're too bloody gutless to accept that."

The air in his SUV crushed down on him, icy cold and searing hot at once.

"Fuck you, Singleton." His pulse pounded in his ears. "What the hell do you know about love, about living for someone else apart from yourself? In the four years I've known you, you've had what? One serious relationship. And you ended that when she went out and bought a fucking dog."

"I know a hell of a lot about love, mate. *And* about losing it. One of these days, when your head's not so far up your arse, I'll tell you about it. But right now, all I'm thinking about is you. Fuck, not even you. I'm thinking about your girls. Do you have any idea how gray they've been since Bridget's death? You've spent the last two years sacrificing everything to make them happy, and how's that worked out? When does Willow do anything for fun? When does Sasha giggle? She's six, for fuck's sake, and until Randi came into your lives, I thought that little girl had forgotten how to laugh. And now you've pushed away the one person who's brought back the color in their lives for what? To protect them? To protect the memory of their mother? What would Bridget say about this? Would she be happy you're denying your daughters happiness?"

"I'm not—"

"Your younger daughter rang me from her school to ask for ice cream, Thorton. Think about that."

Something cold wrapped around Brody's chest. Constricted.

"And not just any ice cream," Singo went on, his voice calmer now. Gentler. Like he was aware he was talking to someone on the edge. Was he? "Triple-chocolate fudge ice cream. I could be wrong, but I'd put my rather sizeable income on that particular flavor having some kind of connection to Randi. Am I right?"

Brody swallowed. Tried to swallow, at least. His throat was too dry. "It was the flavor Randi brought around the first night she came to our place."

"There you go. Bloody hell, mate. Think about that. What does that tell you?"

He scrubbed at his face. "I…"

"What? I don't understand what happened between when I saw you Friday night and now? Surely it's not just Willow throwing a tantrum about catching you and Randi kissing on the front porch? I thought we sorted that out. Hell, you even had a conversation with Alicia about your life, and that ended well. Really well. I was there, remember? And if anyone was going to make your life hell about Randi, it was the Queen of Control."

Brody let out a short chuckle at the nickname.

"So what happened? What made you fuck up so badly I'm going shopping for ice cream this arvo?"

I got so caught up in making love to Randi I completely forgot I had a life, a wife, before her.

His gut, his heart, clenched. He opened his mouth. Closed it.

"Talk to me, mate. Help me understand so I can—"

"I fucked it up." Ha. Fucked is right. "I forgot what the point of my life is now—Willow and Sash. And I can't do that. I won't let myself do that."

A long, shaky sigh sounded through the phone. "Well, I don't know what to say to you, Brody. The way I see it, you have two options. Be courageous and live, or just…exist. Seems like you've decided on the latter."

Closing his eyes, Brody nodded. "I'll…make it work. It'll be okay." It had to be.

"Fair enough, although I think you're a bloody idiot."

"Noted."

Singo grunted out a laugh. "So, do you want me to go buy a tub of triple-chocolate fudge ice cream and bring it around this arvo when I knock off from work?"

"Yeah no. I'll do it."

"You sure?"

Brody nodded and then rolled his eyes. Idiot. "Yeah, I'm sure. In fact, I might knock off work early myself and go get the maniac out of school. Give her an early mark."

"K. Let me know if you need anything." Singo paused. "I mean it, mate. I don't agree with the direction you've decided to go. Think you need your bloody head read, to be honest. But I'm here for you. And your girls. If Sash ever needs to eat ice cream with someone, I'm her go-to guy, got it?"

"Got it." Brody chuckled. Hell, why did he feel like he'd just gone five rounds with a grizzly? "Tell me, what are your *Horizon Zero* skills like?"

"My what?"

"Figured. Maybe I can get Willow back into Lego. She always loved it as a kid."

"Bring 'em both to Legoland on Sunday. The *Star Wars* installation I've been working on has its grand opening at ten. I'll pull some strings and make sure Willow and Sash are the ones to cut the red ribbon if you want."

"I'll let you know." It could be just what they needed. A fun day out with lots of distractions and attention poured on them. Maybe?

"All right. I'll get back to it then. I've got some finishing touches to do to the Millennium Falcon. Talk to you later then, mate."

Ending the call, Brody tossed his phone onto the passenger seat and then rubbed at his eyes. He should feel better. *Why don't I?*

Because everything Singo said is true.

And he'd just rejected it all.

"For the girls," he muttered, turning over the engine. "For the girls."

Pulling out into the traffic, he headed for the closest Walmart. Hell, when was the last time he bought a tub of ice cream?

"For the girls."

He'd find a tub of triple-chocolate fudge ice cream if it was the last thing he did. And he'd sit down with Sasha and eat the ice cream with her straight from the tub if that's what he had to do. If that's what made her smile and be happy.

He would. For his girls.

Because that's all that mattered. Not how much he missed Randi. Not how right Singo had been about it all. Just his girls. And the life he couldn't steal from them.

He'd make it all work.

Somehow.

———✦———

"Has he said anything to you yet?"

Shaking her head at Sydney, Randi closed the door on the kiln. Four days' worth of pinch pots and coil pots made by her freshman classes were ready to be fired.

Fired. Huh. An apt term, given the email she'd received from Dave Pascoe that morning.

It hadn't been as verbose as the one he'd sent to her on Sunday. The one that had read: *I had certain expectations of you when you became a staff member. We've discussed Willow Thorton's placement on the track and field team numerous times, and I think I've been clear on my preferred outcome. If I recall correctly, a promotion to Head of the Arts faculty was also discussed. I will be calling a meeting with you this week so we can discuss how to move forward on this matter. Don't forget, the first district track meet is this upcoming weekend. I hope to see Willow's name on the team list by the end of the week.*

That had been a fun email to read—fired from her promotion before even getting it—especially straight after her clash with Stacey that night.

The email he'd sent to her today, Friday, simply read: *The track team list is missing a name. I will be seeing you shortly.*

Turning from the kiln, she let out a breath. "Do you think Canada would allow me to immigrate there?"

Sydney snorted. "Too cold."

"Me? Or Canada?"

"Canada." Picking up one of the small clay sculptures Randi had removed from the kiln before repacking it, Sydney grinned at her. "You, on the other hand, are a hot mess."

"Thanks. You know, you should quit the whole teacher thing and follow your true gift."

"Which is?"

"Therapist. You're a natural."

Sydney laughed. "I know, right? I'm so good at it."

"Why aren't you freaking out with me? Pascoe is going to fire me."

"He can't fire you. He *can* take away your promotion, demote you from all the good classes. He *can* and probably *will* make your life a living hell here, assigning you to weekly lunch detention supervision, and driver's ed… Oh wait, yeah, we *should* be freaking out. Argh. I'm freaking out."

Randi scowled. "Sydney, I'm serious."

Sydney returned the sculpture to the table and crossed the kiln room to grab Randi's shoulders. "Girl, you're a teacher. You deal with shit and drama every day. Pascoe will bluster and bark about it, but in the end, he *will* give you your promotion because he knows you deserve it, and because you are the best person for the job. The school will be better for you getting it. I'm more concerned with your failure to be an absolute wreck over Brody Thorton."

"I so regret telling you about Brody Thorton."

"Well, when you arrived at work on Monday with the ghost of a hickey on your neck but then spent the rest of this week kind of moping around with no mention of any future date plans with the Adonis from Oz, I made the assumption you and Brody had parted ways."

Randi frowned at her.

Sydney shrugged. "Plus, there was the whole incident in the girl's bathroom this morning where Kiera Wiezorek said Willow won the mascot competition only because her dad was —and I quote—*banging Miss W.*"

"What?" Oh God, *what*?

"According to Kiera, Willow went postal and screamed in Kiera's face that you and her dad had broken up and she should shut the fuck up. And that was when Kiera shoved Willow so hard into one of the toilet stall doors that the hinge snapped. Hence the protracted detention. She really is horrid, that girl. Kiera, not Willow."

"Are you serious?" Surely, she couldn't be—

"Very. See the things you miss when you don't come to the staff lounge for lunch."

Randi slumped to the floor and buried her face in her hands. "Oh God, this is…" She looked up at Sydney. "Has Brody been contacted?"

Joining her on the floor, Sydney shook her head. "Willow begged Shayna not to call. And you know our vice principal is a sweetheart to a fault. But yeah, all the staff now knows you and Brody Thorton were happening." She frowned. "What *did* happen? What made Willow get so angry with Kiera? I must admit, I was thinking you and Brody were a romance movie come to life."

And I did, too.

She pinched the bridge of her nose and let out a sigh. "No dramatic reason. I'm just not a fan of baggage, and Brody Thorton... Well, he has *way* too much—"

"Miranda?"

Randi shot to her feet, collided into Sydney—who was also jolting to her feet—and smiled at her boss. *Ah crap, here it comes.* "Dave."

"Hi, Dave." Sydney smoothed her hands on her thighs. "You're back from the conference early."

Of course he was. It was the day before the first district track meet of the season, after all. He was here to question her on her complete failure to get the school's record-setting long jumper to return to the sport she once loved and now shunned.

Dave scanned the space around him with a puzzled frown. Randi had always suspected he had no real idea how to connect with creative life.

"It's a crazy room, but the students really like it." Why the hell was she justifying the chaos of the kiln room?

Because he was about to take away the thing she'd been working so hard for—her promotion.

The final check on her things-to-fail list.

Dave flicked Sydney a look as if to say she could go now.

"I've got papers to grade." Sydney squeezed her hand. "TGIF, girl. See you at the bar in an hour, okay?"

Yeah, a drink was *exactly* what Randi would need after this. *There goes being a teetotaler.*

Dave waited for Sydney to leave and then pursed his lips with a frown. "I take it you couldn't convince Willow Thorton to compete again?"

"No."

He sighed his disappointment.

"I stopped trying."

Eyebrows shot up.

"When I found out about her mother. It didn't sit well with me, trying to push her into doing something again that clearly would bring back painful memories." She paused. "Don't you agree?"

He had the decency to look uncomfortable. Good. If she was losing her promotion, at least she wanted to lose it on her own terms.

She crossed her arms. "I mean, I'm a fan of school pride and success and all, and I absolutely love it here—go Stingrays—but it just seems callous to hound Willow about something like that."

Wow, so losing it on my terms means getting snarky? Fair enough. She'd lost her promotion, may as well speak her mind now.

"Our great school's reputation is on the line here, Miss Lockwood." Miss Lockwood? *Whoa, he's not happy. Mind you, I have been being particularly snippy.*

"And it all hangs on whether one thirteen-year-old girl competes in long jump or not?" She grunted. "Our school has some serious issues if that's the—"

"Excuse me," a soft female voice sounded from her door. "Miss Lockwood?"

Randi's throat seized shut. *Well, now this is becoming ridiculous.*

Turning, she forced a smile. "Hi, Willow. What can I help you with?"

Willow—hovering at the kiln room door—flicked a frown at Dave. "Hi, Principal Pascoe. I just need to tell Miss Lockwood something if I can."

"Willow. Come in. Come in." He waved her in. "Did you know the first district track meet is tomorrow?"

If I hit him, will I keep my job? Maybe it depends on how hard I hit him.

"That's what I'm here to talk to Miss Lockwood about, sir."

Willow took a few steps into the room and stopped, looking back to Randi. "I was hoping it's not too late to add my name to the team? I brought in my signed permission slip and everything."

"Not too late at all," Dave boomed, throwing his arms wide. "This is—"

"Miss Lockwood?" Willow took a step closer to Randi, ignoring Dave altogether. "Am I too late?"

And there's the final nail. In love with Brody, in love with Sasha, and now with one question, in love with Willow. I'm screwed.

"It's not too late, Willow." She frowned, even as her heart smashed a rabid path into her throat. "Is your father okay with this?"

Willow nodded. "He is. See?"

She held out a slip of paper to Randi. It was a school parental-approval form, signed by Brody.

Randi studied Brody's signature. She'd never seen it before, but just reading his name…

Oh man, it's going to take me forever to get over him.

"Okay." She swallowed, looking back up at Willow. "But are *you* sure about this?"

"I am." Willow nodded again. "I really love long jumping and I…I miss it. A lot. I'm hoping you can help me…help me make it not be a sad thing for me anymore. If that's okay?"

Dave stepped toward her. Is he really rubbing his hands together? Yes, he really is. "That's totally—"

"I'm sorry, Mr. Pascoe, but I want to talk to Miss Lockwood. *Just* Miss Lockwood."

Yep. I love this kid.

Dave cleared his throat. His eyes jumped between Randi and Willow and back to Randi. "Fine. Fine. I'll leave you two alone to work out the details then." He fisted his hand and almost-but-not-quite tapped it against Willow's chin, smile so broad it was a wonder he didn't strain a muscle, and then plucked the signed permission note from Randi's hand. "Good to have you on the team, Willow. The school will be cheering you on."

He hurried from the room.

Willow frowned. "Am I wrong, or is he far more excited about this than he should be?"

"I think you've made his year."

"Hmm, okay then." Willow chewed on her lip, uncertainty filling her face. "What about you? Are you happy about it?"

Randi held her hand out to the closest stool.

Willow sat, watching Randi do the same. "Well?"

Drawing in a slow breath, Randi met Willow's gaze. "Tell me why you've changed your mind about jumping."

And about talking to me.

Willow plucked at the hem of her shorts. "I realized I haven't been...fair to Dad lately."

"And that's why you want to compete again? Because of your father?"

"No. I was angry. At everyone, but mainly him, for Mom's death. And that wasn't fair because I knew he wasn't to blame. But every time I thought of jumping, I remembered the day Mom died, and a little part of me just...grew emptier."

Randi couldn't hug her. No matter how much she wanted to. Not here. Not in her capacity as a teacher. But her heart was breaking.

"I've been thinking a lot about that emptiness this week." Willow stared down at her feet swinging gently beneath the stool. "And I realized it won't go away. Ever. But I can fill it with the things and people I love. And I love Daddy. So much. And I love long jump. I really do. And I know Mom would want me to grow up doing the things I love, being happy with the people I love. So..." She looked up at Randi, eyes shining, and gave a little shrug. "I know I won't ever be able to replace what Mom and I had, but I'm hoping...if it's okay with you... if you're not too angry with me for how I've been treating you… I hope you will let me join the team again. And maybe…maybe coach me during lunches?"

A wave of warmth rolled through Randi. Wonderful, heart-breaking warmth. "I think I can do that, Willow. I'd *like* to do that. Thank you for asking me."

Willow swung her legs a bit more. "Thank you for always being nice to me, even when I was being horrible."

"Not horrible." She reached forward and squeezed Willow's hand. "Just protective of your family. You're allowed to be that. It's a good quality."

Willow's smile grew wider, and she squeezed Randi's hand back. "You know what, Miss Lockwood? R-Randi?"

"What?"

"I think my mom would have liked you. A lot."

CHAPTER EIGHTEEN

And that's the fourth *time I've hung up before the connection is even made.*

Biting back a frustrated growl, Brody tossed his phone onto the passenger seat.

Okay, so he'd told himself he wasn't going to call Randi. He had no right to call Randi. Randi was out of bounds. Randi was…

She was in his fucking head and heart, and he couldn't bloody well forget her, no matter how hard he tried. And bloody hell, he'd tried.

"It's been only five days," he muttered, glaring at the traffic through his windshield. "Suck it up, buttercup. Try harder."

Try harder. Ha. It wasn't like he'd been sitting around moping or anything. He'd thrown himself into his work and was doing everything in his power to be the best father in the world.

It was a distinct possibility Willow and Sasha were beginning to question his sanity.

There were only so many times he could suggest Chuck E. Cheese for dinner or take impromptu trips to the Safari Park. He'd done both—and then some—since his phone call with

Singo, all in an attempt to prove to himself his sole focus in life was Willow and Sasha and their happiness.

And every fucking time something made him think of Randi—a song on the radio, the sight of cupcakes, Skips sitting innocently on Sasha's bed, the bloody clouds in the sky…

"Jesus, mate." He dragged a hand over his face. "You really are screwed."

He reached for his phone, brought up Randi's number, and then threw it back onto the passenger seat before he could hit dial.

"I can do this."

Chances were Randi wouldn't answer anyway. Apart from the fact she was most likely teaching, why would she take his call after the way he'd behaved?

What way? Respecting the memory of Bridget? Being true to her, to what we'd had?

Yeah, that's exactly what he was doing. For his girls.

So why did it feel so…wrong?

"Stop thinking with your dick, Thorton."

The trouble was, he *wasn't*. It had gone beyond that. Every desire and need to call Randi, to see her, was from the heart.

Because it didn't matter how many lectures he gave himself in the dead of night, how busy he kept himself during the day, how many times he said yes to ice cream demands, or how many impulsive trips to somewhere exciting he made with the girls, he was in love with her.

He just hoped to God he'd stop being in love with her soon. For his sanity. And his credit card balance.

"Maybe," he muttered, turning into the pickup zone of Sasha's school, "it's time to move back to Australia."

Hell, maybe twelve thousand kilometers between him and Randi would do the—

"Hi, Dad." Willow opened the front passenger door and climbed in.

"G'day, Daddy." Sasha leaped into the back seat.

He blinked. "What are you doing here, Will? G'day, maniac."

Willow buckled her seatbelt and smiled at him. "I thought I'd come to Sash this arvo."

Arvo. Such an Aussie term.

He cast her an askew frown. "You seem in a good mood."

She shrugged, smiling.

"Will got into a fight at school today," Sasha piped up from the back.

"Will what?"

"Seriously, Sasha?" Willow twisted in her seat, scowling. "You couldn't wait until we were home?"

A car horn blasted behind them, and Brody swore.

"It's okay, Daddy." Sasha grinned at him in the rearview mirror. "She didn't get into trouble."

"What?"

"Or hurt."

"*What?*"

"Sasha." Willow laughed. Laughed, for Pete's sake. "Shush."

Throwing his SUV into first, Brody pulled out of the pickup zone. "All right, talk. Explain. Now."

Willow smiled. "It's okay, D—"

"Some horrible girl said Will won the mascot art competition only because Miss Lockwood likes you, and Willow told her that wasn't true, and the girl pushed Will into the toilets." Sasha's eyes couldn't get any wider in the mirror.

Brody's gut clenched. *Miss Lockwood likes you.* "Is this true?"

Willow nodded, shrugged again, and then waved her hand in a so-so gesture. She continued to smile.

"Why didn't the school call me?"

"I told them not to."

"And they listened?" Could he get any more surprised today?

Miss Lockwood likes you.

Oh, for fuck's sake, get over it. Over her.

"And that I was okay," Willow went on.

"The horrible girl is getting detention," Sasha stated with sage solemnity. "What's detention, Daddy?"

Brody gripped the steering wheel. *This is the most surreal conversation I've ever had.*

"In other news," Willow said. "I'm competing at the district track meet tomorrow."

"*What?*"

"I went and saw Miss Lockwood today and told her. Gave her the permission note saying you approved of me going back on the team."

A rush of anticipation, relief, and joy flowed through him all at once.

Randi. If Willow was jumping again, he'd have a legitimate reason to see Randi.

"I didn't sign any permission note."

Willow chewed on her bottom lip. "I kind of…of signed it for you. I decided through the day and didn't want to miss out on being on the team."

He could just see her handing the note to Randi, Randi taking it, smiling that smile of hers that was like the sun beaming, filling the world with warmth and joy and—

No," he growled. "You're not going."

"I'm what?" Willow blanched, gaped at him, and then frowned. "Why not?"

"Because…"

Yeah?

"Because you're not…"

What?

He swallowed. "You can't spend all this time saying you've quit and then suddenly change your mind, young lady."

Young lady? Jesus, I sound like a misogynistic old man.

"Are you kidding me?" Willow's voice cracked. "I don't believe—"

"And let's talk about this fight," he said, fixing his stare on the road. "Since when do you get into fights at school?"

"Since you taught me not to let anyone belittle me," she shot back.

"I still can't believe you got into a fight."

Miss Lockwood likes you.

"I can't believe I got into a fight over *you*," Willow snarled. "You are being so unfair."

"Life *is* unfair, Will." He turned his SUV into their driveway. "That's the way it—"

Willow opened the passenger door and scrambled out of the car before he stopped.

"Willow!"

She ran along the side of the house.

"Willow!"

"You messed that up, Daddy," Sasha said softly in the back. "You really *are* a poo head." She scrambled out of the car, slammed her door shut with a solid thud, and ran after Willow.

Scrunching his eyes closed, he attempted to strangle the steering wheel.

What the fuck am I doing? What is wrong with me?

The second Willow had mentioned returning to long jump, he'd thought of Randi. Not Willow, not Bridget. Randi. The very second. He didn't even pause for thought on the fact that Willow had forged his signature on a school note. No, it was all about seeing Randi again.

Instead of being angry about that, or being happy for Willow, being proud of her for moving forward, he'd thought of himself.

He'd thought of Randi's smile, thought of her back in their lives, *his* life…

Not even a week after swearing his daughters were his priority, along with the memory of their mother, and he'd gone straight to thinking of himself.

Guilt twisted through him. Hell, he needed to have his head read.

"But first, you need to apologize to Will."

He'd explain they could take the return to competing slowly. Go back to training—he'd even coach her if she wanted, or he'd find her a coach outside of the school. He'd explain they'd spend the next few months, maybe a year, getting her into peak fitness again, and *then* return to competing.

Or maybe he'd float the idea of moving to Australia. After all, her great uncle Rob was best mates with the head of the Australian Olympic Committee. Joseph Hudson would be the ideal person to help Will find the right trainer.

Yeah, maybe that was exactly what the Thorton family needed to do. Start fresh Down Under. Clean slate. Without the risk of ever bumping into Randi Lockwood any time he might need to go to Willow's school.

"All right." He tapped the steering wheel and climbed out of the SUV. "Let's do this."

He went inside. "Will? Sash?"

Silence.

"Captain Poo Head reporting for duty."

Nothing.

He let out a sigh and headed for the bedrooms. Willow's door was shut.

Sasha's was open. She sat in the middle of her bed, Skips in her hands.

"Heya, maniac." He leaned against the doorframe and offered her a white-flag smile. "I stuffed up, didn't I?"

Without looking at him, she climbed off the bed and went to close the door.

He stepped back just as it clicked shut.

Fuck.

Okay, what did he do next?

Turning, he crossed to Willow's door and knocked on it with a gentle tap. "Will?"

"I don't want to talk to you, Dad."

"If I say I fucked up will that change anything?"

Yeah, that's it. Use the F word to her for the very first time. That'll fix everything. Wanker.

"Not really." The door muffled her response. "But thank you for saying it."

That was something. Not the opening-of-the-door something he'd hoped for, but something.

Closing his eyes, he pressed his head to the wall. "I'm sorry, Will. I really am."

The faint sounds of movement came from inside her room. "Can I go to the interschool competition tomorrow?" Willow asked, her voice louder this time.

His gut clenched. "Can we talk about that? I've got some thoughts—exciting thoughts—on how we can—"

"Yes or no, Dad."

If I say yes, I'll see Randi, Willow will be happy, and so will Sasha.

"I don't think—"

"You can stop talking, Dad." Disappointment laced her voice. "You've said enough."

He stared at her door. He could open it and go in and tell her about his decision to move them all to Australia. He could tell her it was going to be amazing, and it was the way it was going to be because *he* was the father, the one who made the decisions. He could go in there and remind her he was the one who put food on the table and a roof over their heads, and point out that roof was soon going to be in Melbourne, Australia, goddamn it.

He could do all that...

Letting out a shaky breath, he turned and walked out into the kitchen. He opened the fridge and pulled a beer from it.

It was going to be a long night.

Neither Sasha nor Willow came out for dinner. He made their favorite, turkey tacos, and called them to the table, but no one arrived. Five minutes of waiting later, he carried a tray laden with four turkey tacos to their rooms.

Sasha's door was open, but her room was empty.

Soft voices came from Willow's room. He knocked on the door.

The voices on the other side fell silent.

"I've got your dinner."

A few heartbeats later, the door opened.

"Thanks, Dad." Willow took the tray from him.

"Not coming out?"

She regarded him—expression impossible to decipher. "I'm going to stay in here."

Something invisible kicked him in the chest. "What about Sash?"

"I'm staying in here with Will," Sasha called from Willow's bed. "Go away now, Daddy."

Willow gave him a look, the kind Bridget used to give him when he'd done something stupid. God, how could anyone, including himself, ever think he'd forget Bridget when every day she was there with him in their elder daughter?

"Okay." He nodded and turned away.

"He's a poo head," Sasha muttered from the bed.

Christ, if only he had someone to talk to, to help him navigate this.

Call her. Call Randi. Now.

He didn't.

Another beer was his only companion for the rest of the night. Neither Willow nor Sasha came near him. He heard both of them shower, heard both of them getting ready for bed. He heard them talking softly to each other.

At eight, he waited for Sasha to come ask him for their normal goodnight routine.

She didn't.

At ten, when he switched off the television, the house was in silence.

Shit. I really messed up.

"Then fix it," he mumbled, rubbing at the back of his neck. "You know how. Your heart knows how. So fix it."

He straightened from the sofa and retrieved his phone— sitting beside Willow's—from its charger in the kitchen.

Chest tight, throat tighter, he dialed a number. *The* number. The one he knew by heart.

Heart. Ah, shit, he was tearing himself apart.

The phone rang in his ear.

And rang.

And rang.

And finally, "Hi, this is Bridget Lockwood's phone. Don't leave me in suspense. Leave a message."

He flinched at the beep and then let out a weak chuckle. "Heya, Bridge. It's me." His voice cracked. "It's been a while, hasn't it?" He'd never been able to bring himself to disconnect her cell phone account. He just…couldn't. "Sorry about that. I've been…" Another wobbly chuckle. "Busy."

Busy. What a fucking moron.

"I miss you, Bridge. And I've been petrified of losing you, even though I know you're already gone, that I already *did* lose you. Christ, I miss you. But…but I've met someone, and she's amazing, and I think you'd like her. Sasha adores her, and I think Will likes her a lot, but you know Will…it's never easy to tell." He swallowed, a hot dust ball in his throat. "The girls miss you so much, but they are finding their happiness again. They really are. And I think…" He swiped at his mouth. His eyes burned. "I think maybe, just maybe, I've got another chance at…at love, at life. I hope you're okay with that." He squeezed his eyes shut, but that didn't stop the tears falling. "I think, I *know* it's time to say goodbye, Bridge. Thank you for being my first love, Mrs. Thorton. I will never forget you."

Pulling the phone from his ear, he stared at the screen. At the end-call button.

Stared at it.

Stared at it. And pressed it.

———+———

He fell asleep in the armchair.

Neck protesting—*seriously, Thorton, you're too old to sleep in a chair*—he straightened to his feet.

Hell, even his knees were getting in on the complaining act.

Wincing a little, he rolled his neck, rubbed at his knees and hobbled—*hobbled*—into the sunlit kitchen. He flicked on the coffeemaker and squinted at the clock on the oven.

What time was it? Damn it, awake before seven on a Saturday. Maybe he could go grab a quick hour's nap, horizontally this time, before the girls woke. His neck and knees might forgive him if he did.

Scratching at the thickening stubble on his cheeks and jaw, he cracked his neck again and pulled a glass from the cupboard. He'd hydrate and then—

He frowned at the bright yellow Post-it note stuck to the sink tap.

"What the…"

"I've gone to the comp," Willow's neat cursive handwriting informed him. *"Wish me luck. XOX"*

"Ah fuck," he breathed. At least she finished the proclamation with two kisses and a hug.

"Fuck, fuck, fuck." He placed his empty glass in the sink and spun on his heel. Comp. Where *was* the comp? Had she told him yesterday?

She called it the interschool competition. God, where the bloody hell is that being held?

Crap. He was the worst father in the world. He'd denied his daughter the one thing she loved doing, denied his other daughter the new person who made her happy, didn't know where—

Hurrying into the living room, he snatched his phone up from the coffee table. Shit, it was almost flat.

He punched in Willow's number and rammed the phone to his ear.

After five rings it switched to her messaging service. "Hi, this is Will. If you're calling me, you must be old. Leave a message. Or send me a text, weirdo."

He hit end. Of course Willow wouldn't answer his call. What with the way he'd behaved yesterday, with the selfish way he'd dismissed what she'd wanted to do…

"Crap shit fuck poo."

Heart smashing in his dry throat—*yeah, really should have hydrated*—he called Randi.

Ask about Will, that's all. Ask about Will. Nothing else.

Randi's phone cut over to her message service.

"Shit," he muttered as the beep filled his ear. "Hi, Randi. It's me. Brody. I'm just checking that Will is with you. Sorry to be a pain in the arse. Can you let me know where the comp is?" He pulled the phone from his ear, went to hit end, and then rammed it back to his ear again. "It's Brody. Did I tell you that?"

Yes. Idiot.

Ending the call, he hurried into the bedrooms. Maybe Will was playing a trick, getting back at him for how horrible he was yesterday?

Nope. Her bedroom was empty. The neatly made bed mocked him. He strode to the wardrobe and flung it open. Willow's spike bag hung on the hook he'd nailed to the back of the door years ago.

Spike bag. So she is playing a trick. No way she'd compete without her spikes.

Of course, she was two years older now; her feet were two years bigger. Knowing Will, she'd borrow a pair.

Or maybe Randi's bought her a—

"Crap." Spinning on his heel, he rushed into Sasha's room.

"Heya, maniac." He gently shook her hip. "Gotta wake up. We gotta go somewhere."

A sleepy moan answered him.

"Quick, gorgeous." He shook her hip again, scanning the room for her dressing gown. Was that it? Nope. That was her towel from the bathroom. Argh, Sash. How many times… "C'mon, maniac. We gotta go find Will."

"Will's gone to do jumping," Sasha mumbled, waving off his shaking hand and burying deeper into her pillows. "At her school."

At her school. Right. Good to know.

"C'mon, Sash." He peeled the sheets off her and scooped her up. "We have to go."

"I wanna sleep," she complained, wrapping her arms around him, cheek on his shoulder.

"Cool, cool." He hurried out of her room, through the house. "You can sleep in the car, kay?"

"Kay." She hugged his neck tighter. "Will's going to win."

"I'm sure she will, honey." He snagged his keys and his phone and strode to the garage.

"Can we get McDonald's for breakfast after Will jumps, Daddy?" Sasha asked, eyes still closed as he buckled her into her seat in the back.

"Absolutely, maniac."

"Yay." She yawned the word. "I'm sleeping now."

"Sure, sure." He climbed behind the wheel. "It's all good. I'll wake you when we get there."

Way too many minutes for his sanity later, he pulled to a halt outside Willow's school. People were everywhere. Students, supporters, parents, coaches…streaming in and out of the school grounds. A ghost of a life he'd thought long lost to him.

He found a parking spot not too far from the sports field and watched people in the rearview mirror moving behind his SUV.

Christ, he'd actually missed this. Missed it for Willow,

missed it for himself. The atmosphere and the charged energy of the competitors.

Why the hell had he tried to deny Willow this? How could he ever make it up to her?

"Are we there?" Sasha rubbed at her eyes. "Where's Will?"

"Let's go find her, eh?"

"Are you going to yell at her, Daddy?"

He let out a choppy breath and shook his head. "No, Sash. I'm not. Not at all. I'm going to cheer her on and be so proud of her I might burst."

Sasha smiled. "No more poo head?"

"No more poo head."

She beamed. "Yay. Is Randi going to be here?"

A hot knot twisted in his gut. "Let's go find out, what do you say?"

"Okeydokey."

He scoured the grounds. The interschool meet was huge. So many schools, so many competitors. Twice, he thought he spied Randi hurrying through the crowd, clipboard in hand, baseball cap pulled low over her face. Twice, his gut leaped up into his throat, a place his heart had decided to settle when he'd discovered Willow was gone.

Twice, Randi—if it was her—slipped away before he could catch up with her.

Sasha held his hand, giggling and clearly having a great time, despite the fact he'd dragged her here in her PJs. One day, she'd be furious with him for it. Today...

"This is fun! Look, there's cotton candy! Can I get some cotton candy, Daddy? I'm hungry." She squeezed his fingers. "Look, look, there's Will. Will! *Will!*"

And yep, there she was a few yards away on the other side of the long jump runway. She was prepping for her event by stretching and warming up, smiling to herself and her fellow competitors. He recognized some of them, rivals Willow had competed against from the age of eight. Some of them spoke to her, some seemed to be welcoming her back.

He hadn't seen her look so happy, so contented, since before Bridget's funeral.

But she'd found her way back to it. To her happy, to her element. To her space.

"She's going to be okay, Bridge," he whispered.

Sasha tugged on his hand. "Can I go to Will, Daddy? Can I?"

He crouched down. "Check out your big sis, Sasha." He smiled at Sasha as she settled onto his bent leg, and then at Willow, still completely oblivious to their presence. "She's going to be a world-record breaker one day, you know that?"

"Bloody oath," Sasha intoned, sounding for all the world like his father.

He laughed. "We're going to have to have a serious chat with your grandfather about your language, mani—"

Randi walked up to Willow on the other side of the pit and put a hand on her shoulder, and everything in Brody's world stopped.

CHAPTER NINETEEN

"Nervous?"

Willow smiled up at her. "No. Maybe. A little. It's been a while."

Two years. "Have you stretched? I'd hate for you to tear a muscle, or strain a—" She laughed at Willow's rolled eyes. "Sorry. Sorry. I know."

Willow shrugged and smiled wider. "It's okay. It's actually nice. But, yes, I've stretched. I walked half the way here, remember."

Yes, that little nugget of information had left Randi reeling when Willow told her as she'd strolled in with Lyle, the school's track star.

She'd had a hard time not asking if Brody knew, even as she smiled at Lyle and asked Willow if she needed anything.

"You all good and ready to roll?" she asked now. Why was her stomach fluttering so much?

Willow tugged at the laces of her right shoe. "I was worried I'd be competing in normal running shoes, since my old spikes don't fit any more, but Lyle's sister still had her old spikes, and she said I could wear them."

Lyle laughed and gave Willow a gentle nudge with his knee. "You'll get better use from them than she ever did."

Randi arched an eyebrow. "Isn't your sister on a college scholarship for triple jump, Lyle?"

He chuckled. "Yeah. But Will is better than her." And with that, he went off to do his own prep.

Willow let out a shaky breath. "Lots of people here I remember," she almost whispered, looking at the other competitors moving around them. "I hope I don't embarrass myself."

A wave of warmth rushed through Randi. She was tempted to take a photo, to send it to Brody. Instead, she checked out Willow's competition mingling next to them.

"These spikes *are* comfy." Willow said as she looked at her feet. "But I should probably get some new ones before State."

State. God, this girl has confidence. "Probably a good idea. Although the green and pink definitely make a bold statement."

Willow grinned. "They do, don't—Sasha?"

Sasha?

Randi's stomach clenched.

A multicolored, Sasha-shaped blur launched itself at Randi, two small but strong little arms wrapping around her waist. "Hi, Randi."

"What…" She blinked down at Sasha beaming up at her. "Why are you in your pajamas?"

"Daddy got me out of bed and made me get in the car when I was sleeping." Sasha smiled at Willow. "Are you going to win, Will?"

"Hope so."

"I like your spikes."

"They're pretty, aren't they?"

"They are. Daddy was really worried about you. Do you have any food, Randi? I haven't had breakfast."

Randi blinked again and then let out a yelp when Brody—suddenly in front of her—said, "Hi, Randi."

So this is what having a meltdown feels like.

Dragging in a deep breath, she met Brody's gaze. "Hi, Mr. Thorton."

This was neither the time nor the place for an emotional crisis. Not with so many of her students around her and Dave Pascoe hovering nearby at the bottom of the bleachers, ready to swoop in and claim victory for the school if Willow were to break another record.

Brody cleared his throat, opened his mouth, closed it again, and turned his attention to Willow. Had he been about to say something? Sorry for being a jerk? Or sorry for being so wonderful you couldn't help but fall in love with me?

Did he have any clue at all how he'd changed everything in her life?

"So," he said, his voice deep and somehow husky, "I see you decided to come anyway, Will?"

"Yep."

"Are you sure you're ready for this? That it's what you want to do?"

"It is."

He studied her and then scrubbed a hand over his face. "In that case, we better get you some new spikes. Can't have you competing in borrowed ones all the time. We'll swing by the sports store on the way home from here if you like."

Willow didn't answer. Instead, she scrambled to her feet and wrapped her arms around him. "Thanks, Daddy," she whispered, eyes closed, cheek pressed to his chest.

He met Randi's gaze over the top of her head. "Randi…"

She shook her head. "Don't, Brody. Please." She couldn't do it. Whatever it was, she couldn't do it. Failing at this, at being a deep, significant part of the Thortons' lives…she couldn't do it anymore. It hurt too much.

How the hell was she going to survive the rest of Willow's

time at Jefferson Middle School and seeing Brody often? She'd have to learn how to stop reacting to him, otherwise she was going to go insane.

"Willow Thorton."

At the sound of the event official calling Willow, Randi turned away. She had to. It hurt too much. Looking at Brody, looking at him hugging Willow as Sasha hugged her… It was everything she'd spent days telling herself she didn't want. It was perfect and painful all at once.

"Willow's here," she called, waving at the official.

Around them, a few people—some competitors, some adults—murmured Willow's name. She really was something special.

The whole family is. Special and amazing. So stop thinking you deserve to be a part of it, because you—

"Coming," Willow called, pulling away from Brody. She frowned at him. "Dad, whatever you said to Miss Lockwood to make her upset with you, you need to make it better. Say sorry."

"Yeah." Sasha swung Randi's hand. "Say sorry, Daddy."

"Willow Thorton?" the official called again.

Randi touched Willow's shoulder. "Time to jump, Will."

Oh, what was she doing calling her *Will*? She had to stop. Her heart wasn't going to survive any longer.

Willow sighed, shook her head and, with a scowl at both of them, ran to her start marker on the runway.

Randi squeezed Sasha's hand. "I've got to go, little one."

Sasha echoed her sister's frown. "Okay. Bye, Randi."

Randi hurried away. She didn't look at Brody. She had to start shutting down how she felt for him sometime. It may as well be now.

She crossed the runway, ready to take her place near Willow's start marker, chest tight.

She could do this. She was tough. Strong. She was—

"Randi Lockwood." Her name was bellowed across the

ground, the familiar twang of a megaphone emphasizing Brody's Australian accent.

She stopped.

So did everyone else around her.

"Dad," Willow groaned, shaking her head.

Turning slowly, Randi stared at Brody across the runway.

He stood motionless, one hand holding Sasha's, a megaphone in the other.

She raised her eyebrows, her heart a cannon in her throat.

Holding her stare, Brody raised the megaphone to his mouth. "Randi Lockwood, I love you."

"Oh my God." Willow rolled her eyes. "Dad."

"We love you, Randi," Sasha shouted.

Brody nodded and raised the megaphone again. "I'm sorry for being a—"

"*Poo head*," Sasha yelled.

Around them, people laughed.

"*Dad*." Willow groaned again, a laugh threading through the word.

"Excuse me, sir," the official called, glaring at Brody. "You're holding up proceedings."

Brody lifted the megaphone to his mouth.

Randi sprinted across the runway before he could say a word.

He lowered the megaphone and smiled at her. "I love you, Randi. I'm sorry for being a wanker. I want you in our lives, in *my* life, more than I can bloody well say. Please say you—"

"No."

He swallowed.

Mouth dry, throat tight, she shook her head. "I love you, too, Brody. I do. You and your girls, but…" She shook her head again. "Just no."

His chest rose with a ragged breath and then, shoulders slumping, he nodded. "Fair enough."

Randi balled her fists. It was that or tangle her fingers in his hair, pull his head to hers, and kiss him senseless, pausing only to apologize for being so stupid and stubborn. "Sorry, Brody," she whispered. "I just…can't do this."

"Willow Thorton jumping."

Oh no.

Spinning on her heel in time to witness Willow burst into a fluid, powerful sprint, Randi pressed her hand to her mouth. Holy crap, the girl was incredible, so fast, so graceful. Her sprint technique was exquisite.

"Wow," she breathed.

"Go, Will," Sasha yelled.

Willow's right foot hit the takeoff board with a solid thud. Her whole body seemed to coil, and then she was flying through the air in an arc. Her arms swung up and back to propel her farther, her legs extended out in front of her in corded preparation for her landing. She was already past the current record marker, and she was still high in the air.

"Wow," Randi said again.

Willow came down in the pit, the force of her landing throwing her forward. Awkwardly.

She landed on her shoulder. Her hip. A muffled cry came from the pit, and then she rolled into a ball, face down, in the sand.

"*Will!*" Brody sprinted for the pit. "Will."

"Shit." Randi ran after him. Oh no. No, not on her first jump. Oh God, was she okay? Was she?

"Will?" Brody sank to his knees beside her, hand on her back. "Where does it hurt?"

Randi ran around to her other side, dropping to her knees. "Willow? Is it your shoulder? Your knees?"

Willow moaned, mumbled…something.

Randi frowned at Brody.

He looked at her, worry eating up his face. "Will, talk to us. Tell us what hurts."

Willow mumbled something again, louder this time.

Randi swallowed, reaching for Brody's hand, pressing her fingers to the back of his. "We're here, Willow. But you need to tell us what's gone wrong."

Another mumble. Louder. "...each...other..."

Brody frowned and squeezed Randi's hand. "Will? What did you say?"

Twisting a little to the side, Willow looked up at them. "Will you..." she rasped. "Please...just freaking kiss each other?"

Brody blinked. "What?"

Sasha giggled.

Willow rolled her eyes. "Can you two just hurry up and make up so I can get on with the—"

Randi rose up on her knees, leaned across Willow, and—cupping Brody's face in her palms—kissed him.

"That's what I'm talking about," Willow said. "Now, take the kissing somewhere else, okay? Chuck's here, and I want him to see me win."

Face burning, Randi pulled away from Brody and then burst into laughter when he chased her lips with his.

"Way to go, Aunty R." Chuck's laughter rose above the noise around them from the bleachers. "Awesome. Now get a room, will you? It's jumping time!"

EPILOGUE

"**A**re you sure this is the room you want?"

Randi cast a dubious look at the interior of the room decorated in candy-pinks and vivid purples, with butterflies painted on the walls and ceiling. Beside her, fingers holding hers, Sasha nodded. "I like this one."

Brody cleared his throat. "Maybe if we paint it—"

"No." Sasha's eyebrows knitted. "I like it as it is."

"Me too." Chuck bounced on the single bed in the center of the room—also adorned with pink and purple butterflies. "It's an awesome room. Can *I* have it?"

Sasha gaped at him. "You already picked the room down the hall. No fair."

"This is a pretty cool room." Willow dropped onto the bed beside Chuck and grinned at Sasha. "Can *I* have it, Dad?"

"What?" Sasha yanked on Randi's hand. "Randi, stop them. Stop them."

"Okay, you two." She gave Chuck and Willow—clearly trying not to hold hands—a pointed look. "You can't have this room."

"Yeah." Sasha nodded. "You can't."

Randi grinned. "You know this is going to be *my* room. It's perfect for my art studio."

"What?" Sasha's mouth fell open.

With a chuckle, Brody scooped her up. "Ignore them all, maniac. Of course this can be your new bedroom. Will Skips approve?"

"Bloody oath," she answered before twisting in his arms and poking her tongue out at Willow and Chuck.

"Ouch." Chuck grabbed his chest. "That hurts."

Letting out her own chuckle, Randi scanned the hallway and the doors opening from it. "Do you think they are going to accept?"

Brody took in the hallway as well. It was their fourth inspection of the property—a five-bedroom home on Mission Beach, with a massive yard, a home gym in the garage, and an in-ground pool desperate for some TLC—and today they'd made their first offer. "I hope so. I must admit, I'm already starting to see us here."

"I'm going to go check out the gym again," Willow said, straightening from the bed. "Coming, Chuck?"

Randi bit back a groan at the look on Chuck's face as he rose to his feet. That was one gone boy. Hook, line, and sinker. Of course, he hadn't told his parents he was staying in San Diego because of his new girlfriend; he'd told them he was staying because he didn't want to move to France. But when Stacey came home next—sometime before Thanksgiving—and saw how deliriously happy her son was, Randi was probably going to be subjected to a serious lecture.

She was okay with that. Chuck was happy. Willow was happy. Sure, there were interesting complications having two dating teenagers living in the same house, but even those had been easy to deal with so far.

Everyone was happy in her new family unit. She'd defend it and nurture it with every breath in her body. Even against her sister. When it came to what was best for *her* family—Brody,

Willow, Sasha, *and* Chuck—she was so far from being a failure she almost didn't recognize herself.

"Can I go check out the gym, Daddy? Randi?" Sasha asked.

"Absolutely, maniac." Brody returned her to the floor. "Need you to keep an eye on those two for us, okay?"

"On it." Sasha snapped off a salute.

"Dad." Willow rolled her eyes.

Chuck just grinned and followed Willow and Sasha along the hallway and down the stairs.

Smiling, Randi leaned her back to the wall and looked up at Brody. "You sure about this?"

"About Sasha being our spy around those two? Bloody oath."

She laughed and shook her head. "About *this*. Us. Buying a house together. Getting…" She wriggled her left ring finger at him, the square-cut, one-carat solitary diamond ring he'd slipped onto it six months ago still almost too amazing to be true. "Y'know. If we buy this house, you'll never be rid of me."

Nostrils flaring, he smoothed his hands up the wall beside her head and pressed his hips to hers. "Miranda Lockwood, the last thing I'll ever want is to be rid of you, got it?"

"Hmmm…" She gave him a mock frown. "I'm not convinced."

Mischief and desire danced in his eyes. "What if we, y'know, do it right now? Here? In the hallway? Would that convince you?"

"Do 'it'?" She trailed her fingers up his chest to the open collar of his shirt. "Is this some weird Aussie term I'm not familiar with? What's 'it'?"

He chuckled. "You know exactly what I'm talking about, woman."

"I do." She popped the top button of his shirt. "Ready?"

He lowered his head closer to hers. "You better bloody believe I am."

She laughed.

"Love you, soon-to-be-my-wife."

"Love you back, soon-to-be—"

He silenced her with a kiss.

Who knew house-hunting with her family could be so naughty?

COMING SOON

Love and Other Inconveniences
Love and Other Primal Urges

MORE ROMANCE FROM LEXXIE
COUPER...

The Always Series

Unconditional
Unforgettable
Undeniable

The Outback Skies Series

Bound to You
Breathless for You
Burn for You
Bare for You
Better with You
Blindsided By You

The Heart of Fame Series

Love's Rhythm
Muscle for Hire
Guarded Desires
Steady Beat
Lead Me On
Blame it on the Bass
Getting Played
Blackthorne

Stimulated

Blowing It Off
Revving It Up
Switching It On
Rubbing It Out
Pinning It Down

Heart of Fame: Stage Right

Compliance
A Single Knight
Balls Up
Lust's Rhythm

Dangerous Desire

The Bad Boy Next Door
The Good Girl in My Bed
The Bad Boy in Cuffs
The Good Girl in Trouble

ABOUT LEXXIE COUPER

Lexxie Couper started writing when she was six and hasn't stopped since. She's not a deviant, but she does have a deviant's imagination and a desire to entertain readers with her words. Add the two together and you get erotic romances that can make you laugh, cry, shake with fear or tremble with desire. Sometimes all at once.

When she's not submerged in the worlds she creates, Lexxie's life revolves around her family, a husband who thinks she's insane, an indoor cat who likes to stalk shadows, and her daughters, who both utterly captured her heart and changed her life forever.

Lexxie lives by two simple rules – measure your success not by how much money you have, but by how often you laugh, and always try everything at least once. As a consequence, she's laughed her way through many an eyebrow raising adventure. You can find details of her writing at www.LexxieCouper.com